Murder in the Pit

By Erica Miner

Twilight Times Books
Kingsport Tennessee

Murder in the Pit

This is a work of fiction. All concepts, characters and events portrayed in this book are used fictitiously and any resemblance to real people or events is purely coincidental.

Paladin Timeless Books, an imprint of
Twilight Times Books
P O Box 3340
Kingsport TN 37664
http://twilighttimesbooks.com/

First Edition: June 2010

Library of Congress Cataloging-in-Publication Data

Miner, Erica.
   Murder in the pit / by Erica Miner. -- 1st ed.
       p. cm.
   ISBN-13: 978-1-60619-110-1 (trade pbk. : alk. paper)
   ISBN-10: 1-60619-110-1 (trade pbk. : alk. paper)
   1. Women violinists--Fiction. 2. Metropolitan Opera (New York, N.Y.)--
Fiction. 3. Murder--Investigation--Fiction. 4. New York (N.Y.)--Fiction. I.
Title.
   PS3613.I598M87 2010
   813'.6--dc22

                                    2010013804

Cover artwork by Ardy M. Scott

Printed in the United States of America.

Foreword by Valerio Massimo Manfredi

A young violinist, overwhelmed with excitement, about to embark on a career as a member of New York's Metropolitan Opera Orchestra... A great event, the premiere of a classic production of Verdi's *Don Carlo*, about to take place in a high-stakes atmosphere... An audience of refined *glitterati*, waiting with great anticipation... A leading tenor being placated in the wings... A celebrated maestro on the podium in the orchestra pit... All these elements set the stage for the suspense of *Murder in the Pit*.

For naïve Julia Kogan, of humble origins, the protégée of a maestro who expects she will someday ascend to the first violinist position in the orchestra, it is a baptism of fire with a double-edged sword: unimaginable gratification, but at the risk of being exposed to the envy and maligning of resentful colleagues. Not only is she musically gifted; her beauty is no less attractive to women than to men.

But before Julia can truly relish her shining moment, tragedy rips through the grand theater and turns her world on its head.

Erica Miner's novel creates expectations of a powerful, monumental event about to unfold on stage and in the orchestra pit. Then, suddenly, the music changes registers, transforming from harmonious melody and dramatic tension into a tangle of human misery, bringing readers into the world of investigations, suspicions, and motives. Under the author's adept fingers, characters alive and dead are created; then, one by one they are mercilessly dissected and their faults brutally exposed. Intricate tracks are followed, and then improbably vanish.

Just another crime novel? Hardly. *Murder in the Pit* is an adventure of the imagination, a play within a play. The protagonist, a promising but unfinished musical score who at first seems to lose her way and sink like a pearl in turbid waters, page by page pulls herself up from sheer will and determination, allies herself with an opera-loving cop and an ambitious *comprimario* tenor, and reminds us in the end that music itself can be a revelation.

The author's narrative is light and efficient, flowing naturally, and avoids the easy temptation to descend into grandiose special effects. In the end, she has recreated in a fascinating operatic world a tangle of plot twists whose intricacies ultimately unravel to reveal the prose of an author who is sure of her skills.

Valerio Massimo Manfredi is the author of thirteen novels such as the Alexander trilogy, *The Ancient Curse* (Macmillan Publishers Ltd., July 2010), *The Ides of March* and *The Lost Army*.

Acknowledgment

I would like to thank the following people for helping me in my journey with this novel:

Valerio Massimo Manfredi, for his generosity and time in writing the Foreword

Detective Rita Sanders and Sgt. Ralph Garcia, for their expertise in police procedurals

Carol Pinchefsky, Linda Seger, and Devorah Cutler-Rubinstein, for their input on the story

Carol A. Guy and Leslie Holman-Anderson, editors extraordinaire

The Metropolitan Opera, for being my 'home away from home' for twenty-one years

And especially my publisher Lida Quillen, for her belief in me and in this story

List of Characters

Julia Kogan, a young neophyte violinist in the Metropolitan Opera Orchestra

Sidney Richter, her avuncular best friend in the orchestra

Abel Trudeau, conductor of the orchestra, Julia's mentor

Patricia Wells, General Manager of the Met

Charles Tremaine, Met tenor, an admirer of Julia

Matt Reynolds, head stagehand at the Met, and another of Julia's admirers

Frank Bernini, Matt's assistant

Larry Somers, NYPD Detective and opera aficionado

Tony Rossi, orchestra personnel manager and conductor wannabe

Katie Ma, Julia's roommate and violinist colleague

Chapter 1

Quanto hai penato, anima mia!

How you have suffered, oh my soul!

Puccini, *Tosca*, Act II

JULIA THREADED HER WAY through the waiting crowds of patrons in front of the Metropolitan Opera House and headed toward the revolving door. Off to the side, she heard a downtrodden street violinist give a passionate rendition of the fiendish showpiece, *Zigeunerweisen.* Despite his brilliant playing, he was ignored by the throng. Julia stopped to listen to him. She smiled at the man in sympathy and placed a twenty-dollar bill into his violin case.

"You sound great. Keep plugging away."

"Thank you, Miss."

He cast a grateful acknowledgement in her direction and carried on with his impassioned performance. She smiled at him and sent a thankful look heavenward.

How lucky am I to have a real job with a weekly paycheck?

Julia had decided to enter the opera house through the front doors on Lincoln Center Plaza. Her usual habit was to go in through the stage entrance, via the alley off Amsterdam Avenue, toward the rear of the theater. Instead, she chose the revolving glass doors off Broadway, which afforded a much more elegant entrance. This evening, Julia was seized by the desire to be among the glitterati of the opening night gala. It was her first performance as a violinist with the Met Orchestra. All her instincts told her things would never be the same again.

No stage door tonight. I go in with the paying customers.

In front of the Met's massive glass doors, a pair of elegant life-sized, glass-enclosed posters heralded the evening's performance: "Metropolitan Opera, Gala opening night performance: Verdi's *Don*

Carlo, Abel Trudeau, Conductor – Sold Out."

Julia gently squeezed past an older woman, looking chic in a fox stole and diamond necklace, and a younger woman clad in a simple but stylish Diane von Furstenberg frock, and inhaled their heady perfume. From her position in front of the giant glass windows that revealed activity inside the Met lobby, she watched the distinguished crowd sweeping through the doors and up the circular Italian marble staircases, past the red velvet-flocked walls and underneath the lead-crystal chandeliers that had been a gift from the Austrian government.

Julia had overcome every possible obstacle to be there among the *crème de la crème* of New York musicians. But she owed her career to Abel Trudeau.

Abel was the mentor who had nurtured Julia's musical gifts for the past dozen years. Because of his unwavering attention, Julia had developed a single-minded confidence in her ability to perform under pressure in auditions and performances. This gave her an edge, enabling her to outshine her fellow students under duress. Most of them resented her talent, not to mention her beauty. Petite and slender, with a cascade of chestnut brown hair and eyes to match, she inspired jealous glances wherever she went. But Julia decided early on that making Abel proud far outranked the social acceptance of her peers.

Her mind wandered back to the fateful day when Maestro Trudeau had pronounced her "ready" for the Met. A dazzling display of violin mastery in the Juilliard School's production of Britten's opera *The Rape of Lucretia* had brought Julia's achievements to his attention. He didn't hesitate to tell her so afterwards, and when he placed Julia on the list of auditionees for the opening in the Met's first violin section, she was astonished. He then proceeded to coach her on her audition repertoire, most of which she could perform with ease. But the fiendish passage from Verdi's *Luisa Miller* Overture was still eluding her, or so she thought.

"I'll never get it right."

"No. As far as I'm concerned, you've got it right. You're ready for the Met."

"You really think so? Well, if I am, it's only because of you."

"No, it's not. It's because you have the gift of an artist's soul."

The gift of an artist's soul.

His words inspired her. She was so overjoyed at Abel's praise she wanted to hug him. She didn't, of course. She couldn't. Not since her father. But Abel, who had always looked after her, remained closer to her than anyone else. Julia thought since Abel had no wife or family perhaps he considered her his daughter substitute. It was a role she was happy to play. Not even her perennial sadness at the loss of her father could keep her from focusing on her goal: to please Abel and to be a part of his prestigious orchestra.

Abel had looked at her glowing face and flashed her a wise smile. "Remember, never let anyone undermine your confidence in your abilities. And always think *beyond* the notes. You will be true to the music, and to yourself."

Julia made a pledge to herself to follow his counsel to the letter. She wasn't sure what he meant by thinking "beyond the notes." He had taught her about how letter designations of certain notes changed from language to language, such as the note letter "B natural" in English, which was the equivalent of "H" in German. But she was sure his present wisdom about notes referred to something else, something subtler.

Maybe I'll understand better when I'm older and more sophisticated.

Nonetheless she always kept his advice close to her heart, touched to the core that Abel had considered her worthy of sharing such precious information.

Julia had, as he predicted, been ready. She blew away her competition at the grueling round of auditions and won the unanimous praise of the judges. At age twenty-two, she became the youngest member of the Met's orchestra "family."

I'll be in his debt forever. There's nothing I wouldn't do for him...

In the six months following her successful bid for a position in the orchestra's first violin section, Julia rapidly adjusted to the Met. The demanding pre-opening night rehearsal schedule was her first test: five days a week from 9:00 a.m. to 5 p.m., with limited breaks. Music for as many as five new operas was thrown at the musicians at a frenetic pace, and the new players were constantly being scrutinized by the more established musicians as well as the conductor. Once these rehearsed operas came into the performance repertoire, new operas were brought in to rehearse in their place during the day in tandem with evening performances. In the case of new productions, or those featuring famous conductors or opera stars with the most clout, the musicians often were called upon to rehearse after hours, although this practice was reined in by the management to keep overtime costs under control.

In spite of this punishing agenda, Julia kept a good deal of her original ingenuousness, staying upbeat and positive about her adored new job. She loved all the operas, even the five- or six-hour Wagner ones. When other violinists sat down in their chairs groaning at the rich meal before them on the music stand, Julia consumed every note of each page with an insatiable appetite.

Tonight Julia hoisted the strap that held her violin case to her other shoulder, trembling with anticipation. The evening ahead was going to be a long one, but full of excitement. She allowed herself a moment to admire the magnificent Chagall murals, the immense, towering artworks that distinguished the Metropolitan Opera House from all others, renowned as the signature of the Met's façade. Their brilliant colors displayed the French-Russian painter's genius to the world, especially the world of New York's Lincoln Center, much as the Eiffel Tower represented the genius of late nineteenth-century French engineering. The paintings stood as a monument to music, inspiring admiration and awe.

A sudden longing for her father replaced her anticipation with intense pain. A tear escaped her eye and clung to her cheek, glistening in the bright lights of Lincoln Plaza, as she gazed into the cascading jets of its famed fountain.

Why couldn't Dad be here to see me fulfill my dream? It just isn't fair.

Chapter 2

O *dolce notte, scendere*
/*Tu puoi gemmata a festa*

O sweet night, descend/
Starlit on our celebration

Verdi, *Un Ballo in Maschera*, Act I

As she finally stepped through the revolving doors and into the Met lobby, Julia gave one last wistful glance at the patrons ascending the elegant staircase and headed toward her own appropriate stairway, the one leading to the lower level and the alley where the stage door was located.

The servants' entrance.

Life at the opera house appeared glamorous to the patrons and public at large, but Julia knew her place; notwithstanding her well-paying position in this prestigious artistic institution, she and her overworked Met cohorts in the orchestra were just the hired help. The true stars of this exhilarating world were the Domingos and Pavarottis. Musicians were underlings, and no one was better at putting them in their place than Patricia Wells, the Met's formidable general manager whom Julia had dubbed "a barracuda in high heels."

Julia had grudging respect for Patricia's running the Met like a well-oiled machine, but she had no love for Patricia's personality or for her spiteful attitude toward musicians. Patricia had a clear-cut disdain for these "low-class drudges" who were very good at grinding out musical notes night after night but who, she believed, showed no gratitude to the organization responsible for putting bread on their tables.

Patricia, with her high-and-mighty mind-set, did not acknowledge the fact the orchestra was the lynchpin of the opera house and did not appreciate the magnitude of the orchestra's contribution. The majority of Met musicians had been honing their craft since early childhood, and without an orchestra, as Mozart had displayed with such effectiveness in the movie *Amadeus*, there was no opera.

Julia admired Patricia's *chutzpah* in climbing to the top, but she could not abide the attitude: Patricia had actually docked her own pay when she took a day off to attend her father's funeral, just to show how much she disdained the practice of spending the company's money on "personal" matters. Julia thought this behavior a perfect example of Patricia's lack of sensitivity.

If she thinks that's how the other members of the company should behave, she's barely a warm-blooded mammal.

Julia had grown up without parents most of her life, yet still maintained a commitment to compassion. She had lost her father, Sol, when she was ten. His death was sudden and violent. Since then, she never allowed herself to demonstrate physical affection toward anyone. Her father's hand was the last she had ever clasped.

At this moment, Julia imagined the scene backstage, Patricia calming the nerves of the evening's lead tenor, Giuseppe Masini. Julia tried to arrive early for rehearsals to spend time watching the pre-rehearsal activity from the wings. She often observed the way Patricia masterfully controlled such situations, by stroking Giuseppe's ego, as the harried wardrobe mistress fussed with his costume.

"The Maestro will be watching you like a hawk. *Non preoccuparti.*"

"*Grazie*, Patrizia, you are *Regina*, a queen among general managers."

"Ah, you are too generous, Giuseppe."

It was a scene of dramatic proportions rivaling the operatic performance itself and a familiar drill at the Met. Opera, after all, was the epitome of drama.

Putting such musings out of her mind, Julia entered the stage door and approached the security guard's station. She was not surprised when she noticed a number of extra guards patrolling the area. Between the assemblage of stars onstage and rumors of bigwigs such as Rudy Giuliani and Michael Bloomberg in the audience that evening, security was extra tight.

Before the 9-11 attacks, several years before Julia joined the orchestra, she had heard that the guards were friendly and affable and even kibitzed with the personnel who passed through the gate. Now checking people out as they passed through was serious business, and the guards, sequestered in a bunker-like contraption high off the floor, no longer smiled. All personnel were required to swipe an ID card through a magnetic strip in order to enter. This change in procedure and mind-set saddened Julia.

Life in New York City, and at Lincoln Center, has never been the same.

Julia fished for her Met ID in her pocketbook, while doing a balancing act with her violin case, and finally produced her card. As she swiped it through the magnetic reader, Sidney Richter squeezed past her, waving his ID in haste. Sid, her best friend in the orchestra's first violin section, was a jaded veteran, though Julia could never figure out how he still managed to bypass the security procedure required of most "normal" personnel. And he complained about everything.

"The pay is too low, and the hours are too long. And why did Abel have to add the extra forty-five minutes of music?"

Don Carlo was Julia's favorite Verdi opera, but though she agreed it was too long, she still defended Abel. "He's a stickler for doing operas uncut."

Sidney had reason to object. Sitting through the longer operas often irritated his diverticulitis, causing him to get up and head for the men's room. From the back of the pit where he sat, he was able to slip out without too much notice from the audience. The other musicians griped, but Julia felt both sympathy toward him and fondness for his protectiveness of her. Nonetheless, she frowned at the guard with mock bravado.

"How come he gets in with a wave but not me?"

Sidney flashed her a hurried smile. "Stick with me, kid, you might get in with a wave, too. Someday."

Julia rolled her eyes at Sid and pivoted back to the guard. "Is that fair?"

But when she turned again in Sidney's direction, the older violinist had already dashed through the gate and disappeared down the stairs toward the orchestra level. Like a modern-day Alice neophyte trying to keep pace with the more experienced inhabitants of Wonderland, she scurried to catch up with him.

Oh, Mister Rabbit…

൪ൠ

After convincing Giuseppe he was the twenty-first century's answer to Caruso, Patricia Wells made her way to Abel's dressing room and peeked in the door.

"I just wanted to wish you *'merde'* for tonight, Maestro." Wishing someone *"merde"* was the operatic equivalent of saying, "break a leg."

Abel stopped her from retreating. "Just a moment, Patricia. About that interoffice mail I sent up this afternoon, I just wanted to make sure you received—"

She stepped inside. "What? I didn't see anything cross my desk from you."

"You're certain?"

She ignored the dark shadow crossing his face. "Quite certain. Now if you'll excuse me, I have a baritone to appease."

Patricia withdrew, closing the door behind her, unaware that as soon as she was gone, Abel hurried over to the piano, picked up a piece of music and started to scribble on it.

ಬಂಚ

Julia negotiated the dimly lit stairway and passed through the noisy, fluorescent-lit area one level below the stage, which was alternately called A-level, pit-level, or orchestra-level. This was the hub of the orchestra's workspace, where musicians signed in on a list posted near the men's locker room and milled about during pre-performance frenzy and intermissions. The conductor's dressing room was close by the pit so the musicians could also observe whoever visited the maestro. Patricia was seen there frequently, as were nervous solo singers, management types, and others who felt welcome in the conductor's inner sanctum. The pit entrance was a few strides away, though it was necessary to pass by the men's locker room on the way there. The women's locker room was discreetly separated from the men's by a long hallway. The pit was also accessible from the opposite side, close to the company cafeteria, one of the few places in the opera house where musicians mixed with choristers, stagehands, ballet dancers, and solo singers. Even the illustrious tenor Domingo had made appearances there. Julia had confided her excitement to Sidney the first time she saw the star up close.

"He smiled at me, I'm sure of it."

"Those Latin types can smell a young, inexperienced chick a mile away."

Julia bristled. "What makes you think I'm inexperienced?"

"Just a hunch."

Most of the time however, orchestra members were sequestered in their own little world, a planet apart, in Julia's opinion, from the real guts of the opera house.

Sidney was nowhere to be seen. Julia glanced at the date at the top of the sign-in sheet and scanned the list of orchestra personnel to see if he had signed in.

September 29. One I'll always remember.

She was embarrassed to find a small "heart" symbol scrawled next to her name. She looked around. Matt Reynolds, the cute head stage-hand, smiled at her from the opposite corner of the hallway. Julia turned away from him, wondering how to react.

A familiar, scolding voice interrupted her thoughts. "Haven't I told you not to let him deface the sign-in sheet with his little love notes? People are beginning to notice."

Tony Rossi, the orchestra's personnel manager, was glaring at her. A wannabe conductor, he walked around waving a baton in practice gestures, tapping the skinny little stick on a music stand before each performance, trying to corral the musicians.

"It's not my fault, Tony. Why don't *you* tell him?"

"Is that any way to talk to your boss on your first night?"

"Should I wait until my *second* night?"

He didn't laugh. "I don't have time for this." Tony turned on his heels, flapping the baton in her direction as he took off. "Just tell your boyfriend to cease and desist."

"He's not my boyfriend."

Julia turned around. Matt had disappeared. She would have liked to protest more strongly, but realized she couldn't afford to anger her boss so early in the game.

Tony, too preoccupied to hear her protest, grumbled to himself just loud enough for her to hear, "Miserable stagehand. Just because he played clarinet as a kid, thinks the Met owes him a living."

Julia, intent on escape, slipped on the well-polished floor and felt her feet go out from under her. She clutched her violin with the protective instinct of a mother holding tight to her baby. As suddenly as he had vanished, Matt reappeared at her side and grabbed Julia around the waist, preventing her from tumbling to the floor.

"You okay, Julia?"

Blushing, Julia gently pulled away. "You shouldn't worry so much about me."

"I was just afraid you might hurt yourself."

"Me? I've been taking care of myself most of my life." She tried to regain her composure. "It's just opening night jitters."

Matt lowered his voice. "Still, an opera house can be a dangerous place. You'll find out after you've got a few more years' experience."

There it was again, that word. "Experience."

Someday I'll show all these guys I can hold my own with any veteran.

Matt flashed his famous sardonic grin. Julia took off before she could do any further damage to herself or her violin.

Chapter 3

Non esser, gioia mia, con me crudele:
lasciati almen veder, mio bell'amore

Don't be cruel, my treasure:
I beg for one glance, my beloved.

Mozart, *Don Giovanni*, Act II

ON HER WAY to the women's locker room, Julia passed Abel's dressing room, where the *Maestro Trudeau - Do Not Disturb* sign was posted on the door. She felt a little flutter of excitement and glanced at her watch.

Fifteen minutes, and he'll give the downbeat for my first performance.

Even with the door closed, she could easily distinguish the raised voices from behind the closed door as Abel's and Sidney's.

"You son of a bitch!"

"For God's sake, Sidney, keep it down."

"You said you'd leave her out of it!"

Abel lowered his voice. "I had no choice."

"Over my dead body."

Julia couldn't fathom what caused the personality conflict between the hotheaded Sidney and the self-assured music director. It made her uncomfortable.

They're only the two most important men in my life.

Sid continued at top volume. "If I find out you've done something stupid, I'll...I'll write a whole new finale to your opening night!"

"The trouble with you, Sidney, is you think you're too damned important." The contempt in the maestro's voice distressed Julia. "No one is indispensable around here. Now get the hell out of my dressing room. We've got a show to do."

A whole new finale—what does that mean?

The booming sound of the P.A. system made Julia jump.

"Curtain for *Don Carlo* in fifteen minutes."

She took a tense breath and let it out with a sigh of relief as the door opened. Sidney stormed out of the dressing room, slamming the door behind him, and ran right into her.

"How long have you been there?"

His dark tone alarmed her. "You know I get concerned when you and Abel—"

"Who are you, my mother?"

"What's going on, Sid? Why were you going at it again?"

"Since when do you answer a question with a question?"

"Since I'm Jewish." Julia tried to charm him with a smile, but his expression remained grim. "Can't you two just call a truce already? Please?"

His rage softened. "Look, kid, it's what parents do."

"But it's so distressing." She attempted a smile. "You're acting like a jerk."

Won over, he returned the smile, until Tony disrupted their caring moment.

"Time's getting short 'til curtain." Tony tapped his baton against his palm in short, tense gestures. "You two better hustle."

Sidney glared at Tony. "Don't you ever get tired of ordering people around, Rossi?"

As Sidney turned to walk away, Julia turned and saw Charles Tremaine appear, balancing a full cup of coffee in each hand.

"Coffee, *Maestro?*"

Julia knew Sid had never picked up a baton, but she tried not to stare at the movie-star looks of the tenor understudy, who had a tendency to hang out with musicians and stagehands. According to rumors, he did this to fend off his own bitterness at constantly being passed over for big roles despite having more talent in his left thumb than tenor star Giuseppe had in his entire body. Julia sympathized with Charles's plight, but she couldn't understand why he blamed Abel for his own lack of recognition in the opera world. Still, eavesdropping on Charles and Sidney's conversation helped Julia endure Tony's scolding.

"It's an understudy's duty to provide overworked musicians with their 'fix.'"

"Right, that's all I need, Charlie. Something to make me even more hyper." Nonetheless, Sidney took the cup and gulped it down.

"And don't worry about paying me back. I'll think of something." Charles's grin made Julia's heart quiver, but she kept nodding at Tony.

Sidney scowled at Charles. "And don't call me 'Maestro.' I'm no conductor."

"It's a term of endearment." Charles flashed his best Rat Pack smirk.

Julia suppressed a smile. She, too, felt the term "maestro" should be reserved for conductors, the great ones at that. But she couldn't help thinking Charles's misuse of the phrase was apt. Sidney's strong opinions on everything gave him an air of authority.

The door to the maestro's dressing room opened. "Julia, come in please."

Abel did not look at the others. They all stood still, caught off guard by his unexpected appearance. Tony walked off, miffed. The rest of them continued their conversation as if nothing had happened. Julia walked into Abel's dressing room, and the door closed behind her.

Chapter 4

Zdes chto-nibud ne tak!
Yevo ochei bluzhdane sulit ne dobroe

There's something wrong here!
The wild look in his eye bodes nothing good.

Tchaikovsky, *Pique Dame*, Act II

In the intimacy of Abel's world, arguments and overbearing orchestra personnel managers were easy to forget. Julia gazed at the beautiful marble chess set the maestro always kept on a low glass table near the door. As usual, a game was in progress. She knew he expected her opinion and studied the board only a second or two.

"*Rook* C-5, C-7."

Abel picked up the black King's rook, positioned it two rows away and removed a white pawn. "Your powers of observation are as keen as ever, Julia."

Julia's father Sol had taught her to play chess when she was five. Like Sol, Abel was a true renaissance man, gifted in both music and chess, and also found time to pursue his hobby of amateur photography. Julia's admiration for him was limitless.

"Maestro, I was wondering…about you and Sidney—"

He waved away her concern. "I called you in for a more important reason."

Abel checked the door to make sure it was shut. Then he regarded Julia, his expression both serious and pleased.

"Mental acuity aside, your playing during the pre-season has been outstanding. I have every confidence you will be the Met's number one violinist someday, our concertmaster." He paused and lowered his voice. "Your father would be so proud."

She bit her lip to maintain her composure. "Thank you, Maestro."

Abel plucked a small box from his desk. "A modest gift, for your debut. May it give you what you need, for this memorable night, and for many more."

Julia was overwhelmed. She felt as thrilled as Sophie when she received the silver rose from Octavian in Act II of *Der Rosenkavalier*. Accepting the box with a trembling hand, she managed to find her voice after a brief speechless moment.

"I...I don't know what to say. It's just...I'm so...so flattered."

Abel motioned to her to open the box. Hands shaking, she lifted off the cover. Tucked inside was an elegant, beautifully wrought pin in the shape of a violin, enameled in bold colors and outlined subtly in gold, nestled in delicate tissue paper.

She gasped, awestruck. "It's...it's stunning."

His smile made her heart sing. He lifted a folder from its perch on the piano and handed it to her. She read the cover sheet. *Song to Julia*, by Abel Trudeau. Overwhelmed, Julia struggled to find words.

"Maestro, I don't deserve this."

"But you do. Even if I hadn't promised your father to look after you, I would still consider it an honor."

She fixed her gaze on the page, hearing the music in her head as any musician would. A few scribbled notes at the bottom caught her attention. She looked up at Abel.

"I had to make some last-minute changes. I hope you can read them."

"Of course..." Julia stared downward at the music to avoid his penetrating gaze.

"Just remember, Julia. You're brilliant technically, but you need to bring more of who *you* are to your playing."

"Yes." She looked up, expectant. "But how?"

"Just think about it. We'll talk more next time."

"Then will you also tell me, 'next time', what it means to 'look beyond the notes?'"

Abel smiled. "Yes, Julia. I promise."

Julia hugged the music. "Thank you for the gifts. And for being my mentor."

Abel returned her gaze. At that moment, Patricia, her icy beauty emphasized by the dazzling diamonds in her ears and at her throat, waltzed in.

"Corrupting minors, Abel?"

Julia felt herself blush. Gathering up the box, the music and her violin case, she thanked Abel once again and hurried away, her eyes sparkling as brightly as Patricia's diamonds. In spite of her embarrassment, Julia still felt elated.

Whatever Patricia thinks about me, or my relationship with the maestro, this is my special moment, and neither she nor anyone else can spoil it.

଼ଠଓଷ

"Is knocking not in your job description, Patricia?"

She dismissed his query with a wave of her bejeweled hand. "I certainly don't think bickering at full volume with orchestra musicians is in yours."

Patricia poised herself atop his desk, crossed her legs, and adjusted her carefully coiffed hair. She narrowed her eyes at Abel, a signal to him that she expected his agreement.

"If you're referring to Sidney, he's my problem. I'll keep him in line. Now if you'll excuse me, I have to warm up."

The maestro sat down at the grand piano and began tinkling the keys with assurance. Patricia didn't budge but remained silent. Ignoring her, he played on, running through his arpeggios with an ease that would make any novice pianist weep.

After a time he spoke. "Do you want something else, Patricia?"

She replied evenly. "You've told me before that you had him under control."

"I do have him under control."

"Then why were you heard all the way down the hall, arguing before a performance, with the orchestra and stagehands milling about… is *that* controlled?"

"Stop worrying."

"Oh, but I do worry." She pulled a monogrammed silver cigarette case and matching lighter from her purse. "I worry very much. Especially about you."

"If you're referring to the latest missive from my 'mystery non-admirer'…," he hesitated, frowning. "*that's* not your problem, Ms. General Manager."

He shot a venomous glance at the cigarette and lighter. She returned the items to her bag with an elegant flick of the wrist. "Oh? I beg to differ, *Maestro*."

"Excuse me, Maestro. Ms. Wells."

Patricia looked up to see Abel's valet, a handsome dark-haired young man named Damon, enter from the bathroom toward the back of the suite carrying a neatly pressed tuxedo jacket. She raised her eyebrows and slid off the desk. "But I see you're in good hands. And in case we don't see each other later, *merde*, darling. Or should I say, '*in bocca al lupo?*'" She glanced at the valet and flashed a provocative smile. "He's cute. We should share him."

೮ಅ

Patricia didn't need to see Abel's grimace follow her as she swept out of the room, closing the door behind her. Once outside the forbidden zone, she pulled cigarette and lighter from her bag and lit the cigarette. With a toss of her head, she made her way down the empty hallway followed by a wisp of smoke, her heels clicking on the slickly polished concrete floor.

Chapter 5

È aperto a tutti quanti…
siam grati a tanti segni di generosità

A welcome to you all…
we thank you for your generous greeting

Mozart, *Don Giovanni*, Act I

THE WOMEN'S LOCKER ROOM was Julia's oasis. A spacious, well-lit carpeted room with rows of lockers, mirrors, and overstuffed sofas, it was a safe haven from the bare concrete floors, sterile fluorescent lighting and overall cacophony of the rest of pit level.

In spite of the female musicians changing clothes, adjusting their makeup and chatting together, the space was relatively tranquil. Tony allowed his female musicians to add a touch of white to their all-black dress code as a way to avoid disgruntlement in the ranks. Julia preferred to stay monochromatic, at least for her first year. Her black silk blouse and close-fitting velvet pants were neat and elegant enough for the pit, and she kept several other tops and a black dress in reserve in her locker.

Julia placed her violin case on the bench in front of her locker, then perched herself on a sofa in a quiet corner away from prying eyes. She got along well enough with the women to work in concert, but was not willing to share such a private moment.

Opening the box Abel had given her, she gazed again at the pin.

Easily visible but not ostentatious—how typical of Abel's impeccable taste.

She fastened the pin carefully to her blouse, noting with pleasure that its gold outline matched the delicate gold "*J*" pendant she always wore at her throat. Then she looked over the sheet music, breathless with wonder, her eager eyes drinking in the notes, excited at the thought of playing through the piece and savoring its content.

A song, for me! How will I ever find a way to thank Abel for this honor?

She noticed at the top of the page a note: *Page 1 of 2.* But when she turned the page, she was puzzled to find page two missing. She was too excited to let this bother her.

I'll just have to ask him—next time.

Julia gathered up her treasures, took a moment to admire the pin in her little hanging mirror, then arranged her hair and makeup and adjusted the belt on her velvet pants. She was scrupulous about her appearance, especially in the orchestra pit. Despite the advice of the more experienced women musicians, she had never felt a need or desire to wear makeup but allowed herself a little mascara and lipstick.

She placed Abel's song in the zippered compartment on the outside of her violin case, alongside her libretto for *Tosca*. She was committed to learning all the words to all the operas in that season's repertoire, and having a libretto always on hand assured her of an opportunity to study, in case she had an extra minute or two. Then she headed out the door and toward the pit, ready for anything.

ഇരുൽ

Julia negotiated the path through the tangle of chairs and music stands crammed into the pit and passed by Abel's conducting podium. Noticing his baton positioned at the top of his musical score was a bit askew, she stopped and adjusted the baton so it was straight and perfectly centered. Satisfied with her deed, she continued on to her chair in the first violin section, taking a deep breath to quell her butterflies.

She opened her violin case, glanced briefly at the photo of herself at age ten with her dad, and bowed her head in reverence. Then, sighing, she extracted her violin and bow and started to warm up on the most difficult passage in the first act of *Don Carlo*, determined to perform it with the perfection Abel demanded. The pit began to fill up with other musicians, who all took their seats and started to warm up as well. Soon every chair in the pit was occupied, except the one next to Julia. She paused her warm-up, frowning at Sidney's absence.

With a dejected sigh, Julia extracted a sugar-free candy from her purse, unwrapped it and popped it into her mouth. This was her main method of relieving tension. She rationalized it as not as bad a habit as smoking, or "emotional eating," as Met people referred to the habit of chomping on a Danish during intermissions.

The candy melted, but Sid did not appear. Julia placed her violin and bow in the case with great care, got up and headed for the hallway to look for him. She was so distracted she dropped the candy wrapper on the floor, a gesture that under ordinary circumstances would have gone against her fastidious nature. But when it came to her dear friend, her feelings took priority.

Sid isn't here, and I need to find out why.

Chapter 6

Un nobile esempio è il vostro…
Al cielo attingete dell'arte il magistero che la fede ravviva!

It is a noble example you give…
You draw from heaven the mastery of art to revive
the faith of men.

Puccini, *Tosca*, Act I

"Eight minutes to curtain for act one of *Don Carlo*. This is your eight minute call, ladies and gentlemen."

Disregarding the P.A. system's urgent call, Julia looked around and was relieved to see Sidney coming from the direction of the men's locker room. She hurried to him, concerned about his haggard face and agitated expression.

"Are you okay, Sid? You don't look too well."

"Yeah. Just my diverticulitis kicking up again."

"Oh, no." Julia's anxiety escalated when she spied Tony striding toward them. "Are you going to be able to make it through the performance?" she asked.

"I hope so, kid."

"Wandering around the hall when the show's about to start?" Tony came out of nowhere to scold Julia, his eyebrows arched. You may be Abel's favorite, but in the pit I'm your boss. Remember?"

"I'm sorry, Tony. I was just worried about Si—"

Tony waved away her protest. Anxious to avoid another confrontation, Julia flashed him the most ingenuous smile she could muster and hurried off to the pit, leaving Tony grumbling.

೮೦೮ಃ

"She thinks that attitude will work with me? She's a piece of work," Tony snapped.

"She's an artist, Rossi, get off her case."

The disembodied voice living in the P.A. system interrupted Sidney's invective. "Five minutes. Orchestra to the pit, please."

Tony raised an eyebrow. "What are you standing there for?"

"Up yours, man." Sidney grumbled under his breath.

Tony's annoyed tone turned menacing. "What'd you say?"

"I said it must be tough because we have talent and you have squat."

Snarling, Sid strode into the pit, leaving Tony shaking his head in exasperation.

₧‘’

When he arrived, panting, at his chair next to hers, Sidney found Julia struggling with her tuning pegs, candy wrappers at her feet.

"You shouldn't let Rossi get you so upset, Julia."

"It's not *him*, it's *you* I worry about. All this arguing with Abel couldn't be helping your health."

"There's nothing you can do about it. Let it go."

He reached for her violin. "Here, let me fix that. When are you gonna get new pegs that work?"

"When you stop nagging me about the old ones."

Julia's magnificent 1720s violin had one flaw: ill-fitting pegs. But she was not about to make any changes in the instrument her father had bought for her, so she endured the inconvenience. Sidney, always ready to help, made the appropriate adjustment with a few quick movements and handed the violin back to her.

"What would I do without you, Sid?"

"Forget it. Just get off my case about Abel."

Sidney opened his violin case. Julia peered at the photo displayed inside of a rotund, smiling couple, inscribed in Russian cyrillic script: "Come home to Odessa soon, Shepsel. Love, Mom and Dad."

"How come you never go back? Don't you miss them?"

Sidney did not respond, merely grabbed his violin and bow and snapped the case shut while Julia tried to swallow her uneasiness. The concertmaster, Daniel, ascended the podium to tune the orchestra, interrupting the uncomfortable silence between Julia and Sidney.

Julia always paid close attention to Daniel, the first violinist and concertmaster, whose role in the orchestra was of prime importance. A key player, he was responsible for leading when the conductor was occupied with happenings on stage, or in the case of a "train wreck" type disaster in the orchestra or with the singers. In observing the concertmaster, Julia was also practicing for her future.

After a brief moment of tuning, Julia and Sidney looked at each other, knowing they couldn't stay angry, and clicked the bottom ends of their violin bows together in a grinning wish for good luck. This was their pre-performance ritual, developed during pre-season rehearsals and dress rehearsals. No one in the orchestra could duplicate it.

"Here goes, Sid."

As the house lights dimmed, Julia watched the famed crystal chandeliers ascend to the ceiling of the cavernous opera house. The glorious moment of her Met orchestra debut had arrived, and it was impossible to contain her excitement. But the butterflies in her stomach shifted to her throat when she saw Tony coming toward her once more.

She groaned. "What have I done now?"

"Last minute change. Third chair just went home sick. Move up."

Julia peered at the front of the first violin section, panicked. "What? Me, one row away from Abel? But I can't—"

"Evidently he thinks you can. Get going, it's almost curtain."

As a neophyte, it was normal for to Julia to be placed toward the back of the section. She aspired to moving up in the ranks gradually, but she never expected to be chosen to replace a key player on her very first night. She had no choice but to obey. Overcome with trepidation, she rose, reached for her violin case, and followed Tony to the front of the first violin section, trying to avoid the resentful stares from the other violinists she passed on the way. Julia glanced back at Sid, who flashed her a "you can do it, kid" grin. Then she took her new position and focused on the work at hand.

This is definitely turning out to be an opening night to remember.

Chapter 7

Die Hoffnung schon erfüllt die Brust,
mit unaussprechlich süsser Lust

Hope already fills my breast
with inexpressibly sweet delight…

Beethoven, *Fidelio*, Act I

"CONDUCTOR'S CUE, EVERYONE."
The stage manager announced his orders from his microphone at stage right just as Patricia stationed herself in the position reserved for the person who ran the show. Moments later Tony ushered Abel into the pit. The audience burst into thunderous applause as the maestro mounted the podium. Motioning the orchestra to rise, Abel turned to the audience, acknowledged them with a gracious bow and turned back to the orchestra. When he noticed his musical score with his baton perfectly in place, he flashed a knowing wink to Julia, who returned the look with a smile and a happy gesture toward her violin pin.

The musicians took their seats. Once the theater became silent, Abel raised his baton, and as the orchestra began to play the Prelude to Act One, the curtain rose. The audience stared, transfixed, at the stage.

Afraid of being distracted by the presence of the audience and the tension surrounding her, and terrified of being anything less than perfect in such an exposed position, Julia had to concentrate extra hard. The poignance of the scene, where sixteenth century French peasants bemoan their hopeless, poverty-stricken existence, was reflected in the aching pull of repeated anguished notes from the stringed instruments. These opening tones tugged at Julia's heart and captured her soul, and before long she became immersed in the depths of the characters' despair. With her emotions now a part of her performance, her nervousness dissipated.

Giuseppe sang the title role of *Don Carlo*, the tragic prince whose father, King Philip of Spain, steals away Carlo's intended, Elisabetta, to be his queen. Carlo never gets over losing her, even when his closest friend, Rodrigo, urges him on to the nobler endeavor of liberating the Flemish people from Philip's tyrannical rule. Eventually Philip conspires with the Grand Inquisitor, who suspects Rodrigo and Carlo of plotting to incite a Flemish riot, to kill both Rodrigo and Carlo. But the strange and mystical intervention of the ghost of Carlo's ancestor, Carlo *Quinto*, saves Carlo from that fate.

The scene that takes place in a medieval Spanish monastery was Julia's favorite. Its opening unison French horn melody accompanying a backstage male chorus had a haunting quality. She waited for her next entrance mesmerized by the sound of the horns, immersing herself in the mournful music. While Giuseppe was making his entrance, however, she spied Charles watching Giuseppe from the backstage wings.

Am I just imagining resentment in his eyes? Well, I can't blame him.

Julia had heard Charles's lush, sensuous voice and exquisite phrasing when he filled in for missing tenors in rehearsals. She was convinced Charles deserved to be seen and heard in performance, but it didn't look as if he would get his chance anytime soon. Giuseppe was too powerful a presence, too protective of his territory at the Met.

"*Al chiostro di San Giusto, ovè fini la vita l'avo mio Carlo Quinto.*" Giuseppe sang with all the soul he could muster.

"*At the monastery of San Giusto, where my ancestor Charles V finished out his life.*" Julia repeated silently to herself, ever conscious of the libretto she had studied.

Julia was as meticulous about knowing the intimate details of every opera plot as she was about her personal appearance. After hours of rehearsing and studying the libretto on her own, she had committed most of the dialogue to memory. The music was sublime, full of rich, sensuous tones and exhilarating drama. Julia poured her entire being into her performance, anxious to fulfill her adored mentor's expectations. By the time the company was deep into Act Three several hours later, in the prison scene, Julia's energies had flagged, but her admiration for both Verdi and Abel had not.

How does Abel do this night after night? Does he take some magical potion to keep his physical and mental strength up? Or is he just super-human?

Julia was not surprised at this point to hear a shuffling sound several rows behind her. Taking her eyes off the music for a brief instant, Julia glanced back with anxiety as Sidney, clutching his stomach with a wince, got up and left the pit. She couldn't blame him. Five hours of performance was grueling under any circumstances.

But for someone with Sid's condition, it must be unbearable.

ଧ୦ଓଃ

The viewing room was the exclusive domain of directors, set designers, and other company members who were not needed either onstage or backstage during performances. Perched in the highest reaches of the theater, these upper-management non-performers observed the onstage spectacle in complete privacy, either for critical purposes or just for their own entertainment. The sliding glass windows at the front of the room allowed a bird's-eye view of the stage and theater but were built so that outsiders could not easily see inside.

This opening night, the viewing room was closed for repairs and off-limits for everybody, making it easy for the shadowy figure to break the padlock during the third act without being seen or heard, unfold a VAL Russian Sniper rifle, poke it through the sliding window, and aim it toward the pit.

ଧ୦ଓଃ

Julia always had to gird herself for the moment in the story when Don Carlo's best friend Rodrigo comes to warn him of a dangerous plot against Carlo's life. An assassin wielding a medieval rifle called an *arquebus* moves stealthily onstage to fire at Rodrigo, just as Rodrigo sings the words, *"ed io morire per te –* and I to die for you." Rodrigo falls to the floor wounded mortally, and Carlo rushes to him. The dramatic and powerful moment always caused Abel's impassioned conducting gestures to increase in urgency and intensity. As much as she felt for Sidney, Julia snapped to attention when she realized it was time for the gunshot heralding the assassination of the baritone's character onstage.

The first time the shot was fired onstage, during rehearsal, Julia had gasped, startled. Worse, she'd missed several notes while she recovered.

"Why do they make it so loud?" she'd asked Matt one day during rehearsal break.

"The decibel level of stage rifles is impossible to control. You never know how loud it's going to be. It's just the nature of the beast." He'd grinned. "At least they're shooting with blanks. Imagine the uproar if they used real ones, especially from the insurance company."

Armed with this knowledge, Julia prepared herself in advance for the shock. But as she steeled for this one, she thought she saw a glint of something metallic from high atop the Family Circle, or the "nose-bleed seats," as they were known amongst patrons. For a brief moment, her eyes darted up into the far reaches of the theater. Worried about losing her place, she went back to her music, and when the crack of the rifle came a moment later, it sounded twice as loud as usual, and she reeled from the blast. But her discomfort turned to terror when she looked up at Abel and saw him slumped over the podium, blood trickling down his neck.

༄✿༄

The disoriented musicians stopped playing one by one; a stunned silence pervaded the theater. Patrons who were not close enough to see that Abel was bleeding looked about, wondering what had happened, whispering to each other. The first to comprehend was the concertmaster, who leapt up from his chair and stared at Abel.

Julia didn't know what was going on, only that Abel was in trouble. Thrusting her violin aside, she jumped up and rushed to him, gaping at the blood gushing from a wound in his neck. Horrified, she touched him for the first—and last—time.

"Oh no! Abel – *Abel?*"

Abel toppled to the floor. A woman in the first row of the audience screamed, realizing at last what was occurring directly in front of her. Julia gasped and cried out. She looked around pleadingly, then placed her hands on Abel's neck to stanch the gushing blood.

"Someone call an ambulance! Get help! Please!"

Instantly, the pit was thrown into utter pandemonium. A cellist screeched in terror. Musicians, some comprehending that Abel had been shot, others reacting to the fear that the opera house might be under terrorist attack, jumped up from their chairs and fled from the pit, clutching their instruments.

ഏരു

At first the patrons in the audience stood up in bewilderment. Then a man cried, "Terrorists!"

Someone else shouted him down. "Calm down, people. Don't panic!"

But the audience did panic, believing themselves under terrorist assault. They ran for the exits, screaming. Ushers tried frantically to calm them and stop the mad rush—all in vain.

Unlike her colleagues, most of whom had by this time escaped the pit, Julia just knelt beside Abel, cradling his head in her lap. She stared at him in disbelief until a security guard rushed to her side and tugged at her arm.

"Please, Miss. It's not safe."

She clung to her mentor, shouting at the guard. "No! No! I'm not leaving him!" The blood spouting through her fingers slowed to a trickle.

But the guard, far stronger than Julia, pulled her away. "It's too dangerous, Miss, you have to come with me. Here ..."

He offered her his handkerchief to wipe the bloodstains from her hands. She waved him away, dazed beyond reason, looking back at Abel. She knew he was dead.

How could this happen? How?

The house doctor and EMS personnel entered the pit just as Julia managed one last fleeting glance at her adored maestro. She later wished she had been able to keep something, anything belonging to him, like his baton, or his musical score. But it was just as well she hadn't, for his baton had been shattered beyond recognition. And Abel's musical score, which Julia had glimpsed for a brief moment while the guard was tugging her away from the scene, was still opened on the podium, with Verdi's masterful notes bloodstained. Her mind was forever imprinted with the image of her beloved *Don Carlo* tinged with the crimson blood that had flowed from her beloved fallen maestro and mentor, Abel Trudeau.

Chapter 8

Mal qual mai s'offre, oh Dei, spettacolo funesto agli occhi miei!...
Ah! l'assassino mel trucidò.

Quel sangue...quella piaga...quel volto...
tinto e coperto dei color di morte...
Ei non respira più...fredde ha le membra...

But, oh God, what dreadful sight confronts my eyes!...
Ah! The assassin has struck him down!

This blood...this wound...
his face discolored with the pallor of death...
He's not breathing anymore...his limbs are so cold...

Mozart, *Don Giovanni*, Act I

THE BENUMBED, SHOCKED group of orchestra members sat in silence in the orchestra lounge after the police arrived. Some musicians lay prostrate on the sofas and cushioned benches positioned around the large carpeted room. Some paced, while others poured themselves cup after cup of spring water from the cooler near the entrance, slaking their anxiety-driven thirst. They whispered about Abel, and about whomever the next maestro might be.

Julia, paralyzed with grief, sat on a sofa in a far-off in a corner, barely aware of Sidney at her side. She ran through the events of the evening in her mind again and again, until she realized she had been wrong about not having anything of Abel's. She had the violin pin and the song, the offerings he had bestowed upon her before the performance.

I'll never have the gift of his nurturing and caring again. I'll never know what he meant by "look beyond the notes." I'll never find out what was on the missing page...

She held back a sob, refusing to give in to the emotions threatening to make her break down in tears.

"Next time," he said. But now there won't be a next time, nothing but memories.

It was all gone, lost to her, disintegrated into nothingness as surely as the breath had departed from Abel's body.

Meanwhile, Sidney was trying to comfort a completely desolate Julia. He couldn't squeeze her shoulder or give her a supportive hug; he knew she never allowed anyone to touch her. He could only gaze at Julia with sympathy, and use his most soothing voice. "I know you loved him, kid."

Julia nodded. She tried to speak, but her sobs caught in her throat. "Shh, don't talk. Just let it all out, if that's what you feel like."

She shook her head, choosing instead to grit her teeth and dig her thumbnail into her palm.

೮ುಯ

Patricia appeared at the doorway of the lounge and looked around the room. Tony followed her in. She murmured to him in a low voice.

"How are the musicians reacting to the events of the evening, Tony?"

"How do you think, Patricia? They're in shock." Tony noticed Patricia's look of annoyance. "Unlike you, who seem to be taking this all in stride."

"Oh?" Patricia flashed him an irritated look. "Well, I'm not. Not at all. Reporters are clamoring to get inside the house and question me. And those two obnoxious detectives from the Twentieth Precinct are already making my life miserable. They want a list of all the personnel in the opera house, hundreds of employees. Musicians, choristers, stagehands, wardrobe people and dancers. It's unconscionable."

"It's their job. How hard could it be to get a computerized list?"

"Even so, it's still a royal pain in the ass to obtain. Computers notwithstanding, who has time for such things? Impossible." She sniffed. "As if I didn't already have my hands full, trying to calm down my stars and placate the board members. Did you know they're on the verge of canceling the entire week's performances?"

Tony shrugged. "That's no surprise."

"Well, it's not acceptable, and I am determined to block their initiative. The Met has only cancelled twice. The blizzard of '96 doesn't count."

"Whatever you say, Patricia."

The only times in the history of the Met that shows had been cancelled were when legendary baritone Leonard Warren had collapsed and died onstage back in the sixties, and in '96, when a little-known tenor had keeled over from a heart attack during the first act of *The Makropoulos Affair*. During the blizzard of that year, Mayor Giuliani had closed off the city of New York, but it wasn't the Met that cancelled. Even when a patron had committed suicide by throwing himself off the top of the Family Circle in the middle of a performance of *Macbeth* (though he had been thoughtful enough to wait until the intermission), the show had gone on to its finish, albeit after an extended interval.

"And as for the reporters ..." Patricia shook her head. "I suppose I'll have to allow them in."

Patricia cleared her throat to get the musicians' attention. "The detectives will be here to interview each of you personally in a few minutes." She glanced around, taking note of who showed interest and who did not. "They may want to come back during rehearsals and re-question some of you as well."

ଅଓଓ

Julia turned her face up to Sid and winced. He returned the look.

"Rotten luck. I for one could use a drink right about now. You look like you could, too, kid."

She found her voice but replied haltingly. Yes... But if we have to stay here..."

"Not to worry. Once we're done, we can hightail it across the street. I'll buy."

Nodding gratefully, Julia contemplated getting up but thought better of it. She was still too shaky. She felt torn between her grief and her determination not to let this disastrous turn of events undermine her usual rock-solid exterior.

Now is not the time to let any chinks show in my armor, even to Sid. Julia thought for another moment. Then she spoke hesitantly. "Sid, I meant to ask you, where were you...I mean, when you got up and left the pit?"

"My diverticulitis..."

"Yes, but—"

He grimaced, his face darkening. "What's the matter, you suddenly suspicious of me? You know me better than that, Jul."

"Of course I do, don't be ridiculous." She unclenched her hands and made an apologetic gesture. "I'm just worried that, well...the police don't know you like I do."

"That's not your problem. It's between them and me."

Feeling the sudden need to throw some water over her face, Julia rose with some effort, moved toward the doorway and faced Patricia with a weary expression. The general manager feigned concern.

"You look upset, Julia. Anything I can do?"

Julia answered in a soft voice. "Actually, I need to go to the ladies' room."

Patricia nodded her agreement and watched the young violinist move with slow steps past her and through the door, her eyes never leaving Julia's velvet-clad ass.

Chapter 9

Il duolo estremo la meschinella uccide…

Her great sorrow has killed the poor girl!

Mozart, *Don Giovanni*, Act I

NYPD DETECTIVES AL Cummings and Buddy Cruse snaked their way through a swarm of officers who held back the mob of patrons in the Met lobby. They followed the medical examiner, along with a plainclothes officer with his camera and two uniformed officers, into the orchestra pit. Abel's body lay on the floor by the podium, where the police photographer began his task. The M.E. studied the gunshot wound.

"Shot from behind, high angle. Can't be sure yet, but I'd check the balconies."

Al whistled. "Whew. Perp must' a been one helluva a shot."

"If the perp was actually aiming at Trudeau," his younger partner opined.

"Who else could he have been aiming at?"

Buddy shrugged. "You never know."

৪৩০৪

Backstage, traumatized company members wandered about, speaking in anxious whispers or chattering nervously. The only calm demeanor in the vicinity was that of Giuseppe's understudy, Charles Tremaine.

When the gaggle of reporters found him, Charles was in a huddle with Frank Bernini, assistant to head stagehand Matt Reynolds. Frank was older than Matt and nowhere near as affable. His unmistakable rough Bensonhurst accent and gruff manner put off most people, Julia included. He had a tendency to belittle the musicians, whom he considered the undeserving spoiled brats of the opera house hierarchy. Julia was happy to keep her encounters with him to a minimum.

She felt sure this attitude would lead to some confrontation between them at some point, as—unfortunately—the musicians had occasion to ask for a stagehand's help. She couldn't afford to ignore him completely.

She had also noticed Frank and Charles huddled together on numerous other occasions, sometimes gabbing in full view of others but usually whispering off in a corner of an out-of-the-way hallway or corridor. Julia couldn't fathom what the handsome, talented, and very patrician tenor had in common with a plebeian like Frank, but she supposed the stagehand lent a sympathetic ear to Charles's gripes about Abel, and probably about Patricia, too.

Having just consoled a shell-shocked soprano, Charles now took it upon himself to be the self-possessed representative to the press who had been allowed inside the opera house and were clamoring for information. Julia watched as Charles fielded the reporters' questions.

"Were you backstage when it happened, Mr. Tremaine?" asked one from the *New York News*.

"Would you care to make a statement?" queried another from the *Daily Sentinel*.

"Yes, I would." Charles looked poised and self-assured. "The Met has suffered an incalculable loss in Abel Trudeau. This event has saddened all of us deeply. Its shock-waves will reverberate in New York's cultural community for years to come."

The reporters, evidently impressed with Charles's unruffled exterior, continued to compete for his attention. He smiled sadly and carried on like the trooper he was. He'd been waiting month after frustrating month as an understudy for his chance, his moment in the limelight. Now it had finally come, and Julia had the feeling he was going to revel in it no matter how horrific the event that had provided the opportunity.

ഇരുന

Al and Buddy, leaving the M.E. to his work, pushed their way through the masses of NYPD cops who clogged the hallways and into the lobby. Officers were having a difficult time managing impatient crowds of frightened, irate patrons and helpless ushers who were milling about in mass confusion. The officers formed a barricade across the glass exit doors leading outside to Lincoln Center Plaza, preventing the patrons—the witnesses—from leaving.

Al asked around, found out who the head usher was and approached him. He had to shout to be heard above the din. "What time did people start to arrive this evening?"

The usher, William, shouted back. "These doors open a half-hour before curtain. But people enter from the stage door at all hours."

Al grimaced. "That's a load of help."

A matronly woman rushed up to Al and Buddy, her face red in annoyance. "When are we going to be allowed to leave?" she bellowed in tones of outrage. "My chauffeur is waiting."

"Then you might have to give him a raise, Ma'am. This may be the longest opening night in Met history," Al informed her.

"Not as long as the last act of *Die Meistersinger*, if you know what I mean," offered William.

"Huh?" Al glared at him, waiting for an explanation.

William sighed. "I was referring to the lengthy Wagner opera with a third act as long as the first two acts combined. Close to six hours total."

"Right. Whatever," said Buddy.

The woman strode away. Al turned back to William and noticed Buddy pop a piece of chewing gum in his mouth. Even in the gravity of the situation, Al couldn't suppress a wisp of a smile. Buddy, the most orally fixated kid Al had ever seen, was always chomping on something. Sometimes this habit irritated Al, but in general he found it amusing and somewhat endearing. Once well into his chewing, Buddy proceeded to grill William.

"Which usher was stationed in the balcony?"

"You mean, 'Family Circle'?" William regarded Buddy and Al with mild disdain. "That would be Sergei."

William pointed out a nervous-looking young man standing in a corner. Al thought for a moment.

"Sergei. Isn't that... a *Russian* name?"

"Yes, he's our token Russian Mafia member." Al and Buddy's collective glare told William his quip was not appreciated. "Just a joke. He's new, so he gets to deal with the 'peanut gallery', the Family Circle."

Al and Buddy walked over to the novice usher and took him by the arm. "How would you like to show us to the Family Circle?" Al asked, making an effort to be polite. The police department was getting flak these days for being disrespectful to suspects.

Sergei led them through the lobby to the interior, where they took the elevator up several levels. The mile-high Family Circle, Al and Buddy noticed, was cramped, the seats close together.

"I tell you, this is for me first night," Sergei's accent was heavy, and the detectives had to pay close attention to his words. "I do not notice anyone enter after curtain is up."

"Get real, how could that be?" Buddy unwrapped another stick of gum.

"Giuseppe Masini, great tenor, when he sing, nothing else important."

Al flashed Buddy a smirk. "Any true opera aficionado would agree with that, right?"

Al took in the sight of the immense theater surrounding him and eventually looked up toward the pinnacle of the seemingly infinite expanse of ceiling. There he noticed a large cubicle, so high up it looked suspended in air. In spite of its panel of clear glass windows in the front, the booth looked intimate and apart from the rest of the theater. "What's up there, Sergei?" he asked, pointing to it.

"Viewing room, for company officials to watch operas. But is closed for renovation since for several weeks."

"We'll see about that." Al turned to Buddy. "Got any more of that gum?"

Taking Sergei by the arm once more, Al nodded his head in the direction of the viewing room. The usher let out a deep breath and led on.

༄༅

The first thing Al noticed about the viewing room was that the lock on the door had been clipped off. "So much for renovations." He turned to Sergei. "Who has access to this place while it's closed?"

"Only construction workers and stagehands."

The two detectives donned surgical gloves. Buddy inspected the broken lock on the door.

Al motioned to Sergei to wait just outside the door, entered the viewing room with Buddy and examined the floor. They proceeded methodically around the perimeter for a few minutes, the room silent except for the occasional pop of Buddy's gum. A glint Al spied from something stuck in a crack in the uncarpeted floor sent him kneeling to get a closer look. He picked it up gingerly. "VAL Silent Sniper."

Al had been first in his Police Academy class in ammunition recognition. Not only was he adept at determining a type of ammunition from the casing, he was also well versed in identifying the more uncommon varieties. "Pretty sophisticated weaponry, very distinctive ammo. Russian, just as I thought." He eyed Sergei. The usher blanched.

Looking up, Buddy eyed the casing. "Perp must' a been in a real hurry, to leave that behind."

"I'd be willing to bet this matches the murder bullet."

Al placed his find in a small plastic bag and pocketed it. "Even so, this perp knew what he was doing." He assessed the extreme distance between the viewing room and the pit. "Trained in the military, special ops, maybe. A real pro."

"Yeah, nothing else here, boss, not even foot scuffs," Buddy said.

"Yeah, the guy knew his way around this opera house for sure. Even knew when the floor'd been dusted."

"But even with a silencer, couldn't someone've heard the rifle discharge?"

"Not nesh…necessar…sarily." Sergei tripped over the word. "There is shot on stage, very loud, then *fortissimo* passage in orchestra right after."

"Let me get this straight." Buddy stopped chewing for a moment. "The guy knew exactly when to shoot so the noise, the loud music, I mean, would cover it up?"

"It's beginning to look that way." Al nodded his agreement. "Now, moving on, Buddy boy, I want you to get names, numbers of everyone who isn't a musician, bartenders, program hawkers, whatever. I'll start interviewing the orchestra."

"I'm on it. I already asked that, uh, manager lady for a list of personnel."

"Good work, kid. Have the crime techs sweep the door for fibers, and for fingerprints, just in case the perp wasn't wearing gloves."

"Prints?" Buddy whipped out his notebook. "With all the other people coming in here?"

"From the looks of it, there hasn't been anyone else here for a while. Maybe we'll get lucky."

Buddy's notebook slipped from his hands. As he stooped to pick it up, a violent sneezing fit overcame him. "Man, it's dusty here. Hard to get prints when it's so covered with grit. Are opera houses always so dusty?"

"Who are you, the EPA?" Al shot back. "Find out who has criminal records, too. I'll start interviewing the orchestra. Got that?"

Buddy seemed to recognize that he was outranked. "Right."

As they made their way out of the room, Al took one last look toward the extreme angle between the viewing room and the distant orchestra pit. "One way or another, it's hard to believe this could be a random hit."

"What makes you say that?"

"Someone went to an awful lot of trouble. Those VAL rifles are not easy to get, and that ammo has to be special ordered."

"Yeah?" Buddy resumed his chewing.

"Yeah. This took planning. Mark my words, Buddy boy. This wasn't the work of some nut loaf out to get his fifteen minutes. It was done by a pro, hired by someone who wanted the maestro dead."

Al paused for an instant's thought, and continued, "No, this wasn't random. This was personal."

Chapter 10

Fia lunga tal notte!

It's going to be a long night!

Verdi, *Rigoletto*, Act III

WHILE BUDDY WENT as instructed to interview stagehands, choristers, and soloists, Al set his sights on the orchestra members. Tony ensconced the detective at a table in the orchestra lounge with a list of personnel. Whipping out his notebook, Al began to interview the musicians one by one.

From what he gathered by asking the orchestra members to describe their duties, they had the least interesting jobs in the opera house. They were like factory workers, grinding out the notes day after day and night after night.

"I just play the trombone."

"I just saw away at the cello."

"Think of me as a plumber. I bring in my tools and do my work, then I go home."

Thus, not one of them had anything of interest to say, until Harold, a violist of unspecified advanced age, sat down. Al sensed Harold had something to tell, but that he'd have to drag it out of the uncooperative musician. He started innocuously enough, by commenting on the way the violist was gnawing on the metal ferule of his pencil.

"Aren't you afraid of breaking a tooth like that?"

"Beats getting TMJ, like our tight-ass concertmaster."

It had never occurred to Al that string players, who spent countless hours with their instruments squeezed under their chins, would encounter teeth-clenching problems. When he thought about it, it made perfect sense that musicians, especially ones working in the Met's high-pressure atmosphere, would be prone to gritting and grinding their teeth to the point it became painful. He restrained his curiosity in order to get down to the business.

"Are you sure you don't know anyone who might have had it in for the maestro?"

Harold shifted with discomfort, hesitating. "Well...okay, if you're looking for clues, go talk to that drug pusher, Sidney."

"You mean..." Al peered down his list and spotted the name under the violinist column. "Sidney Richter?"

"Uh,...yeah, well. He was always fighting with Abel, too. Hated Trudeau's guts, in fact. Everyone knew about it."

"Was the feeling mutual?"

"Yeah. I guess so." Harold lowered his voice. "They almost threw it down once in the men's locker room."

"And how do you know Sidney's a...drug pusher?"

Harold affected an arrogant expression. "I've seen him with sleazy guys. You know, shifty types that hang out in bars."

"But did you ever actually see him selling or buying or using drugs?"

"Well, uh, no." Harold's guard went up. "But it was kinda common knowledge...in certain circles."

Al frowned and penciled a note in his book, then looked again at the list. "And Richter's, um ..." He fumbled over the odd pairing of words. "Stand partner, Julia Kogan?"

"Yeah, he's real thick with her." Harold, suddenly nervous, broke the end off his pencil. "But she's a straight shooter. Just does her job, all business-like, ya' know? If there was one person who didn't know about Sid's, uh...'activities,' it would' a been her."

"Oh?" Raising his eyebrows, Al jotted down the info and waited for Harold to continue.

"She was Trudeau's protégée. Whenever anyone criticized him, she took it personally. She knew all about the problems between him and Sidney." He paused. "But mostly, she just keeps to herself, doesn't trust or rely on anybody. Don't know why. I guess I wouldn't trust anyone either if I had been raised in foster homes."

"I see." Al reflected for a moment but decided it was more important to keep the dialogue focused on Sidney right now than do a character study of Julia Kogan. "Anybody else who might have had it in for Trudeau?"

"Well, there's a lot of back biting around this place, but…I'd talk to Sidney."

"Okay." Al looked up from his writing. "Thanks for your time."

"Don't mention it."

Harold, broadcasting his toothy grin, got up and sauntered away. The next to sit opposite Al was Tony, who fidgeted with his ever-present baton, as though dreading the invasive and personal questions sure to come.

Al stopped writing to look up at him. "Can you show me the closest men's pit stop?"

Tony's face flooded with relief. "Follow me."

ಬಂಞ

Tony watched as Al leaned over a men's room sink, splashed water on his face, and toweled himself dry.

"It's gonna be a long night. Mind if I ask you some questions, since we're here?"

"Shoot." Tony immediately regretted his word selection. "Oh, sorry."

To Tony's relief, Al overlooked the gaffe. "Did you see all the musicians before the show tonight?"

"Sure, it's my job to make sure they're all here."

"And where did you first see Sidney Richter?"

"He was coming out of Abel's dressing room after the last orchestra call. Hopping mad, to say the least."

"Oh?" About what?" Al reached for his notebook.

"Looked like they were having an argument. No surprise. Sid and Abel had a major personality conflict."

"Do you know why?"

Tony shrugged. "They just rubbed each other the wrong way."

"Did you hear their conversation?"

"Not really, it just sounded like shouting behind the dressing room door. But I could definitely make out the word 'sonofabitch.'"

Al paused to write. Then he looked up at Tony. "Anyone else in the orchestra have problems with Abel?"

"Nah, are you kidding? They were all in awe of Abel, me included. The man was a genius. Had the whole music world in the palm of his hand." Tony watched as Al scribbled with a vengeance. "Am I done?"

"Oh…Yes, thanks for cooperating." Al paused. "By the way, where were you when Abel was shot?"

Tony swallowed hard and girded himself. "I was…" He hesitated, then plunged in. "If you must know, I was in Abel's dressing room." Al's sharp look demanded an explanation.

"He had some custom-made batons, I liked to practice my conducting with them." His face reddened. "It made me feel like…a real conductor."

ℭℭ

Al scrutinized Tony's humiliated expression and felt badly for him. It couldn't have been easy for the personnel manager to admit such an intimate detail about his fantasy life. But then again, criminals sometimes confessed to petty crimes to cover up the larger ones.

"I'll take that under advisement for now."

Al headed for the door, realizing he would never find his way back through the maze of hallways. He looked to Tony for help. Nodding his understanding, Tony led Al out of the locker room and back down the hallway. Just as they had reached the lounge, Buddy appeared at the entrance and stepped toward Al, leaning toward his ear. They spoke softly.

"Too many people in this opera house, boss. I've called for backup. You got anything yet?"

They entered the room. "Not much." Al kept his voice low. "How 'bout sitting in on this one?"

He pointed to Sidney's name on the list. Buddy pulled up a chair next to Al's. Al gestured to Tony.

"Send Sidney Richter, over, please."

Tony motioned to Sidney. The violinist grimaced and, taking his time, shuffled over to sit in front of the two detectives, regarding them with a glare.

Out of the corner of his eye, Al noted that a young woman carrying a violin case under one arm had entered the room and now lingered by the water cooler, acting nervous and on edge. When she filled a paper cup with water, he saw that her hand was shaking. He'd be willing to bet she was Julia Kogan, even though he hadn't been introduced to her yet. No doubt she was trying to listen to the exchange between him and Sidney.

Al lost no time in cutting to the chase. "You were heard arguing with Abel before the show. What was that about?"

"We had...artistic differences."

"Like what?"

Sidney narrowed his eyes and frowned. "Like, I personally don't think we should be playing Wagner on Yom Kippur. I wanted him to know."

Al rolled his eyes as Buddy eyed Sidney with suspicion.

"What's so bad about that?" Buddy asked.

"Because Wagner was an anti-Semite. It was his music they played when the Jews marched into the concentration camps." He shot Buddy a scowl. "Want more detail, Mr. Detective?"

Al cut in. "Was that the only thing you were fighting about?"

"Yeah. That's all." Sid grumbled, his expression defiant.

"Were you the only one in the orchestra who had that kind of disagreement with him?"

"I was the one who told him to his face. You got a problem with that?"

"So..." Al ignored Sidney's confrontational tone. "You and Trudeau had personality conflicts, yes?"

"Yeah, so what? It happens. A lot of musicians do battle with the conductor. It doesn't mean they're going to kill him."

"I didn't say anything about that."

"You didn't have to. Your attitude is obvious. Can I go now?"

Al knew his questioning was going nowhere. "Yeah. But stick around, just in case. And maybe you could point out your stand partner, Julia."

Sidney did what he was asked to do, then flashed Al a look of discontent. "She doesn't know anything."

"Oh? How do you know?"

"Why don't you ask Tony-the-*wunderkind*-up-and-coming-Toscanini where *he* was during the murder?"

Before Al could reply, Sidney pushed back his chair and, with a scowl at Buddy, got up and walked over to Julia. Al could see that her hands were still shaking. Sid gently plucked the paper cup from Julia's trembling hand.

"You're next, kid," Al heard Sidney say. "Don't let them get you down. I'll wait for you in the hallway, and we can blow this joint, okay?"

Julia nodded.

Al motioned her toward the chair opposite him and cleared his throat as she carefully positioned the violin case upright by her right arm and held tightly to its upper end. "Was there anything special about your relationship with Abel Trudeau?"

"He was my mentor. I wouldn't be here if it weren't for him."

"Did he ever talk about any enemies, any threats to his life?"

She shook her head, her frayed nerves already starting to show.

"What about Sidney? Are you, ah…close with him?" Al regarded her shrewdly.

"If you mean…physically…" Julia bristled. "It's none of your business."

"I wasn't implying that."

"Oh, weren't you?" Julia's face colored. "If you must know, Sid's like a big brother to me. That's all. Took me under his wing when I first got here. Okay?"

There was an uncomfortable silence as they locked stares.

Buddy got up and motioned to Al. "I gotta go back upstairs. Whaddya' think so far?"

Al murmured in Buddy's ear. "Not much to go on here, except maybe Richter. Didn't believe a word he said."

They exchanged glances of understanding, and Buddy walked off. From Julia's anxious look and the way she was clutching the violin case, Al could tell she was worried about Sid, even if she hadn't been able to hear what he and Buddy had said.

Al cleared his throat again and addressed her in a normal voice. "Abel and Sidney were arguing before the performance. Were you aware of their personality conflicts?"

"Yes. But if you think Sidney—"

"Forget Sidney for the moment. Is there any reason why you might want Abel Trudeau dead?"

Julia quaked with shock. "Are you accusing *me?* For God's sakes, Abel got me this job. Why would I want to do him harm?" Her voice became more agitated. "Look, I know where this is going. First my mentor is murdered, and then you want to accuse my best friend of being involved, and now me."

Julia stood up abruptly, misery etched in her face, spilling the contents of her water cup all over her sweater. She burst into tears. Sensing she was sincere in her distress, Al felt sudden sympathy for her. "We can finish this later, Julia. You can go now."

Without a response, Julia rose, shoved the violin case under her arm and fled the lounge, shaking her head. Abel's last words again echoed in her ears.

"Just think about it. We'll talk more about it next time."

But there wouldn't be a next time. And this was turning out to be the worst night of her life.

Chapter 11

Vissi d'arte, vissi d'amore, non feci mai male ad anima viva!...
Nell'ora del dolore, Perchè Signore, me ne rimuneri così?

I lived for art, I lived for love, I've never harmed a living soul!...
In this hour of suffering, why, oh Lord, do you repay
me this way?

Puccini, *Tosca*, Act II

AT TWO A.M., Julia and Sidney were still sitting at the bar directly across Lincoln Plaza on Broadway. The bar was a favorite haunt of Lincoln Center musicians, though Julia, who was compulsive about her work and made a point of staying away from booze and late-night carousing, was not a regular patron there.

Sidney, however, certainly was, and his frequent hits from his glass of scotch reminded Julia of a needy baby with its familiar bottle. She nursed her own glass with care, not saying much, then turned to her colleague and spoke with slow deliberation to keep herself from breaking down.

"It's my fault he was killed."

"How do you figure *that*?"

Julia turned and gazed at him, her lip quivering. She began fidgeting with the zipper on the violin case, which was leaned upright next to her bar stool. "He was supposed to go on sabbatical to Vienna. I asked him to stay for my first season. He changed his plans for me. I'm responsible for his...his..."

"Don't be so hard on yourself, Jul."

But Julia wasn't listening. "Here I am worrying about myself, when Abel...Oh no!" She cried out suddenly. "Sid! I saw it!"

"Saw what? Julia, you're not making sense."

"Something glinting from the top of the house, like…metal from… a…" She broke down, sobbing. "It could have been a gun, Sid! I could have done something! Oh, my God!…"

"Julia, stop berating yourself. There was nothing you could do. Shh." Sid reached for her but abruptly pulled his hand away as she recoiled oh-so slightly. "Kid, Abel's gone now. But wherever he is now, he'll be watching out for you. All you can do for him is to be the best violinist, the one he wanted you to be."

Accepting Sidney's proffered handkerchief, Julia blew her nose until she became calmer. Then she gazed at Sidney in gratitude. He gave her a reassuring smile.

"He had high hopes for you, kid. And so do I." He took a chance and patted her hand in a comforting gesture. She withdrew her hand with haste. "You shouldn't blame yourself. You idolized him, and he appreciated it more than you know."

"Oh, believe me, I know." She leaned over him and spoke in a confidential tone. "I haven't told you, Sid, but…before the performance, Abel gave me a song he'd written for me."

"A song? What kind of song?"

"It was—"

But she was interrupted by a man - he could only be called sleazy-looking - approaching from the opposite end of the bar. She couldn't keep herself from staring. His five o'clock shadow gave a Cro-Magnon cast to his grizzled features, and he looked as if he had been sleeping in his clothes since 1982. Sidney shot the man a lethal glance, looked briefly at Julia, then back at the interloper. "Not now, Geraldo," he hissed.

Geraldo grimaced. "But we need to talk about—"

Sidney cut him off, his tone menacing. "We need to talk about *nada*. Now beat it. And leave the girl alone."

He waved Geraldo away. But as Geraldo turned on his heel, muttering under his breath, Sid leaned over to him and murmured something.

That little exchange went sailing over Julia's muddled head. Watching Geraldo slink away, she turned to Sidney and grabbed his arm.

"Who was that?"

Sidney dismissed her concern with a wave of his hand. "Sometimes I give him a handout. Now he thinks I owe him every time he sees me." He paused, looking at her with a furrowed brow. "But you look beat, kid. I think I'd better get you home now."

"You're right."

It was 3:00 a.m., and Julia suddenly felt as exhausted as a bag lady limping across Broadway. She wanted to sleep, very badly. In a daze, she followed Sidney out of the bar and stood without saying a word, clutching her violin case under her arm, as he hailed a cab. Julia knew better than to protest. She was capable of walking the few blocks to her apartment without a problem, but decided to accept Sidney's offer to drop her there.

When they arrived at her building, Sidney asked if she wanted him to stay with her awhile.

"Thanks, Sid, but I…I need to be alone."

Nodding in sympathy, Sidney gave the cabbie an address. Julia watched as they took off. Then she let herself into the entrance and mounted the stairs to her abode, the weight of sorrow pressing down on her slim shoulders.

ဆာလ

Julia entered her tidy bedroom, laid the violin case on the bed, opened the outside zippered compartment, extracted Abel's song and placed it on her music stand. Regarding the music with profound sadness, she pulled out her violin and bow and tuned. Slowly, she started to play the music, fighting back tears. After a few notes, however, she found herself unable to control her weeping. Overwrought, she placed the violin back in the case, too paralyzed with grief to remember to close it, and set the case and the music on the floor.

Collapsing onto her bed, she turned toward her nightstand, reached for a delicate music box and opened it. An engraving on the inside cover read: "Love always, Dad." Tears welled up again as the familiar, graceful melody wafted from the box. *The Anniversary Waltz* was the tune her parents had danced to on their wedding night.

With a mournful shake of her head, she thought of her mom and dad, both of whom were beginning to fade from her memory. Her mother, Sylvia, had preceded Sol to the grave when Julia was five.

Most of the young girl's memories of her mom had been fed to her by her dad. At least the music box, which her father had given her for her tenth birthday, kept those memories alive. But she still relived those horrific moments shortly afterwards, when he'd been shot to death on the streets of Manhattan…

ଡ଼ଠଷ

The mutual adoration between Julia and her father was well known to her classmates at Juilliard Prep School. Julia's violin teacher, famed pedagogue Dorothy De Lay, had often remarked to Sol how rare it was to see such affection flow between father and daughter, nor could she remember seeing a father so willing to participate in his daughter's weekly violin lessons. Julia's most fervent wish was to make Sol even prouder than he already felt on the radiant autumn day when he and his ten-year-old daughter emerged from the school at midday after her lesson. He had told her many times about his imagined vision of her up onstage in a top professional orchestra, or performing in the pit at the Metropolitan Opera, and this day was no exception. When he gazed at her with pride, she returned his look with wide-eyed innocence.

"Did I do good on the 'Meditation' Daddy?"

"You did well, Precious. Very well."

Massenet's "Meditation" from the opera *Thaïs* was one of the most celebrated solo pieces in the violin literature.

"Julia, dearest, your ability to interpret that music astounds everyone who listens to you play, even me," he told her with pride. "And do you know why I'm so amazed? Because in spite of losing your mother five years ago, you've continued to devote yourself to your music and to mastering the violin." Sol went on, beaming. "In fact, I told Maestro Trudeau about how everyone is so impressed with the way you play it."

"You did, Daddy?" Julia knew her father and Abel Trudeau were close friends.

"But if, when you grow up, you decide to audition for the Met, I'm not going to ask him to help you. You'll have to do it all on your own."

"I know, Daddy." She paused, thinking. "Do you think I can?"

"I think you can do anything you set your sights on, Precious."

Julia kept her hand grasped tightly in his as he led her across the traffic-choked intersection to the opposite side of Broadway. She and Sol both hated this intersection, with its multitude of streets crisscrossing at angles and badly timed traffic lights. They always breathed a sigh of relief after dashing precipitously across to avoid being hit by cars or taxis. Julia dreaded the thought of ever negotiating the dangerous junction by herself. Once they had crossed safely, Julia looked at him again and smiled. She trusted him unfalteringly and loved him so much.

In their mutual endearments, they hadn't noticed the swarm of NYPD cops jumping out of patrol cars, the confusing throng of onlookers staring in fright. And when the hirsute man came tearing out of the revolving door of the Chemical Bank on the corner of Sixty-Fifth Street and came close to knocking Sol down, he reacted immediately, oblivious to the man's drawn revolver. He did as any father would do to stop someone from doing harm to his little girl. Shoving Julia out of the way, Sol grabbed the man by the arm.

Julia watched, horrified, as the bullet slammed into her father's chest at close range, and he collapsed on the sidewalk. Before anyone could stop her, she rushed to her father and sank down next to him, her violin case tumbling to the ground beside her. Within seconds, an officer felled the offender with a shot to the shoulder. But it was too late.

Cradling Sol's head in her arms, tears streaming down her face, Julia sobbed as her father's life was extinguished before her eyes.

"Daddy... Daddy!"

In a minute, it was all over. The bank robber, now incapacitated, was not going to hurt anyone else. An officer tried a gentle tug to wrest Julia away from her father's prostrate form. Several other policemen gathered around her, trying to help, asking if she was hurt. Julia remained on the ground, unwilling to move. Reaching for her violin case, she clung to it and rocked herself back and forth, eyes glazing over in shock. In her view, the cops were all useless. They couldn't bring back her dad...

ഇ౦ങ

Now Abel was gone, too. Julia listened for a brief moment to the music box, her eyes glistening. Then she unclasped the violin pin from her blouse and made a silent vow.

I'll wear it every day, Abel, I promise.

She thought of washing the blood off the pin but reconsidered. The blood was the symbol of her pain and her loss. It was more appropriate to let it remain, at least until tomorrow. She placed the pin on the night table, taking care not to touch those drops of blood, the last vestige of Abel's ebbing life. Then, blinded by tears, she shut the music box and curled up in fetal position on the bed, drowned in grief.

৯০০৪

The NYPD swat team burst through the door of Sidney's apartment, guns drawn, at 3:30 a.m. Cops armed with revolvers and protective gear tore through the place. Sidney and his "guest" for the evening, Geraldo, had had no chance to flush their coke down the toilet, and just stood by in helpless shock. But when an officer threw open a closet door, revealing a cache of assault weapons and boxes of ammunition, Sidney's astonishment rendered him speechless.

Another officer opened a box of ammo, removed a bag the size of a paperback book from underneath the bullets, and inspected the white powder inside it. Underneath the bag was a packet of letters, which he handed over to a colleague. Then both officers hauled Sidney and Geraldo from the apartment in handcuffs. Fear transformed Sidney's face into a wide-eyed mask of terror.

"I'm innocent! This was a set-up!" Sidney shouted.

The officer holding tight to Sidney ignored his protests. "You have the right to remain silent …"

It wasn't long before the officers dragged Sidney and Geraldo through the entrance of the Twentieth Precinct and upstairs, where they shoved them into separate interrogation rooms. Bedraggled and dazed, Sidney slumped into a chair and leaned, head in hands, over a table. Within seconds, Al and Buddy appeared. In spite of the late hour, Al seemed to be on a roll.

Not too hard to figure that out. I could tell he suspected me, and now he feels vindicated.

Al bent over Sidney and glared at him. "It'd be easier on you if you cough up a statement now, Richter."

"Yeah." Buddy registered his agreement. "Your pal in the next room might beat you to it, and where would you be then?"

"Statement? About what?"

The detectives weren't buying Sidney's bewilderment.

"And about those letters. You and Trudeau were lovers, and he was about to throw you over. That's motive..." Al raised his eyebrows. "For murder."

Sidney grimaced in silence as his attorney, Herb, swept into the room.

"Herbert Cafferty, defense attorney for Sidney Richter. I want my client released immediately."

Al was quick to jump on Herb's demand. "Not so fast. He's in major trouble here."

"What kind of trumped-up charges are you trying to pin on him?" Herb tapped his foot with a lawyer's impatience.

"Possession of unregistered weapons and controlled substances." Al paused for effect. "And murder."

"What!" Herb and Sidney shrieked simultaneously.

Buddy smirked. "Ammo found in his apartment matched the type and lot number of the casing from the murder weapon—"

"It wasn't mine!"

"Shut up, Sidney, I'm the lawyer here."

Al continued. "And he was hiding love letters from Trudeau, who was about to dump Richter for another guy. A jealous lover, killing for revenge."

Herb faced Al. Despite the late hour, he still managed an indignant expression. "Ammo notwithstanding, you still don't have the murder weapon itself. The letters are circumstantial. And on what grounds did you raid my client's apartment? He has no previous record."

"FYI, we got an anonymous tip, Mister Attorney. Plus he had a fight with Abel Trudeau before the opera. *And* he has a relationship with a known drug dealer, who happens to be in the next room."

"I'll ask for a bail hearing. Sidney is a respected musician, in a world-class musical organization, a Manhattan resident with ties to the community and a prestigious job."

Al's demeanor remained calm. "Your client is suspected of a major crime. We'll get the judge to deny bail."

"On what grounds?"

"He's a flight risk. Has relatives in Russia."

Herb contemplated Al's pronouncement. "We'll see what His Honor has to say."

"I'd say he's pretty much nailed. Open and shut case. The love letters, the drugs, Sidney's known conflicts with Abel. Those alone are enough to detain him."

Al paused, peering at Herb's cool expression. "But the fact that Sidney was absent from the pit during the assassination pretty much clinches it, I'd say."

"*You'd* say? I think I'll wait for the judge."

Al addressed the attorney, modulating his voice in an attempt to be civilized.

"If he cooperates now, the D.A.'ll talk to the judge about cutting him some slack."

Buddy turned to Sidney. "You're involved in this, Richter, whatever you try to say. And we can't help you if you won't help yourself."

Sidney just hung his head.

Chapter 12

Menzogna! Nego. Le prove? Al fatto. Chi mi accusa?
I vostri birri invan frugar la villa

Lies! I deny that. What proofs have you? In fact, who
accuses me?
In vain your spies ransacked my villa

Puccini, *Tosca*, Act II

GETTING OUT OF BED the morning after Abel's murder was the greatest trial Julia had suffered since her father's death. After a fitful sleep she awakened, groggy, realizing with sudden anxiety why her head throbbed and her lips still tasted of salt from the tears she had shed during the night. Exhausted, she arose and threw on the cuddly terry-cloth robe Sidney had given her for her birthday and her furry "wolf" slippers.

As soon as her eyes opened all the way, Julia spied the open violin case and Abel's song lying on the floor and was seized with a sudden desire to be connected to this last remaining link to her mentor. She grabbed hold of the instrument and the music, tuned the violin and began to play the song. But when she got to Abel's last- minute scribbled notes, she stopped at once.

That's weird. It's so dissonant. Could this be right?

Puzzled, she stared at the music. There was no second page to clarify the strange sound on the first page. But once stopped, she couldn't bring herself to make another attempt. Putting down the violin, she shuffled toward the living room. The morning sunlight pouring through the windows, which she usually welcomed with gratitude, only hurt her eyes, and she squinted in defense.

Thank God there's no rehearsal this morning.

Even the Met allowed the theater to darken in respect for their maestro, but Julia suspected one day's respite was about all the company would get.

As she moved toward the front door of her apartment to retrieve her *New York News*, the familiar clatter of clunky heels on the stairway aroused her from her stupor. Julia threw open the door to find her buddy and roommate, Katie, violin case in hand, plucking the newspaper from the doormat.

"Katie? You're back from tour. Thank God!"

"Yeah, I'm back," Katie said in her usual matter-of-fact manner. "Didja' miss me?"

Outside of Sid, Katie Ma was Julia's best friend. The two young women were like sisters, for Katie's Korean family had taken care of Julia after the efforts of other foster families had failed. The two girls had shared everything, from violin fingering secrets to their most intimate adolescent fears and hopes.

Even at a young age, Katie had been well aware of Julia's determination not to show her vulnerability and had done her best to make Julia feel as if she belonged with an Asian family. But Julia was so insecure, so terrified of losing someone else she loved, she kept her distance and convinced herself she was, and always would be, an outsider. She decided she would never fit in and made little effort to adapt to her new environment.

Katie, meanwhile, adjusted to living with the young girl who always felt the need to prove herself and fight for her own space. She showed infinite patience with Julia's self-esteem issues, recognizing her new "sister" as a spunky, determined girl who would not allow anyone to step on her or come between her and her chosen career.

If not for her closeness with Katie, Julia would have set off on her own when she reached eighteen. Instead, she chose to stay with Katie until they graduated together from Juilliard, at which point they decided to share an apartment. Julia and Katie practiced together, challenging each other. Even though Julia was the better player, Julia inspired Katie to discover and utilize her own talents to the max.

Katie, too, had auditioned for the Met when Julia had won the coveted position. Julia was afraid Katie would resent Julia's success, but she was relieved to find the opposite was true.

"You deserved it, Julia," Katie had told her. "If I had to lose to some-one, it was only fair it be you."

Meanwhile, Katie made such an outstanding showing she was placed on the roster of extra players at the Met and appeared quite often in the orchestra, filling in for absentees. As a result, she was there more often than not. Attendance could be spotty at times, especially during flu season.

Julia's face lit up at the sight of her. "You couldn't have come home at a better time, K.!" Then Julia thought a moment. "Actually, I didn't expect you for a couple more days."

"I was more than ready to bag it. How many weeks in a row can you play *The Producers* without wanting to off yourself?" Her cheer-ful expression turned sober. "Truth is, I asked to come back when I heard about Abel."

Katie, as though sensing Julia needed a hug but would never allow it, just gave her friend a sympathetic grin and casually dropped her violin and duffel bag on the sofa. "What a nightmare! Those scumbag reporters accosted me at the airport trying to pump me for info on Abel. Can you believe it?"

Julia's eyes welled up.

"I'm so sorry about Abel, Julia." Katie softened her voice. "Are you okay?"

"Do I look okay?" Julia responded in her customary manner.

"Sorry, dumb question." Katie hesitated. "Here's your paper. Not sure you should read it, though."

Julia took the newspaper. She had no doubt what the headline was going to be.

Murder In The Pit—Opera Conductor Slain.

Julia stared at Abel's photo next to the front-page article, fighting back tears. Katie gazed at her with deep sympathy, then gently took the paper and turned to page two. "It gets worse."

"What?" Julia's eyes widened in alarm. "What do you mean?"

Katie read aloud. "'Acting on an anonymous tip, NYPD officers ar-rested violinist Sidney Richter of the Metropolitan Opera at his Upper West Side apartment last night at three a.m. A box of 9mm Russian sniper ammunition was found in his apartment, along with a quantity of cocaine, and a—'"

Julia gasped in disbelief. "Oh my God! Cocaine? How is that possible?"

"'… a packet of love letters—said to be from Maestro Trudeau,…'" Katie put the paper down and turned to Julia, her expression sober. "'to Met violinist Sidney Richter.'"

"Abel and Sid were…?" Katie watched Julia's face turn ashen white. "After all the times Sid hit on me, I'm supposed to believe he's …?"

"Those letters don't prove anything, Jul."

"Are you just saying that to make me feel better?"

Katie frowned at Julia but didn't answer.

After a long moment of silence, Julia felt her disbelief turn into determination. "Lovers or not, Sid could *never* have harmed Abel. Those accusations are unfair." She held Katie's gaze. "I have to help him."

"You? Are you about to take up another one of your causes?"

Julia bristled. "So what if I am?"

"Look, Jul, I've always admired your highly developed sense of justice. But it was one thing when we were growing up and you adopted stray kittens and took them to the shelter, or defended kids whose parents were yelling at them in the park. Sid's innocence, well, that's something else altogether."

"Oh? Why?"

"Why? Because it's something you have no control over and even less possibility of affecting." Katie gave Julia an understanding look. "You're also terrified of losing Sid, but you'll still put up a brave front, no matter what."

Julia looked away, confirming Katie's theory.

"Besides, I'd be willing to bet the NYPD won't approve much if you try to do their job."

"Oh, you think so? Trust me, the police only look for the easy solution."

"How do you know that?"

Julia reflected on her bitter experience with her father's death but thought better of bringing it up. "I watch Law and Order and CSI."

Katie groaned. "You're in denial, girlfriend."

"I don't care what you say. Sid's life is on the line, and he's my friend. I have to do my part to clear him, whatever it takes."

"But what can you possibly do?"

Julia grit her teeth in an effort to think beyond her distress. After a moment, her thoughts began to fall into place.

"The cops for sure don't realize this investigation needs special consideration."

"Meaning?"

"Meaning they should put someone on the case who knows something about opera."

"Julia, you can't seriously believe there's a cop in existence who knows about - "

"So we're going to start by calling every musician in the orchestra, and urge them to sign a petition protesting Sid's arrest."

"We?" echoed Katie. "You don't mean…me?"

"He's your friend, too."

Katie groaned. "Oh, Lord."

Julia ignored Katie's misgivings. "Then we're going to go the Met and hand it over to Patricia, insisting she demand the NYPD assign a new detective to the case."

"The last thing we need is to have you rocking the boat with Patricia."

Brushing aside Katie's protest, Julia reached into her desk drawer and fished out a two-page list of orchestra members and their phone numbers. She removed the staple and thrust one of the pages at Katie.

"I'll do *A* through *L*, you do *M* to *Z*." She handed Katie her cell phone. "If we get verbal commitments, that'll be good enough for starters."

"Can't it wait until I unpack?"

But Julia was already punching buttons on her cell phone. She felt thankful at having something to occupy her thoughts, instead of facing endless hours to brood about the loss of her mentor and the distress of her colleague.

She'd always had her music to inspire her, and playing the violin gave her a purpose in life. Now she had a more important cause - saving Sidney. She felt confident Patricia, faced with a legion of reproachful musicians, would have no choice but to put her considerable influence at work in pressuring the NYPD to hire a new detective. Even if it meant going all the way to the Board of Trustees.

ഇൽ

Julia had never been in the Met boardroom, but it turned out to look much as she had imagined it. Intimidating, luxurious, well appointed and wood-paneled, it had floor-to-ceiling windows and was dominated by an immense, rectangular mahogany table.

Poised at one end of the table, Julia and Katie eyed the gathering of board members, who in turn regarded Patricia, standing guard at the opposite end of the table, with wariness.

Clasping the petition Julia and Katie had worked so hard to assemble and have signed by orchestra members, Patricia spoke down her elegant nose to Julia. "How many names are on the petition, Ms. Kogan?"

"Every member of the orchestra, Ms. Wells, except for Harold."

"Very well. Thank you, Ms. Kogan and Ms. Ma, for presenting us with this mandate." Patricia gestured at Julia and Katie. "We will let you know our decision shortly. If approved, you will have the full weight of the Metropolitan Opera behind you."

⁞⁞

Nodding their thanks, the young musicians rose and departed. Once the two musicians were out of the room, Mrs. Tallman, a stately older woman, turned to Patricia.

"Patricia, dear, wouldn't we be overstepping our bounds, intervening for a...criminal?"

As usual, Patricia exuded utmost confidence. "Let me put it this way, Mrs. Tallman. A quick call to the precinct is a small price to pay to avoid mutiny in the ranks." Patricia cast a meaningful glance around the room and smiled. The other members nodded in agreement, Mrs. Tallman included.

Chapter 13

Wer du auch seist, ich will dich retten...du sollst kein Opfer sein!
Gewiss, ich löse deine Ketten, ich will, du Armer, dich befrei'n!

Whoever you are, I will save you...you shall not be a victim!
Surely I will loose your chains, I will free you, poor man!

Beethoven, *Fidelio*, Act II

POLICE COMMISSIONER TED Branson had just finished slipping into his pajamas when he reached for the phone. His private line never rang unless something important was happening. Ted was overworked, but he had assumed that went with the territory when he'd accepted the appointment from Mayor Giuliani after 9-11. He had been in a constant state of raw nerves ever since, and though he had anticipated having to deal with major crises in the late evening hours, he was not a natural born night owl. Despite his choice to stay on with the new administration, calls from Mayor Bloomberg's office always made him jumpy. Who knew the source of this latest calamity would come from the Metropolitan Opera?

Deputy Mayor Jim Earhart's voice sounded regretful but resigned over the phone. "This is a tough one, Ted. High profile case, you know."

"You don't have to tell me that, sir." Ted cleared his throat to compensate for his late-night gravelly voice.

"But I don't want any excuses, and neither does the mayor." Jim paused. "He thinks you should find a detective who knows a little something about opera."

"What difference would that make?"

"You never know. It couldn't hurt."

"Doubtful, sir, with all due respect." Ted paused. "And how the hell am I going to find an opera-loving detective?"

"That's your problem, Commissioner."

℞℞℞

Detective Larry Somers thought he was a closet opera buff, but as far as his colleagues at the NYPD's Twentieth Precinct were concerned there was nothing closeted about Larry's absolute and unquestionable love for opera. He was known to start conducting without provocation to some unknown music when the inspiration hit him. He never burst into song, however. Singing was too intimate, too revealing. He did, however, spend endless hours haunting the Barnes and Noble bookstore at the corner of Sixty-Sixth and Broadway, where he searched for the latest releases of his favorite opera stars.

Although Larry's buddies at the precinct joked among themselves that his "opera habit" had distracted him, he still managed to pass his detective's exam—albeit after several tries. Some of his colleagues riffed him about getting a life, and maybe a date, instead of sitting in the property room after hours night after night with an iPod by his side and headphones over his ears. But Larry felt he could best deal with the stress of his work in the relative quiet of that space at the end of the day.

Larry was there the evening Detective Al Cummings, who had stayed late to work on some supplemental LE2s (offense reports) with his younger partner Buddy Cruse, had gotten the call about the murder at the Metropolitan Opera. Larry knew that Al, like most detectives, detested paperwork. He also knew that these reports, which were the detective's follow up to the ones filed by the first officer on a crime scene, were the most detailed and annoying to write up, and he felt sympathy for Al.

Buddy had stopped by the prop room on his way out. Larry had gotten so carried away listening to Pavarotti let loose on *La Donna È Mobile*, from Verdi's *Rigoletto*, he started conducting along with the music, waving his arms with enthusiasm. He'd noticed the exuberant rookie, Buddy, gesticulating at him.

Larry ignored him in favor of Pavarotti. Buddy waved his hands in front of Larry's face. Larry was so absorbed in his music, Buddy had to yank the headphones off.

"Hey!" Larry was indignant. "That was Pavarotti's high *B* you interrupted."

"Sorry to intrude, Toscanini." Buddy made an inept imitation of Buddy's conducting. "I just wanted to tell you Al and me are assigned to a murder case—"

"What else is new?"

"But this one's at the Met Opera. Conductor's been assassinated."

"What? You mean, Abel Trudeau?!"

"Yeah, I think that's the guy's name."

"JesusMaryJoseph." Larry had been stunned. "Abel Trudeau assassinated. This city has truly gone ape."

Larry's attention finally turned away from Pavarotti's mellifluous voice. He had followed every detail of the prodigious Maestro Trudeau's career. Now, he was dead. How was it possible?

Buddy turned toward the exit. "So when am I gonna hear you sing, Caruso?"

"How many times I have to tell you? I only sing in the shower."

But before Larry could ask about the case, Buddy was out the door.

ಬಂೞ

Larry followed every detail in the New York papers of the case of Abel Trudeau's murder and the subsequent arrest of violinist Sidney Richter, who was being charged with the crime, and he pumped Al and Buddy for information. There was, understandably, a run on Trudeau's recordings in the Barnes and Noble bookstore near Lincoln Center, and Larry was there to snap up any CDs he didn't already own. He assumed, however, his involvement with the Met case would end there.

Larry was careful to stash his headphones and CD of the Vickers-Ludwig *Fidelio* out of sight when he saw his chief, Donald Darnell, approach the prop room several nights later, giving the impression he was hard at work studying for his detective's exam. The music leaked through the headphones, a tinny sound, and Darnell cleared his throat until Larry pushed the stop button.

"So here's the deal, Somers." Darnell made his pronouncement with his customary authority. "You're on the Met Opera case, with Cruse."

Larry peered in disbelief at his boss. "Is this supposed to be a joke? 'Cause if it is, it's not funny."

"It's not a joke, and I'm not toying. Cummings is off, and you're on."

"Can you do that?" Larry was still unconvinced. "Take him off just like that, I mean?"

Darnell's frustration was obvious. "It's been done before. Not often, but when the situation calls for it," Darnell said, frustrated. "In this case, the higher-ups at the Met lobbied for the change. Truth be told, I'm not happy about it, either."

"But Cummings will have my ass. He's not exactly my biggest fan. He'll never let me live it down."

"Cummings doesn't know squat about opera. You do. That's what the Met management has asked for, and that's what we're delivering. Think you're up for it?"

"Yikes," Larry muttered under his breath, then swallowed hard. "Sure, boss."

"And FYI, Cummings threw a fit at being passed over for you." He glared pointedly at Larry. "But there was nothing I could do. When it comes to the power of the Met's influence, there's nothing *anyone* can do."

Larry murmured softly. "Ya' got that right."

"Meanwhile, report to the Met stage door tomorrow morning. That'll be all, Somers."

Larry absorbed Darnell's orders and watched as the chief departed. He wondered when the news was going to hit him.

When it does, I won't know whether to be thrilled or terrified.

He also wondered if, with the evidence against Richter being so compelling, it was possible he was being brought in as a decoy to pacify the Met Management. Even he could recognize, thanks to the inside information Al and Buddy gave him, that the case was pretty much sewed up. To him, it didn't matter. Despite his sadness and anger about Trudeau's demise, Larry had every reason to rejoice.

One way or another, my dream of entering the Met by the stage door is about to come true.

Chapter 14

*Und ist die Arbeit abgetan, dann schleicht die holde
Nacht heran*

And when the work is finished, then blessed night will
creep on.

Beethoven, *Fidelio*, Act I

WHEN HE AND BUDDY arrived at the Met stage door security station the next morning, Larry was showing the effects of lack of sleep. Buddy had brought him up to date, since Al was still sulking about being taken off the investigation, and it had taken most of the night. Despite his red eyes, Larry took in his surroundings with the fascination of a child.

Finding themselves face to face with a surly security guard who seemed to have been chosen expressly for his suspicious nature, Larry and Buddy flashed their NYPD badges. But this guard took his job, keeping the Met backstage terrorist-free, seriously. He was determined to make sure the two men were authentic NYPD detectives.

"Haft'a see ID."

Larry's immediate, hotheaded reaction was to protest. "But I already showed you."

"Lemme see it again."

"We're on the list," Larry said in frustration. "Detectives Larry Somers and Buddy Cruse, for Patricia Wells, the general manager."

"Yeah… Okay." Mumbling, the guard checked his clipboard. "End of the hall, turn left, go past the artists' area, elevator to your right, if it's working and you're not claustrophobic. Otherwise, take one of the three stairways to the sixth floor. She'll be waiting."

Larry sighed, wondering how he and Buddy would manage to locate this sequestered ivory tower. He looked at the guard, bleary-eyed. The guard picked up a phone.

"Detectives Somers and Cruse on their way up, Ms. Wells… Yes, Ma'am, I'll find someone to show 'em the way."

"How hard could it be?" Buddy flashed his affable grin. "Maybe we should go back to the precinct and Map-Quest it."

At that moment a young woman Larry didn't recognize came in carrying a violin. The guard turned to her. "How 'bout you show these detectives how to get to Ms. Wells' office, Julia?"

୫୦୯ଷ

Julia recognized the younger detective as Buddy Cruse. *The older one must be the opera fan. Good to know my request was taken seriously.* She focused her attention of the guard. "You mean I can come in without showing my ID?" Her own sarcasm startled her. She lost no time in chastising herself. *Here I am, facing the opera-savvy replacement detective, and I'm being flip. What was I thinking?*

The guard clucked his tongue in disapproval. "What do you think?"

Peering at Larry and Buddy, Julia extracted her card from her bag. Something made her feel suspicious of the new detective. He noticed this.

"Detective Larry Somers." He afforded her an acid smile. "Don't worry, I won't bite."

He tried not to raise his eyebrows at Julia's apparent youth. Then he addressed the security guard.

"This kid plays the violin?"

But Julia always had a retort ready for "older" skeptics who had their doubts she belonged at the Met.

"Excuse me, but FYI, Mozart was a 'kid,' too, and no one questioned his violin playing," Julia replied haughtily. "I know my way around, Detective. But if you prefer, I could just drop breadcrumbs. Do you want the fast track to the elevator or the travelogue?"

Larry seemed happy to prove himself up to her verbal jousting. "Oh, definitely the travelogue." He turned to Buddy. "One of us should search Trudeau's dressing room."

Buddy had observed the subtle repartee going on between Julia and Larry. "I'll do it," he volunteered. "Meet you later."

Julia tried not to show her annoyance at Buddy's barely suppressed grin as the guard buzzed all three of them inside the gate. None of them saw or heard the guard when he picked up a phone, dialed upstairs, announced, "Detective Somers on his way up," hung up the phone, and sniffed, "Your Highness."

ಬಂಡ

Julia saw that Larry had difficulty keeping up with her as they hastened down a long, winding hallway. Each time they passed a closed-door room, she explained its function with expertise, aware of his wide-eyed fascination.

"Wardrobe, coaching and rehearsal rooms on the right. Green room on the left."

Larry nodded. "How'd you learn about all this? Don't you spend most of your time in the pit?"

"I've been coming here since I was a kid. Abel Trudeau coached me after my dad died."

"Oh. I'm sorry."

Larry's apology was sincere. Julia heard it in his voice and sensed that he himself been there. But she kept her thoughts to herself.

This stranger represents my only hope for Sidney.

Soon they arrived at a carpeted space where a large number of people were rushing about in different directions. Larry watched them, puzzled. Julia continued her tour speech.

"This is the Artists' area. Stage is in that direction, soloists' dressing rooms over there."

Larry watched the activity, awed. "So many people. Who are they?"

"Singers, wardrobe people, stagehands. The usual."

"Where are they all going?"

"With six evening performances and one matinee a week of different operas, and rehearsals for upcoming repertoire during the day, there's plenty to do, believe me."

Julia pointed to a door on one side of the corridor and explained it led to orchestra level, where the pit and cafeteria were. Then she led Larry to an elevator at one end of the artists' area.

"That's it. Sixth floor. She'll be waiting, no doubt."

"She?"

"Patricia, the general manager." Julia couldn't hide her impatience. *This is the sharp new detective who's going to help me save Sidney?*

"Oh, right. Sure you don't want to see me to her door?"

For a brief instant, Julia was tempted to accept his offer. After all, being sequestered in a slow-moving elevator for a few extra minutes would give her an opportunity to plead her case for Sidney's innocence. But she thought better of it.

There'll be time for that later.

"I only go there when I have to, trust me."

"By the way... Thanks."

"No problem."

She smiled at him briefly, determined to be nice to him for Sidney's sake. But the gesture made her suddenly shy. Julia fixed a stray hair and took off, leaving Larry to fend for himself.

৳ಂগ

Larry exited the elevator at the appropriate floor and bumped right into Patricia. He was startled. Something about her intimidated him, and he was rattled for an instant, a rare occurrence for him.

"Uh...Ms. Wells?"

Calm and unruffled, Patricia extended her hand with a supercilious smile. "Generally speaking, yes."

"I... I didn't expect you to be right here to greet me."

"I wouldn't want you to lose your way."

Her brusque manner and air of superiority gave him pause, but he managed a rejoinder. "I'm touched you would go out of your way to help out one of New York's Finest."

"Finest what?" Patricia asked.

But before he could respond, she turned around and led Larry down another long hallway.

"Do you have that list of personnel that Al, er, Detective Cummings requested?"

Without missing a beat, Patricia turned and faced him. Her calm tone took on an icy edge.

"I'm going to need more time, Detective. You don't understand, between performers and stagehands and wardrobe people... Well, there are over three hundred persons working here at any given moment..."

The atmosphere between them was awkward as they entered her office, where the first thing Larry noticed was the floor-to-ceiling window with its spectacular view. Spread out below them were Lincoln Plaza, its celebrated fountain and the microcosm of New York City

populace that passed through the famous square day in and day out.
Larry realized he needed to change the subject. "That's quite a vista.
You must rate."

"Isn't it? And yes, I do."

When will she stop talking down to me?

Larry, uneasy, cleared his throat and tried a different tack. "You've
got your hands full, running the opera at this difficult time, dealing
with a murder on top of your usual problems—"

"Problems, you say? Try notifying an HMO they're going to be
paying for psychotherapy for three hundred employees." She paused.
"Detective Somers, I'm a very busy woman. Did you have some...
specific questions?"

"Ah, of course." Larry spoke slowly, to Patricia's obvious irritation
and his delight. "Did you notice anything or anyone unusual backstage
before the murder?"

"No, I didn't. Frankly, I was too busy trying to calm our lead ten-
or—"

"Giuseppe Masini, wasn't it?" Larry whipped out his notebook and
began to write. "I saw him perform *Ernani.*"

Patricia, Larry noticed, was both surprised and taken aback by his
apparent opera knowledge ability. He continued before she had an
opportunity to react. "I'm an opera buff from way back. My mom
used to listen to the Met on the radio every Saturday. And she and I
did standing room, too, whenever we could get tickets."

"Oh really?"

Ignoring Patricia's apparent lack of interest, Larry allowed himself
a brief moment of nostalgia and continued. "What about Maestro
Trudeau? He ever mention anything about a threat? Did he have any
enemies you knew of?"

"*Entre nous,* who doesn't?" Patricia waved her hand in an offhand
manner.

Larry persisted. "Was he involved in anything shady?"

"How would I know about such things, Detective?" Patricia made
no effort to hide her exasperation. "As you yourself said, I have an
opera house to run."

"Of course, it's not the first time there's been a murder here. For
instance, were you here when, uh, that violinist was killed?"

Patricia raised her eyebrows. Suddenly her quick speech pattern slowed. "If you're referring to that unfortunate incident several decades ago,…yes, I was."

Larry remembered the day at the Police Academy when the sergeant had talked to the trainees about the brutal murder of a young woman violinist at the Met. She had disappeared during a performance, and her unclothed body was found in an elevator shaft the next day. There had been tremendous pressure on the NYPD to find the murderer, without delay. Via his colleagues on the force, Larry had followed the case with intense interest, weighing all the evidence —spurious, in his opinion—all through the sordid investigation and the arrest and conviction of the stagehand accused of the crime. He wondered to this day whether they had locked up the right man…

"Nasty business. Never believed it was properly solved." He paused. "We can wrap this one up, though."

As he said this, he wondered how he could sound so confident.

If she knew I was still catching up on the case, she would eat me for breakfast, and ask for a hand towel.

"Indeed." Patricia picked up a ringing phone and spoke into it. "Yes? She is? I'll be right down." She turned to Larry. "Please forgive, me, Detective, I have to go handle a…a diva problem. Are you familiar with Dorothy Muir?"

"Are you kidding? I have all her CDs."

"Well, as you can imagine, she's a very difficult personality. I'm the only one who can handle her. So if you'll excuse me…"

"You don't mind if I tag along, do you?"

Larry saw that Patricia's lack of surprise at his rhetorical question didn't change the fact she had been hoping to be rid of him sooner rather than later. He also knew she wasn't about to rock the boat any further. It was already tilting.

Chapter 15

Se non muove par la sua dolor, ha non il cuor

If he's not moved by her grief, he has a heart of stone,
or no heart at all

Mozart, *Don Giovanni*, Act II

ABEL'S VALET, DAMON, watched unhappily as Buddy searched through the conductor's effects and pulled photos of Abel with famous conductors and singers off the wall. Buddy eyed the valet with suspicion. Having seen too many Coppola movies when he was growing up, Buddy always had a visceral, and unfounded, reaction to handsome young guys with black curly hair who stood behind him silently.

As Buddy inspected the portraits, the valet scowled, exasperated. "Be careful how you handle his things, will you? Try not to paw them to death."

Buddy ignored Damon's nasty tone. "I recognize the Three Tenors, but who are these other ones?"

The valet sniffed at Buddy's apparent ignorance about opera and pointed at two of the photos. "Why, Giuseppe Masini and Dorothy Muir, of course. Naturally, we change them according to who the guest artist is for any particular week."

"Naturally." Buddy didn't have a clue what the valet was talking about and gestured at a third picture. "And this is...?"

"Charles Tremaine. Tenor."

"Another biggie?"

"Actually, no. You might say second-string."

"Then why'd Trudeau have his photo taken with the guy?"

"Maestro Trudeau was kind, magnanimous," Damon said with exaggerated impatience. "He was happy to be photographed with even the most insignificant of artists. Charles was just an in-house *comprimario* who got lucky."

"'Comp'… what?"

The Valet's irritation mounted. "*Comprimario.* That's what we call the singers who do secondary roles. Charles eventually became an understudy."

"Right." Buddy was doubtful but didn't share that with Damon. "So where's the one of Trudeau with you?"

Damon snatched back the photos, glowering, and muttered something under his breath about "nerve" and "philistines." Taking a small dust mop, he whisked the pictures with a delicate gesture and replaced them on the wall, frowning with disdain.

Buddy, oblivious to Damon's distress, continued his search.

A fruitless hour later, Buddy huddled with Larry in a corner backstage, comparing notes. "I did Trudeau's dressing room and Richter's locker, too. Couldn't come up with much. Though that valet was acting pretty weird."

"No problem. It's open and shut with Richter, unless he can explain his way out of those jealous love letters," said Larry.

Buddy was incredulous. "You mean…you know? I mean, about the case being—"

"I wasn't born yesterday." Larry flashed a crooked smile. "I can recognize irrefutable evidence when I see it. Or in this case, read about it."

There was an awkward silence as Buddy lowered his voice confidentially. "And how do you feel about—?"

"Being a walking, talking detective replacement?" Larry again finished Buddy's thought. "It got me into the Met, didn't it?"

ಬಂಜ

The memorial gathering that evening took place at Charles Tremaine's apartment. Located a short walk from the Met, in a landmark building off of Central Park West and up the street from the ABC network studios, the spacious, upscale co-op was a perfect venue for such a ceremony. The company considered it a generous gesture on Charles's part to volunteer his home in their collective time of need.

Inside the elegantly furnished living room, a glossy photo of Abel was positioned on a dais surrounded by flower arrangements. In the background, somber operatic music played, Siegfried's Funeral Music from Wagner's *Götterdämmerung*, which Charles thought appropriate for the fallen hero. Musicians, choristers, stagehands, and other company members hung about, downcast, conversing in subdued whispers.

Ever the gracious host, Charles circulated through the crowd, alternately offering drinks and solace, whichever seemed suitable for the situation and the people he addressed. Seeing Julia lingering in a corner by herself, he approached her, gazing with concern at her eyes, swollen from crying. Julia's devotion to Abel was legendary.

"Anything I can get for you?" he asked in a gentle voice.

Charles saw that his kindliness had touched off a threat of tears from the overwrought violinist, even though she was putting on a brave front.

"Oh...thanks, Charles. I...just need to find the powder room, I think."

"Of course. Why don't you use the one in my bedroom? It's more private."

Julia acknowledged him with a grateful smile. He pointed toward the rear of the apartment, and she moved off, looking relieved to have kept her composure, at least in public.

Larry and Buddy, having been ushered in by a maid, remained at the entrance, scrutinizing the action and taking discreet notes. They had agreed even if the case was open and shut it wouldn't hurt to get a sense of the feelings, positive and negative, of the attendees toward their departed maestro. Thus, they both watched closely as Patricia moved to the dais and waved her hands to get attention.

"I'd like to make a few announcements," she said in a subdued tone.

All faces turned toward the general manager, and even Charles stopped what he was doing. Calm and self-assured as always, she gave off a vibration of confidence, a result of years of experience as an important figure accustomed to addressing boards of directors as well as rich patrons.

"I'd like to start by thanking you all for coming." She looked around as if to check on who was, and who was not, in attendance. "If anyone has a problem with performing at tomorrow's rehearsal, please inform me, and I will see an alternate is found for you."

A number of people raised their hands. Patricia acknowledged them with a nod. Her face turned somber.

"On that note, I'm sorry to report our tenor, Mr. Masini, is unable to sing and will have to be replaced..."

At this, Charles started to step forward toward Patricia, a stalwart expression on his face. Patricia waited for the appropriate disappointed murmur from her listeners. Then she continued.

"Fortunately, however, as a special favor to the Met, Mr. Andrea Bocelli has agreed to sing in Mr. Masini's place."

The crowd reacted in surprise, gasping and whispering to each other. Charles stopped still, his expression darkening. Patricia cast a canny eye in his direction.

"I also wish to thank Charles Tremaine for so graciously offering us his home as a venue for this gathering."

Patricia gestured toward Charles, applauding, and the others joined in. Beneath a gallant smile, his face was etched with frustration. Larry and Buddy looked at each other. Buddy muttered to his boss.

"Hey, even I know who Bocelli is. Guess he's gonna be the next one to have his face plastered on the dressing room wall."

Larry responded with a sober nod. The detectives gazed around the room once more and left without making a sound.

৪৩೮೩

Julia emerged from the bathroom adjoining Charles's bedroom and sank down in a chair by his desk, dabbing at her eyes.

I should have known how hard this would be. I should have taken some kind of tranquilizer. If only Katie were here.

Julia knew Katie's AA meetings took precedence over everything else, even death. But she missed her just the same.

At that moment, Charles hurried in and closed the door behind him. He chugged half the contents of a tall glass of scotch in one gulp.

Julia, noticing his distress, cleared her throat, and when Charles noticed her sitting at his desk, his face flushed a bright red. He set his glass on the wet bar by the door and turned to her, anxious to cover up his embarrassment.

"Are you all right, Julia?"

She replied with as much conviction as she could muster. "Fine, thank you, Charles." Then she noticed his unhappy expression. "What's wrong?"

Charles took another gulp of his drink. "Oh, nothing…" Her questioning look gave him pause. He hesitated for a brief moment, finally deciding to reveal the cause of his discontent. "Giuseppe cancelled tomorrow's rehearsal, and Bocelli is replacing him. Which leaves me odd man out. Again."

Julia's face fell. She felt his pain. "That's a shame. But don't worry, you'll be in the limelight soon, I'm convinced."

She smiled her encouragement through misted eyes. He responded with a grateful look and approached her, perching on the ottoman by her chair.

"How sweet you are to worry about me in your time of grief. No wonder Abel was so fond of you."

Julia blushed and sighed. "I miss him so much, Charles. He was the best mentor I could have ever asked for."

"He was my mentor, too," he confided. "My very first coach."

"Oh. Really?"

They looked at each other in mutual understanding. She was seized with a sudden urge to confide in him and gestured at the violin pin fastened to her sweater.

"He gave me this for my first opening night, the night he…died."

He leaned in close to her, eyeing the pin with admiration. "He must have had immense faith in you."

"Not only that. He wrote a song for me and gave it to me that night, before the performance."

She cast him a bittersweet look, as if trying to bring back the glow of the experience before it had turned into a dark nightmare.

"Oh? What kind of song?"

"That's a good question. I tried to play it, and it's just…weird sounding."

"His composing style was rather…well, different."

"And, there was a page missing."

This statement seemed to pique his curiosity. "Oh? Well, I could take a look at it, if you think it would help."

"That's very generous, but—" She hesitated, somewhat embarrassed. "It's kind of personal."

"I understand. I didn't mean to pry," Charles said.

"You weren't."

Uncomfortable at his closeness, Julia shifted in the chair. Charles responded by moving back several inches.

"I could use some help, though, with something else…" Julia paused. "I mean, if you wouldn't mind."

"Anything for you, Julia."

"It's Sidney, he's in trouble." She groped for the words. "I…I tried to help him by getting a new detective assigned to the investigation. But now I don't know if it will do any good at all. He's been in that horrid Tombs place for a whole day now, and—"

"What can I do?"

"I'm not sure. But if you hear of anything, any gossip around the opera house that has to do with Sid, please let me know."

Charles flashed her a smile. "I'd be happy to."

With a great effort, Julia rose and turned to go. Charles took her arm in a caring gesture. She pulled away from him.

He gazed at her in sympathy. "I'm sorry. I should have been more sensitive. You're obviously in pain."

"No, really, it's okay."

"No, it's not. I know what Abel meant to you and how close you are with Sidney. I can only imagine how you're suffering right now," Charles said sympathetically.

"Thank you," she said.

"I'll do whatever I can, even if it's only to offer you consolation."

Nodding her gratitude, she moved toward the door. She noticed him watching her, admiring the way she walked. It made her nervous.

How could he look at me that way, when he knows how vulnerable I am right now?

Suddenly aware of how clingy her black jersey skirt was, she chastised herself.

It's probably my fault.

She quickly slipped through the door, resolving to be more careful about her attire from now on.

Chapter 16

Dolce signora, che mai v'accora?...
Darei la vita per asciugar qual pianto

Oh gracious lady, whatever is it that grieves you?...
I would give my life to wipe away those tears.

Puccini, *Tosca*, Act I

JULIA SAT BY A WINDOW in the visitor center of The Tombs—more properly, the Manhattan Detention Complex—the next morning, staring at the slate gray sky.

How appropriate for a visit to jail.

She was not a morning person, but in order to see Sidney before getting to rehearsal at 11:00 a.m., she had to arrive at the prison by eight o'clock, what she considered an ungodly hour.

She looked around, trying not to be disturbed at the brutal, low-life atmosphere surrounding her. But it was difficult. The place reeked of human misery and unhappiness. She could not deny it, even in her befogged state.

The first thing she noticed when Sidney came in was his haggard, sweating face. There was something wrong with him, something beyond the customary wretchedness of an imprisoned man. She could tell by the way he avoided her gaze when he sat down opposite her. She focused an anxious look on his face.

"Are you okay? You don't look too great," she said, feeling anxious and afraid all of a sudden.

He finally looked at her. "I...I think someone is trying to poison me."

Julia cried out in distress. "What! Why? Oh, Sid—"

"Haven't got a clue. I just suddenly got sick, and it's not my diverticulitis." He spoke with difficulty, shaking his head. "Hell, I should'a been outta here by now."

Julia jumped up, as if there were something she could do in sympathy. Even though she disliked being touched, right now she only wanted to take his hand, or stroke his forehead to see if he had a fever. But the barrier between them prevented her from accomplishing this, and she sat back down.

Sidney waved away Julia's look of concern. "Rossi overheard me calling Abel a sonofabitch, and suddenly I'm a murderer."

"It's crazy. They'll never prove it."

"I was set up. Someone planted that ammo and those love letters."

Julia looked Sidney straight in the eye. "What's going to happen to you, Sid?"

He avoided her gaze at first. Then he returned the look, speaking in a low voice. "They're talking about…the death penalty."

Julia felt the color drained from her face as she struggled to comprehend. "They? Who?"

"The D.A. She was elected on a so-called 'death penalty' ticket. Wants to make an example of me, show the assholes who voted her in that she means business."

"Oh my God, Sid. That's not possible."

"Believe it." Sidney's panic began to show in his wild-eyed expression. "The grand jury meets tomorrow. If they indict, I'll be arraigned. The D.A.'ll pressure me to make a deal, otherwise I go to trial with the death penalty hanging over my head."

Sidney suppressed a sob. Julia had never seen him so vulnerable.

"Jul, I can't make any deals. I'm innocent."

"I know, Sid, I know." Julia thought for a moment. "But there's a new detective on the case. He can—"

"He can do squat. He's just a patsy, to shut up the Met management."

Julia gasped as the impact of his words hit her. "How do you know that?"

"Trust me kid, words gets around. Even in this joint."

She spoke slowly, "If that's true, then…is there anything left for you to do?"

"Plead guilty. But I can't, I didn't do it!"

Suddenly Sidney's breath started coming in halting spurts. He doubled over, groaning. "God, I feel so nauseated."

Julia leapt up and made a frantic gesture at the guard. "Help! Come here! He's... he's..."

Seeing Sidney collapse on the floor, the guard rushed over. Within seconds, another guard joined him. Julia stood motionless, watching in disbelief as the two men dragged Sidney off, and felt the beats of his life ticking away like the pendulum on a metronome.

‽ϫ

When she returned to her apartment, Julia was still upset. She had not been allowed to stay long enough to find out the details of Sidney's condition and was told to call the prison later if she wanted to find out. She had had no choice but to reclaim her violin and stalk out of The Tombs, trying to keep her outrage in check.

On the subway coming home, she had racked her brains for some means of helping Sid, but she came up with nothing. Back in her bedroom, facing her music stand with Abel's song still staring at her, she decided to clear her head by trying once more to play it. But the strange, incongruous notes with their puzzling dissonance stopped her just as before. She was poised in front of the music in confusion when Katie peeked in.

"Practicing before rehearsal? Are you obsessed or what?"

Julia ignored the question. "Did you hear those notes? Do they sound as skewed to you as they do to me?"

Katie thought for a moment. "Yeah. Obviously there's some mistake. Maybe when Abel was copying it, he—"

"But there wasn't." Julia was adamant. "Abel told me they were some last-minute changes. He must have known what he was doing. And that missing page —"

"Look, he was in a rush. It was opening night. Really, don't you think you should just bag it?"

"What, give up trying to play it? How can I, with Sid in prison, wasting away?"

"What does this song have to do with Sid?"

"Abel gave me this song for a reason, K. My gut tells me there's something tying it to Abel's murder, and maybe I can use it to prove Sid is innocent. I'm going to keep at it until I figure out what it is."

Julia eyed Katie's dubious look. "Maybe you could help me make sense of it."

"I was afraid of that."

"You will help, won't you?"

Julia gave Katie a puppy dog gaze. Katie groaned in surrender.

Chapter 17

E perche piangi...onde contanta senti pieta della mia vita?

But why do you weep...why do you feel such pity for my life?

Verdi, *Un Ballo in Maschera*, Act III

Even with Katie's help, Julia's efforts to decipher Abel's composition proved fruitless, and before long she gave up in frustration. But since there was still an hour remaining before rehearsal, she hid the music away in the zipper compartment of her violin case, in the event she found an extra moment to practice. Soon she was marching down Broadway, her fiddle case strap hitched to her shoulder, and when she found herself in front of the Barnes and Noble located diagonally across from Lincoln Center, she could not resist stopping there.

After witnessing the disturbing spectacle with Sidney that morning in The Tombs, Julia felt a need to indulge herself in a bit of music store exploration. In times of stress, she often escaped to the comforting womb of Barnes and Noble and lost herself amidst the myriad of comforting favorites in the classical CD section. It soothed her to be sequestered among the plastic discs representing her dear friends Mozart, Beethoven, Brahms, and Verdi. As a child, one of her favorite treats had been wandering the bookstore aisles with her father after her violin lessons at Juilliard Prep.

Sol Kogan had been Julia's first violin teacher. Though he never became a professional musician, he had enough mastery of the violin to start her off in the right direction. But within the first two months of his tutelage, he realized she would quickly surpass him, and he lost no time in sending her to Juilliard Prep, the Lincoln Center institution famous for preparing talented young children for their musical careers. He always accompanied Julia to her lessons, and the two of them spent hours afterwards searching through the bins at Barnes and Noble for "little bargains," as Sol called them.

The display in the familiar window at the northeast corner of Broadway and 66ᵗʰ Street commanded her attention. All of Abel's recordings, labeled "Homage to a Fallen Maestro," were there, beckoning to her. The word *fallen* again brought into sharp focus the realization that Abel was dead. At first Julia did not know whether she could handle the emotional pangs of being surrounded by these reminders of Abel, another mentor who had passed from her life with such violence. But her indecision disappeared when she overheard the conversation of the two shoppers next to her.

"Do you think we should snatch up some copies?" one asked.

"Of course. Trudeau's recordings may be worth a lot of money someday," the other replied.

Without waiting to hear another word, Julia hurried into the store, headed for the opera section, and began to scoop up a number of CDs of Abel's performances. But as her distress about Abel came bubbling up toward the surface, she put the CDs back with sigh of defeat, berating herself inwardly.

Julia, you're being ridiculous. You're acting like a child. When are you going to get your inner strength back?

In the midst of her diatribe she spied Larry Somers approaching her from a few rows away, and her self-punishment shifted to a sudden desire to flee.

The last thing I need is to chitchat with this guy in the middle of a public place. Especially after what Sidney just told me about him.

She decided it was better to pretend not to see Detective Somers. But it was too late. He was already at her side, flashing her a look of mock bravado.

"You're buying them all? Damn, I was gonna buy some."

Julia couldn't resist a retort. "I'm not going to let a bunch of philistine thrill-seekers snatch them all up because they want a piece of scandal they can sell on eBay."

"Hey, not all of us want to profit from the maestro's death."

His crooked smile made her feel regret for her hasty response. "Oh…sorry."

"Apology accepted."

There was an uncomfortable silence as Julia picked up a CD with Abel's picture on the cover and gazed at it. She saw Larry look at her from the corner of her eye.

"*Fidelio* is sublime, don't you think?" he asked. "One of my all-time favorites, in fact."

Despite her hostile feelings toward Larry, Julia was impressed. In general, even self-professed opera aficionados stuck to the so-called bread and butter of the repertoire, like Verdi, Puccini, Donizetti, and Bellini. Most devotees proclaimed Beethoven's only effort at writing opera to be inferior to the Italian school. But Julia loved *Fidelio* as dearly as any other.

"It was one of my Dad's favorites."

"Right. I knew that."

Julia was taken aback. "You did?"

"He was also partial to '*Thaïs*,' wasn't he?"

The sudden memory of the last piece her father had ever heard her play brought Julia wistful thoughts. But Larry's knowledge of her and her father startled her.

How can he know about this?...

"You're a graduate of Juilliard, worked at the Willowstream Music Camp as a teenager, were mugged on upper Central Park West last year. You've volunteered to teach some kids in Harlem about opera..."

His voice trailed off as he paused to let these facts sink in. Julia was aghast at his knowledge about the intimate and all-too public details of her life, but she had to admit he did his research.

Larry broke the silence. "I lost my mom when I was a youngster, too."

"Oh...I'm sorry." Julia exchanged looks of mutual understanding with Larry.

"She was the one who tuned me in to opera. Met opera broadcasts every Saturday, like clockwork. The only opera I can't listen to is *Don Carlo*. That's the one they were playing when my dad was killed in the line of duty. He was a cop, too." He paused to take in Julia's look of sympathy. "But in general, I'm a cheerful sort. Now I sing with Pavarotti. In the shower, of course."

Julia managed a smile. For the first time, she took a good look at

Larry. Like her father, he was not too tall, maybe 5' 9, and slender. She figured he was about forty. Something about him made her feel comfortable, relaxed. It was as if a link had been uncovered all of a sudden, allowing them to reveal their private lives to each other. *Maybe there's hope after all. He might be open to discussing Sidney's innocence.*

Julia decided it was time to ask about Sidney. "Is it true that Sidney's case is closed?"

Larry sighed, shaking his head, and Julia immediately regretted her question. He looked as if he had some sad truth to tell her and felt badly about having to do so. She girded herself.

His look was full of sympathy. "Look, I feel for you and your friend. But the evidence against him is pretty compelling." Julia's expression elicited a look of sympathy. "Sidney was a rejected lover. He and Abel were at each other's throats. They found letters, they found ammo."

"I don't care, Sid's not capable of murder."

"How do you know?"

"He's my best friend. He's looked out for me ever since I joined the Met."

"Hey, you think you know somebody, then it turns out you don't. You've got to be careful who you trust, Julia. Look what happened to Abel."

Julia looked at him in distress, and his face softened. He spoke in a firm but gentle tone. "My hands are tied. They sent me here because they wanted to comply with Met management's request, and they knew I wouldn't rock the boat."

Julia felt nauseated by each harsh word. All her efforts, to collect the musicians' signatures on the petition, to sway Patricia and the board, to plead Sidney's case to this new detective, were for nothing. He would be found guilty, and there wasn't a thing she could do to help.

And to make things worse, this guy is trying to be nice.

"There's going to be a Grand Jury hearing soon, maybe even today. It's a high profile case, and it'll be on a fast track. I...I'm really sorry, Julia."

He really does seem sorry. But I still wish I'd run when I had the chance.

"I…I have to get to rehearsal."

"How 'bout I tag along with you? I have to go there, too."

Julia had second thoughts about Larry's sincerity. "Oh? I thought the case was closed."

"I still have to show up."

"Suit yourself."

Julia reached over and plucked the Fidelio CD from a bin and proceeded to the cashier. Larry followed.

"Once you make up your mind, you're off and running," he said.

Julia was too mired in thoughts of Abel and Sidney to hear him and within seconds had paid for her purchase. She declined the offer of a bag and instead placed the CD in the zipper compartment of her violin case. As she unzipped it, Abel's song fluttered to the floor. Larry bent down and retrieved it, eyeing it with curiosity. He whistled.

"Ooh, impressive." He examined the title. "Dedicated to you?"

"Abel gave it to me the night he was murdered."

"Have you played it?"

"Of course. But—"

She snatched the song from him, pointing out the scribbling at the bottom of the page.

"These notes don't make sense. I…I think he put them there for a reason. Like he was trying to tell me something."

Larry looked skeptical. "That's a bit of a stretch, don't you think? Messages in music?"

"That shows how much you don't know about music history, *Mr. Detective.*" Julia considered another tack. "If I can prove it's not a 'stretch', will you consider the chances of Sid's innocence?"

Larry hesitated. "I'll think about it."

Julia mused on the mixture of admiration and resentment she felt for this cop, whose intelligence was disarming.

"So how about we call a truce?" Larry asked.

Julia was reluctant to ally herself with the enemy, but she also felt it was unwise to give up her efforts to convincing Larry of Sidney's innocence. "I'll think about it."

Chapter 18

La vita mi costasse, vi salverò!

I'll save you, even if it costs me my life!

Puccini, *Tosca*, Act I

WHEN JULIA AND LARRY appeared at the stage door, company members were gathered around a sign tacked to the bulletin board near the security post, which proclaimed, "*Tosca revised rehearsal time, 11:30 a.m.*"

Larry excused himself and headed through the gate to the backstage wings. Charles, who was retrieving an envelope from the mail cubbies on the wall, approached Julia.

"Who was that?" he asked.

"The new detective on Abel's case."

"Oh. He doesn't much look like a detective." Charles gazed into what Julia supposed was an exhausted, stressed face. "Haven't slept?"

Julia shook her head. "I've mostly been trying to play through Abel's song."

"Oh, yes, of course. If you'd like me to take a look at it, I have some time this afternoon."

Julia didn't know what to think. On one hand, the song was deeply personal and intimate. On the other hand, Charles was an accomplished musician and might have some insight into the strange, bewildering notes eluding her own expertise.

Or maybe even help me find the missing page.

Regarding Charles with reluctance, Julia unzipped the special compartment in her violin case, carefully pulled out the music for Abel's song, and handed it to him. She waited, anxious, searching his face while he studied the notes. Then, remembering she also wanted to talk to Matt before rehearsal started, she glanced up at the wall clock. She turned back to Charles and reached out for the music.

"I've gotta go, Charles."

"How about letting me keep the song today so I can look it over? We can discuss it later, maybe over dinner. If you're off tonight, that is."

Julia's guard went up. *Is he asking me out?* She knew the Met stayed out of employee's dating affairs. They weren't thrilled when people dated "in-house" but didn't interfere either. A number of marriages had taken place, usually between employees of the same genre: musicians with musicians, singers with singers, ballet dancers with other ballet dancers. Daniel, the orchestra's concertmaster, had married a well-known solo singer, but no doubt his prominent position helped him cross the genre line. The one unwritten rule was not to accept couples that were already married. Nepotism, at least on the surface, was frowned upon. Better to support two families than one, was the policy. The stagehands were an exception in this case, but they were part of the Teamsters, and no earthly rules applied to them. They were a "family" in every sense.

Paranoid, Julia looked over at the people around her, but no one was listening. "Well, I am off, actually, but I—"

Charles must have intuited her reluctance. "Just a get-together, no strings. Okay?" He waited patiently while she considered and flashed her a grin. "How about if we meet at the Ginger Man at eight?"

She hesitated another moment, but his smile won her over. "Okay."

In spite of her misgivings Julia managed a smile and a nod to Charles. "Wonderful. See you tonight."

Charles remained with her as she pulled out her ID and showed it to the guard. With a final backward glance at Charles and her precious song, she allowed the guard to buzz her inside.

୫୬ଓଃ

Matt was supervising the placement of sets for the day's rehearsal when Julia arrived at the busy backstage area. The stage manager, his assistants and other assorted company members, worked at their respective tasks. Solo singers and choristers warmed up their voices. Stagehands made adjustments on scenery and props.

Positioned behind a group of his charges, Matt shouted orders to them. "More to the left. Lower it slowly!"

With a groan of effort, the stagehands let down a backdrop with great care and stopped for a much-needed breather. They all managed to smile, however, when they spied Julia coming toward them. She returned the greeting.

Because she was new, they were nice to her, and Julia didn't perceive their appreciation of her as a threat or sexual innuendo in any way. She got along well with all of the stagehands except for Matt's assistant, Frank, who seemed to have been born with a nasty disposition. After a number of attempts at being friendly with Frank, she'd given up and decided to stick to the more genial members of the International Alliance of Technical and Stage Employees contingent.

Even if their union is part of the Teamsters, at least they're nice to me.

Striding toward Matt, Julia didn't notice the cloth-covered table placed in her path. She bumped right into it and found herself face-to-face with the bloodied head of Saint John the Baptist on a silver platter. She looked around and saw Frank smirking at her. Suppressing a shudder, she limped toward Matt with as much dignity as she could muster. He gave her his usual affable grin.

"Hey, Julia. What's up?"

Julia got right to the point. "Matt, can we talk…about Sid?"

Matt's face darkened. He narrowed his eyes at her, lowering his voice. "Let's go somewhere else."

Matt motioned to Frank, who darted a questioning look at his boss. "Take over for a minute, will ya', Frank?"

Frank frowned. "We're awful busy right now. It's not a good time."

Matt shot Frank a disapproving glance. Looking uncomfortable, Frank relented, though he still fired an unpleasant look at Julia.

"Sure thing, boss."

As Frank took Matt's position, Julia noticed him watching her and Matt out of the corner of his eye as they walked off. Julia thought Frank probably knew about the little love notes Matt penciled by her name on the sign-in sheet and resented Matt's crush on her. She sensed there was something about her that grated on his nerves, but she couldn't fathom what it was. He was either jealous of Matt, or thought she was distracting Matt from his job. But Matt had never mentioned that Frank had made any complaints about her.

I'll never understand the world of stagehands.

As usual, the backstage wings area on stage right was a zoo. Stagehands, the stage manager and his assistants and lackeys, and other assorted company members were all jockeying for space and attention. Matt led Julia to a dark, quiet corner near the stage manager's desk.

Julia nodded in Frank's direction. "He doesn't like me."

"Don't take it personally. He's like that with everybody. It's his army training, to be suspicious of people."

Army training? That explains a lot. The military is even more incomprehensible than stagehands. Some sort of feral tribe.

There was a tense silence as Julia tried to summon up the courage to broach a difficult subject, one she knew Matt was not looking forward to discussing. Nonetheless, he smiled his usual sympathetic grin.

"So…Sidney. Gee, Julia, I'm disappointed. I was hoping you wanted to maybe suggest dinner and a movie."

"This is serious, Matt. He needs your help."

Matt's smile lost its luster, but he pretended bravado. "Me? What could I do?"

"Find out who framed him."

With a furtive look around, he knit his brow. "What makes you think—" Julia's pointed look stopped him in mid-sentence. "This isn't the time or place, Julia."

"Then when? Or where?" Julia's voice became frantic. "Sid's chances of beating the charges are fading away as we speak. He's sick, too, thinks someone in the jail is trying to poison him."

"Oh, man…" Matt groaned.

Julia held his gaze, her expression pleading. "Will you help, *please?* I don't know where else to turn. You're his friend, you've known him, like, forever, right?"

Matt hesitated. "Okay, we'll talk, but later. And anywhere but here." He lowered his voice to a faint whisper. "The walls have ears."

"It has to be soon. There's going to be a Grand Jury hearing at any moment."

"ASAP, I promise. I'll find us a time and place. And I'll ask around about Sid, don't worry."

Julia struggled to maintain her composure. "I've never been so scared, Matt."

"You need to let go of things you have no control over, Julia." Matt returned to his upbeat smile. "Now get into that pit and be the violinist you're meant to be."

He reached over to give her shoulder a reassuring squeeze. Julia instinctively stepped back to avoid his gesture and noticed Frank hurrying toward them, eyeing them with distrust.

"Sorry to interrupt, boss, but the stage manager's on my case."

"I'm on top of it, pal. One minute, okay?"

Julia made her best effort to return Matt's smile. "I'd better go. Catch you later."

With an uneasy glance toward Frank, Julia walked off, narrowly avoiding a collision with a floor rail. Matt started toward her, but she held up her hand. "Thanks, Matt, I'm okay," she said. "I can take care of myself."

"Oh. Right. I knew that."

She flashed him a smirk and continued on her way.

છાલ

Matt returned to Frank, who was watching Julia with a disdainful sneer.

"Can't figure why you hang around with those snooty musicians. Under-worked and overpaid, if you ask me."

"Oh? They're not all bad, you know," Matt told him.

Frank scrutinized Matt for a moment. "Yeah, I have to admit she is a piece of ass." He flashed Matt a canny look and sauntered away.

Anxious to complete a final check of the stage before the first act curtain, Matt hurried off. He wasn't watching where he was going and accidentally brushed against Patricia, who was making her way to the wings to watch the beginning of the rehearsal.

She glared at him. He knew she was ready to pounce, but was glad to see she restrained herself. Instead, she muttered, "Watch where you're going, Matthew."

"Sorry, Patricia." He blanched and rushed away, aware that she was probably following the sway of his boyish shape as she took her position in her favorite observation spot.

Just before he reached the wings, Matt spied a book of matches lying on the floor. Without hesitation he leaned over and picked them up, as Frank was approaching him. He straightened up and grimaced at the assistant. "So much for a 'smoke-free' environment, right, buddy?" Frank nodded his agreement. "Those guys will never learn until they burn down the place."

Stagehands sneaked cigarettes wherever and whenever they could, demonstrating a reckless attitude toward the smoking ban in the opera house. It was something even Matt was powerless to control. In response, he kept a collection of all the matchbooks he had accumulated over the years and displayed it in its full glory on a bulletin board in the stagehands' locker room. His "guilt board," he called it.

"But did they have to leave this where the general manager can see it? Just one more reason for Patricia to be on my case," Matt added.

"Nah, she's got a few other things to tick off her list first. No worries."

"If you say so."

With a hopeless shake of his head, Matt pocketed the offending matchbook, intending to add it to his ever-growing collection, and sped away to survey a newly repainted backdrop.

৪০০৪

When Julia darted into the orchestra pit Katie was already sitting there, tuning her violin. Most of their colleagues were seated in their chairs, looking up with apprehension toward the balcony. The news had spread quickly that the shot that killed Abel had come from there. The substitute conductor stood on the podium, tapping his baton on his music stand, waiting for the stragglers to take their seats for rehearsal.

At the sight of Katie, Julia's face lit up. "If anybody was going to replace Sid, I'm glad it could be you."

Katie flashed Julia a supportive smile. "Aw, you say that to all the subs."

Julia ignored Katie's flip tone. "Rumor has it everyone's going into therapy, you know. After seeing Abel— "

Her voice choked. Katie stopped tuning, made a quick, discreet sign of the cross and fingered the small gold crucifix around her neck. "Shhh, Jul, let's tune."

As they started to warm up their fingers on some difficult passages, Katie gestured toward Larry, who was sitting in the first row of orchestra seats. Julia glanced in Larry's direction and frowned.

"There's a guy up there staring at you, Jul."

"He's the new detective."

"Oh? You mean the opera one? He's cute."

Julia was about to retort when the stage manager, a beanpole who walked with the most effeminate gait Julia had ever seen, appeared onstage. He waved his hands, glancing with apprehension toward the wings.

"Quiet, please, ladies and gentleman, quiet."

As if on cue, Patricia strode toward him and positioned herself at the apron of the stage. She scanned the stage, pit, and theater and cleared her throat. "I understand the difficulty of working in these stressful circumstances and applaud you for your courage in this time of grief." She paused as of gauging the effect of her words. "I want you to know I have faith in your ability to overcome your distress and to make sure the show will go on. Thank you."

Patricia exited to murmurs and whispers among the company. Julia turned to Katie. "She seem nervous to you?"

"Nervous? How?"

"I don't know, maybe, like, she's being even more 'business-as-usual' than usual."

"Jul, you're imagining things. *As usual.*"

With a brisk clapping of his hands, the stage manager shushed the Company. "Quiet, please. *Tosca*, Act One. Places."

The conductor tapped his baton on the podium. A collective sigh emanated from the reluctant musicians as they poised themselves to play. Julia could tell that, like her, they weren't quite ready to plunge back into work after the recent trying events.

Julia and Katie sat at attention, responding to the conductor's ample downbeat with as much enthusiasm as they could muster. The tragic irony of the situation struck Julia. Whatever the circumstances, she and her cohorts were expected to play their instruments as if nothing had happened.

And the show goes on.

Chapter 19

Akh! Istomilas, istradalas ya!...Istomilas ya gorem...
nochyu-li dnyom, tolko o nyom dumoi sebya i terzala ya

Oh! I am weary and worn out with suffering!...
I am weary with sorrow...
night and day only of him I think and worry.

Tchaikovsky, *Pique Dame*, Act II

As soon as the curtain drew to a close after the first part of the rehearsal, the stage manager appeared in front of it. "Twenty-five minute break, ladies and gentlemen."

He disappeared behind the curtain, and the conductor climbed from the podium through the small door in the pit wall and into the theater. The musicians placed instruments in cases and raced out of the pit, like horses at a starting gate, to beat the lineup at the cafeteria.

Julia clambered up on the podium and followed the conductor's path into the first row of seats, where Larry was watching the goings-on. She peered at him, skeptical. "I see you're doing your job."

"How kind of you to notice. By the way, has that guy conducted at the Met before?"

She shrugged. "Who, the substitute conductor? Yeah, I guess."

"How often?"

"I don't remember exactly. Why?"

"Do you think he was after Abel's job?"

"You mean, you're thinking of someone else to pin the murder on?"

"You never know. So, the conductor—?"

Well, this is encouraging. At least he's thinking of suspects other than Sid.

"Very self-involved, like most conductors. But capable of planning a murder? I don't know ..."

"Okay, how about you be the musician, and I'll be the investigator. Deal?"

"Good for you. And while you're at it, how about looking into a few other things."

"Such as?"

"Such as, the general manager is acting funny, in my opinion. So is that assistant stagehand guy, Frank. Have you checked them out?"

Larry waved his hands in protest. "Whoa, slow down. Let's take this one step at a time."

"I mean, for instance, everyone knows Patricia resented Abel."

"They do?" Larry pulled out his notebook and started writing. "How come?"

"Simple. She wanted all the power."

"Oh. I see. And the 'stagehand guy'—what's his name?"

"Frank." Julia watched Larry write. "He's always lurking around, shooting nasty expressions at people."

"That's no reason to suspect him of murder, Julia, now, is it?"

Julia didn't miss a beat. "What about the creep that was arrested with Sid? I bet you didn't even read his file."

"I don't have to. He's a small-time pusher, already copped a plea. Your friend Sidney, on the other hand, refuses. Meanwhile, I found out he learned to be a crack shot with a rifle when he was a teenager after he left Russia, from hanging around with his uncle Upstate. That's all I need to know."

"What?" Julia reeled from yet another setback.

Bad news about Sid just keeps piling up. What else hasn't he told me?

As she struggled to overcome her dismay, she noticed Larry's expression softening, as if he were a concerned brother or uncle.

"Surprised?" A tinge of sympathy crept into his voice.

Julia returned his look with a defensive glare. "Fine, so Sid knew his way around a rifle. But what if someone else in the company is a...a crack shot?"

"Not bloody likely. At least, we haven't found any evidence of that."

"As I said, you should look into the assistant stagehand, Frank..."

Avoiding her accusing glare, Larry picked up the conductor's musical score from the podium and started to flip through the pages.

Julia flashed him a look of outrage. "What do you think you're do-ing?"

Taken aback at her sudden reaction, Larry replaced the score to its rightful place. "Whoa, take it easy—"

"A conductor's score is his private realm. You don't just invade it."

Larry shrugged an apology. He turned his gaze on the lavish sets onstage. "You may not believe it, but this is a real treat for me. So close to Puccini, live." He turned back to Julia. "Do you think *Tosca* is a perfect opera?"

Julia said nothing and turned to go.

Larry glanced down into the pit where she had been sitting and eyed her violin in its open case. "How about playing something for me?"

"What?"

This is the ultimate hassle. Not only does he waste away my break, he wants me to play for him? With Sidney in prison?

"No way. I'm…I'm on break."

"Please, just a little excerpt? It would mean a lot to me. I love the violin."

"But I don't like playing for strangers." She searched her mind for an excuse to stop his begging. "When I was a little kid, my dad always roped me into playing for company. I hated it."

"He probably just wanted to show you off."

"Yeah. And like I just said, I hated it." Julia climbed back into the pit, put her violin in the case and snapped it shut, and grabbed her small libretto of *Tosca* from the zippered compartment. "If you ever sing for me, Detective, I might consider playing for you," she said with finality. "Now if you'll excuse me—"

"Oh. I understand. Some other time." Larry leaned over the pit rail, grinning. "And you can call me Larry."

"Oh? How unpro—" She stopped and reconsidered her abruptness. She couldn't afford to be nasty to him, with Sidney's life on the line. "That's really nice of you."

"No problem. Have a nice break."

"Thanks." Julia began to walk away but stopped to check out the bottom of her shoe. "Damn!"

"What is it?"

Her sudden outburst surprised her. It was so out of character. She noticed Larry staring at her, curious. "Why are you looking at me like that?" she asked.

"You're always so controlled," said Larry.

Julia gave him a look. "What do you mean?"

"What is it that made you use a four-letter word? You don't seem like the type."

"You're right, but whenever I get another nail in my shoe I get frustrated. This place is like a hazardous waste site. Nails, splinters, frayed carpets everywhere."

"Really? The venerable Met?"

"Are you kidding, it's a jungle back here. If you knew how many times I came close to falling flat on my face, tripping over tattered carpeting. It's not as glamorous back here as it is on the patrons' side…"

She extracted the nail from the bottom of her shoe, taking great pains not to injure herself. "There's even stray scenery blocking fire exits near the orchestra rehearsal room downstairs. And there are exposed wires everywhere, and asbestos practically dripping from the stage curtain, and… Oh, what's the use!" Julia suddenly felt guilty. She loved her job so much, yet here she was, besieged with rage and frustration.

It must be the stress of the murder, of Sid's being arrested …

"Yeah, dangerous, I have to agree with you. How come nothing's done?" Larry asked.

"The prestige of the place makes inspectors turn a blind eye. They order corrections, then conveniently forget about them."

"Fascinating. How come you know so much about this place?"

"I already told you about that. You have an awfully short memory for a detective." She tried to say this in a joking manner, so as not to offend him.

She suspected he wanted to know more, but she'd had enough of idle chatter. The precious few minutes of her break were ticking away. Her stomach was growling and she needed to do something about it. She held the nail at arm's length and looked at it in disgust.

"Yeah, we musicians do suffer for our art. To quote the late, great Beverly Sills, 'What a way to make a living!'"

He pointed to the offending piece of metal in her hand. "Can I keep that, as a souvenir of the Met?"

"Nah, there's not enough room for me to sign it. See ya'."

೮ಖ

Larry watched with concern as Julia departed with haste. He was beginning to worry about the safety of this young artist with the surprising rebellious streak.

I better look out for her. Doesn't look like anyone else will.

But he couldn't suppress a smile at the thought of a new name for her.

Drama Queen.

Chapter 20

Egli e innocente, voi sapete

He is innocent, and you know it.

Mozart, *Le Nozze di Figaro*, Act II

JULIA DROPPED THE WAYWARD NAIL in a trash barrel outside the company cafeteria and slipped into the lunch line. Charles sidled up to her, smiling. She smiled back, though not in too friendly a manner. She was beginning to regret having agreed to meet with him that evening. She had heard through the opera house grapevine he had a thing for the ladies, dark-haired, petite ones in particular.

Such knowledge made it easier for Julia to resist the advances of this reputed Lothario, though only a bit, for he was as handsome as any male she had ever met. She had promised herself, when she won the Met audition, to stay away from men in general, since her first priority was to prove herself in the big leagues of the musical world. But for the most part, Julia couldn't deal with the thought of physical intimacy. Since her father's violent death, she had shunned the touch of anyone, even her best friends Sidney and Katie. So she contented herself with being in awe of Charles's musical talent, which he had demonstrated with distinction in a number of rehearsals.

The only man Julia trusted, now that Abel was dead, was Sidney. He was like a "big brother" to her, in spite of the fact he had hit on her constantly when she first arrived on the scene. Sidney was on the auditioning committee and heard her play, albeit from behind a screen. Using a screen or curtain in orchestra auditions had been the practice since the early 1970's, to counteract the sexual discrimination pervasive in the male-dominated world of orchestras.

It was no coincidence that after this change in procedure, the number of women in orchestras rose dramatically. Julia later learned that Sidney was so impressed at the musical gifts of the particular violinist whose identity was hidden he was convinced the player would win the position. Sidney's hunch proved correct, and once Julia had been chosen and was presented to the committee as the new first violin member-elect, Sidney was just bowled over by the winner's being female - and attractive. This did not stop him from offering to coach her over the next six months to help prepare her for grueling pre-season rehearsals.

Julia was thrilled to have an experienced violinist for a mentor and accepted Sidney's offer. He spent time with her, going over the music she would need to learn for the coming season and giving her a heads-up about the difficulties, both musical and personal, she was apt to encounter as a brand-new violinist in the pit of the Met Orchestra. But it didn't take long for his hormones to take over, and at that point he wasted no time going in for the kill. Julia was taken aback at first, but once they had become close enough for him to admit his reasons, she had no problem understanding.

"My ma told me all my life to find a nice Jewish girl."

"And that would be…me?"

"Well, you did admit to me that your father was from the *shtetl.*"

"Yes, but that was from behind the privacy of the music stand, Sid."

"Hey, you don't fool me with those WASP manners and that turned-up non-Jewish nose and your non-New York Jewish accent. You're a JAP waiting to happen."

Julia had taken Sid's flirtations in stride at first, bemused that an "older man" thought he had a chance with a twenty-two year old girl. But when he started asking her out on a daily basis, she had no doubts as to how she could put him in his place. A lifetime of avoiding physical contact and developing the toughness of a Manhattanite fending for herself had prepared her for that.

"You. Me. Not going to happen." She softened the blow by adding, "But you know I adore you, right?"

After some time she managed to set Sidney straight, and once she made him understand he had to refrain from hugging or other demonstrations of physical affection, they became close friends. Sidney, happy enough with a platonic relationship, began in earnest to cultivate Julia's potential as a violinist. He also looked after her with avuncular concern, and she returned his caring with true devotion. After years of feeling abandoned, not able to trust or rely on anybody, Julia at last had found someone whose loyalty she could count on.

Once the issue of sex was ruled out for their relationship, he demanded nothing of her except a friend's devotion, and she was glad to depend on him for moral support. Other than Sidney, Julia was afraid to let anyone else into the deep recesses of her heart. She had allowed her father and Abel there, and they had both left her bereft. Now she kept her feelings hidden away and enclosed in a protective shell. She didn't want to take a chance at being hurt again.

"So what are you up to today, Charles?"

"Oh, you know, the usual. Covering Giuseppe." Julia felt for Charles as he shrugged off his discontent with false bravado, barely able to hide his disappointment. "My best-known role is 'frustrated understudy.'"

"You'll get your chance to shine soon, I'm sure of it. You're very talented."

He grinned. "Oh, yes, do keep the flattery coming. He paused. "Sometimes I wish I were a baritone, so I could sing the role of 'Scarpia' in *Tosca*."

"Oh. Really?" Julia recalled a classic passage with which to impress him. "'*È avanti a lui tremava tutta Roma*' ...And before him, all Rome trembled.'"

As if reacting to a conductor's cue, Charles sang his response. "'*Tosca - finalmente mia*.'"

ଉଓଷ

As they chatted, Larry came in and watched, unnoticed. There was a slight tinge of envy in Larry's glance as he eavesdropped on their conversation. He was physically attracted to Julia, but something about her also made him want to protect her. Larry recognized a Don Juan when he encountered one, and he saw right through Charles's affability.

I hope Julia won't fall for it. But of course, there's nothing I can say. At Charles's "'*Tosca - finalmente mia*.'" declaration, Larry grumbled to himself. He knew what it meant. *Oh, right. In your dreams, Casanova.*

ଉଓଷ

Julia noticed that Charles was eyeing the *Tosca* libretto she held close to her breast. "I'm impressed," he said. "Most violinists don't bother with words."

Having studied the libretto in detail, Julia knew that the phrase *finalmente mia* translated as "finally mine." She also knew it was the villain Scarpia's declaration just before he's about to rip Tosca's clothes off, though in the action onstage, Tosca murders him before he can accomplish the deed. Julia smiled, uncomfortable and embarrassed at the sexual innuendo behind Charles's quote, and tried to steer the subject into more secure territory. "In opera, words and music are equally important. Abel always taught me that."

She was relieved when Charles moved on. "Can I join you?" he asked. "For lunch, I mean."

She found his self-effacing grin appealing and imagined he was using his most non-aggressive tone because of her discomfort. She also realized she had not been breathing for an indeterminate amount of time and let out a lungful of air. "Thanks, but I'm just going to grab a sandwich and eat with Katie."

"Oh." Charles made no attempt to hide his disappointment. "But there's tonight, remember?"

"Yes, of course. Have you had a chance to look over the—?"

Julia spied Tony on his way over and left the question unfinished. *Uh-oh. Trouble ahead.*

In general, personnel managers never bothered with pleasantries. In her experience so far, Julia suspected they lived for the opportunity to stick it to the poor slobs who labored in the pit. Tony lost no time in handing Julia the bad news.

"Patricia wants to see you in her office."

Julia groaned. "Now? What does she want?"

"She didn't say." He fidgeted with his baton. "Just go, you've got time."

"Oh, right." Charles's tone was both sympathetic and exasperated. "What's ten more minutes out of a twenty-five minute lunch?"

Tony glared at Charles, but Julia, hoping to avoid further conflict, concealed her aggravation with a mask of self-assurance. She smiled her gratitude to Charles for defending her, paid for her sandwich, and moved toward the exit.

Just as well, putting some distance between Charles and me. He's much too attractive.

୨୦ଓଃ

Charles eyed Julia hungrily as she left. He had noticed Matt slipping into the line and eavesdropping on his conversation with her. But Charles did not feel threatened. He knew Matt was reaching for something he would never have, for he was steeped in the nitty-gritty world of wrenches, nails and splinters. How could a stagehand, even the head stagehand, compete with a real stage performer?

Whereas I... well, my major role may be pinch hitter, but at least I'm backing up the big guns.

୨୦ଓଃ

When Julia knocked at her door, Patricia was seated at her desk reading *Opera News*. For a general manager of a major opera house, keeping up with the trades was *de rigueur*, much as for the Hollywood set. In Patricia's case, as the first female general manager of the Met, she was under more scrutiny than any male would have been in that position. Julia saw that Patricia rather enjoyed staying on top of her game, since no other opera company in the world held a candle to the Met in terms of prestige. And everyone who worked there reveled in seeing the Met name glorified in print.

As soon as she caught sight of Patricia's acid smile, Julia knew the encounter was not going to be a pleasant one. She felt mentally and emotionally depleted from the week's events and didn't have much mental stamina in reserve as a buffer from further onslaught. She gathered every possible shred of her remaining calm, stepped inside and closed the door.

"Is there a problem, Patricia?"

Patricia laid down the magazine, her smile fading, tension written on her face.

"I don't like the musicians hanging around backstage."

Julia was taken aback. "People go backstage every day. Since when is that a problem?"

"Since Abel's unfortunate murder."

There was a brief, uncomfortable silence. Julia steeled herself for her own defense. She knew she had to be as diplomatic as possible. She was, after all, a novice, a mere cog in the colossal wheel propelling the Met ever forward. And now, Abel was not there to back her. Still, Patricia was being unnecessarily harsh, even for Patricia.

"But I don't understand. The stagehands all know me. I wasn't bothering them."

"Frank told me you waylaid Matt, taking up his valuable time, getting in the way of the scene changes."

"Frank's exaggerating." She hesitated, wondering if it was wise to express her unfounded doubts. "He…he doesn't like me."

Patricia ignored Julia's protests. "Your job is to play the violin, in the pit, not to loiter backstage. Any deviation is just cause for dismissal, your musicians' union notwithstanding."

"Are you threatening me?"

"Let's just say I'm advising you, shall we?"

Julia eyed Patricia, her eyes narrowing. "Why are you so concerned about musicians going backstage all of a sudden?"

"There are dangers in this situation. Things you don't understand."

"You mean, like Sidney's being framed?"

"No." Patricia paused. "Perhaps you were not aware that several decades ago a young woman violinist was brutally murdered here?"

Julia's face turned pale. "No. No, I wasn't." She detected Patricia's inner glow of gratification at having at last penetrated her tough exterior.

"I wouldn't want anything to happen to you, Julia."

"I'm touched by your concern." Julia bit her lip to stop it from trembling. "May I go now?"

Patricia nodded, and Julia departed without another word.

ജ∝౿

Once alone, Patricia pulled a silver vial from her desk drawer and shook some white powder from it onto a small mirror on her desk. She inhaled the powder and sighed with relief, speaking aloud to her inner demons.

"What a way to make a living."

In a few minutes the fine white granules took their effect, and Patricia forgot why she had allowed herself to become so upset about an insignificant little neophyte.

ജ∝౿

In a secluded corner of the backstage area, Matt was having a hushed conversation with several stagehands.

"Any of you guys remember who was the last stagehand in the viewing room the night of the twenty-ninth?"

They all shook their heads.

"Well if you remember, get back to me, okay?"

Nodding, the stagehands dispersed and went back to work, as did Matt; unnoticed, Frank watched closely from the opposite corner.

Chapter 21

La ci darem la mano…
Vorrei, e non vorrei, mi trema un poco il cor

Let's give each other our hands…
I want to, and yet I don't, my heart just won't be still

Mozart, Don Giovanni, Act I

AFTER REHEARSAL was over, Julia put away her violin with an un-characteristic hurry and haphazardness. She was preoccupied with thoughts of Abel and worries about Sidney.

"Whoa, you're in a rush. Is prison closing early?" Katie asked.

Julia noticed her friend's concerned expression. "Oh. Sorry. I guess I just want to get there. Don't look so worried."

"Me, worry?" Katie's smile seemed forced. "Say hi to Sid for me."

"Sure, K. I will."

Julia ran off in haste. She knew Katie would understand her abrupt departure. Julia had received word that Sidney's condition had deteriorated, and she wanted to get to him as soon as possible. As she was the first one out of the pit, the hallway was still empty, and she was able to sprint toward the locker room unimpeded by other musicians. As she passed by Abel's former dressing room, however, a familiar voice she couldn't ignore popped into her head.

You're talented, but you have a lot to learn. I can help you…

Julia's eyes misted over. It was as if Abel were with her again, out of the blue.

Or maybe he never left me…

On impulse, she stepped inside the dressing room door and walked around the room slowly, taking in the atmosphere. Everything was just as Abel had left it. Other conductors had been using the room since he had been killed. Yet it still resembled a shrine. Julia gazed at

Abel's photos, still on the wall, his chessboard, with the pieces just as he had left them, and lightly ran her fingers along the keys of his piano. *Remember, look* beyond *the notes.*

Her promise to herself and to his spirit that she would do her best reminded her she had not yet made sense of the piece he had written for her. She resolved to go back to it after she saw Sidney. Meanwhile, she glanced around the room, searching the walls, the cabinets, and the hidden corners.

Isn't there a clue here somewhere, Abel, something that will point me to your murderer? If so, please...please tell me.

But silence alone was her answer. She turned to leave but had a suddenly realization. The chessboard. There was something weird, different, about it.

Julia scrutinized the board's configuration and noticed the king was in "check-mate" position. Puzzled, she contemplated the change, and out of instinct began to remove the king. Then she realized she had better leave things as they were and instead alert Larry to her discovery.

If I can ever get his attention long enough. Now, what else ...can I find?

A sudden urge to look inside the piano bench overcame her. As she did, she looked around, anxious about someone interrupting her. Satisfied there was no one in the vicinity, she leafed through the pages of sheet music she found underneath the bench cushion and was astonished to discover a hand-written piece buried among them. She removed the sheet and gazed at it. Her heart quickened.

Song to Julia, page 2. The missing page! But did he leave it out...on purpose?

Suddenly she realized she was going through a dead man's things, and that man was Abel. She felt a profound sorrow and a need to flee. She quickly squirreled the page away in the zippered compartment of her violin case and left the room. Now, at least, she had another part of the puzzle, which could help her make sense of the song.

First, see Sid. Next, try to play the song, with the new page.

☊☉☋

A throng of exiting musicians now filled the hallway. In her hurry to reach the locker room, and as agitated as she was, Julia didn't didn't particularly notice the man in the stage-door phone booth as she passed him on her way out.

"I don't think she took anything," the man murmured into the telephone. "She was just snooping around. Let me know if you want me to do something about it."

He hung up the phone, just as Julia rushed by.

ഇരുഖ

Julia watched impatiently as the prison security guard inspected her violin case for contraband, but she couldn't keep silent when he would not allow her to take it in with her.

"But you've already checked it inside and out," she protested. "And it's extremely valuable. Too valuable to let it out of my sight."

"It's against the rules to bring anything of that nature inside the complex. Sorry." He flashed her a crooked smile. "But not to worry, we'll lock it up for you. If you can't leave valuables locked up here, where can you leave 'em?"

Julia knew better than to argue, and she reluctantly handed over her treasure. "Be very careful, it's —"

"I know. Extremely valuable."

The security guard summoned another guard, who walked Julia through a locked cage into the sick ward and stood watch at the foot of Sidney's bed. Aghast at the sight of his pale and worn face, and his much thinner-looking body tossing in a fitful sleep, Julia approached, then bent over Sidney's ear, whispering.

"Sid...Sid."

"Sorry...I'm...not too...together." He struggled to open his eyes. They were bloodshot. "...Medicine...makes me woozy."

Julia tried not to show her alarm at his woeful state. "I...I tried to bring my violin, in case you wanted to play. But they wouldn't let me." She gestured with her empty hands.

He reached toward her but stopped short of touching her. "That's okay, kid. Thanks for trying."

Hiding her worry, Julia thought for a moment. Then she began to hum a lush Verdi melody from *La Traviata*, while making violin movements with her fingers and arms. When she had finished, she looked at Sidney. "Abel coached me on that for my Met audition."

Sidney smiled with pleasure. "I know, kid, I was there."

"Oh, right. I knew that."

He managed a feeble nod of approval and tried to focus his heavy-lidded eyes on her. "Beautiful singing, kid. Abel'd be proud."

"Sid—" Her voice trailed off. She wanted to ask the nagging questions in her head, about his relationship with Abel, about his drug dealing, about where he was during Abel's murder. Unable to bring herself to question her beleaguered friend, she could only gaze at him with anxiety.

Sid made an enormous effort to raise himself up to return her look. "Yes, Jul?" Then his eyes began to droop, and he fell back on the pillow. "Can't talk anymore. Talk...later." He groaned.

In an instant, he closed his eyes and fell asleep. Julia bit her lip, distressed and confused.

I wish I could ask him why someone would frame him. I wish he would get better. I wish none of this had ever happened.

ജരു

Julia thought she owed her admirer, Matt, a peace offering. His fast reaction to her almost falling flat on her face in front of the sign-out sheet the night of Abel's murder wasn't the first time he had saved her butt, nor was his most recent rescue backstage. He always looked out for her in ways even Sidney never had. Plus he had pledged to help her find a way to clear Sidney. She wanted to show Matt her gratitude, without giving him the idea she had any romantic interest in him.

Food is always a safe bet.

She also wanted to ensure that the other stagehands were still on her side. She hoped some of them would help her to gather more information for Sidney's defense. After her visit with Sidney, she stopped by the stagehands' locker room with a large pizza box in hand, hoping to find Matt. When no one answered her knock, Julia opened the door a crack and peeked in. Then she tiptoed in. There was no sign of life. She had been inside the orchestra men's locker room, which was open at one end, but she had never been inside the stagehand's private, closed-off hangout and could not resist taking a look around. The room was Spartan and exuded testosterone, just the opposite of the sophisticated comfort of the women's locker room.

Different in every way.

The one wall devoid of gray metal lockers held Matt's infamous bulletin board of matchbooks. She approached the board and read the label: *Matt Reynolds' matchbooks, collected exclusively at the Metropolitan Opera House. You are guilty as charged.*

Chuckling, Julia plucked a matchbook from the board and flipped it open with her finger as she roamed around the room. A locker with a *Gulf War Vets, '92* sticker stuck to it caught her attention, and she stopped to inspect it more closely. A sudden tap on her shoulder made her jump out of her skin. The pizza box careened to the floor, as she pivoted around to find Frank glowering at her.

"This locker room is off limits. For...musicians."

Frank's menacing tone caught Julia off guard, but she recovered in a heartbeat. She showed him the matchbook she held clutched in her hand.

"I've been hearing about Matt's bulletin board for so long, I just had to check it out."

"That piece of crap?" He sneered. "He's always messing with it, like he probably was the night of the murder, when he should' a been backstage with his crew."

Blanching at the mention of that night, Julia quickly stuffed the matchbook into her pocket and stooped over to retrieve the disheveled food donation. "I...I thought you guys might like some pizza."

Eyeing the disorderly array of slices, he smirked. Julia watched as he opened the locker with the Gulf War sticker and proceeded to take off his shirt. Bare-chested, Frank turned to her and backed her into a corner, an intimidating gleam in his eye. She flushed with embarrassment.

"What's your real business here, anyway?"

She held his gaze without flinching. "I already told you, I just brought some pizza."

"And didn't *I* already tell *you* it's off limits for anyone but stagehands?"

Julia opened her mouth to voice a reply, but seeing him start to stretch his hand toward her, she realized she needed at all costs to avoid a confrontation about the "touch" issue.

"I'll just leave this here."

Laying the box down on the bench, she left the room, too soon to see Frank dump the box into the trash, strip off the rest of his clothes, and head for the showers.

෫ Craft

Sidney slumped in a chair at a table in the interrogation room of the infamous Tombs, sweat pouring down his gaunt and haggard face, which still showed signs of his recent bout of illness. A grim Buddy leaned over him.

"Ballistics report came back. The murder bullet came from your box of ammo, Richter."

"I already told you, I was set up…"

Sidney's voice trailed off as Herb Cafferty, his attorney, entered, a smug look on his face.

"The Judge has set bail and agreed there's no further reason to detain my client."

Buddy ignored Herb's pronouncement and kept his attention on Sidney. "Set up? By who?"

"I don't know." Sidney's voice was tinged with desperation.

Buddy, recognizing a suspect about to cave in, upped the menace in his tone. "I think you do."

Herb sighed with impatience. "Let's go, Sidney. You don't have to say another word."

Sidney got up with great effort and glowered at Buddy. "I shouldn'a had to spend one night in this place, much less pay bail."

Sidney staggered out, followed by Herb. As he watched them leave, Buddy cursed under his breath. Once he had left the room, Assistant District Attorney Richard Magnus turned away from the two-way mirror and intercepted Buddy in the hallway. "We kept him locked up as long as the law allowed. There was nothing else we could do. I'm sorry."

Buddy gritted his teeth and growled. "I thought he was a flight risk."

"He's also been a member of one of Manhattan's most prestigious arts organizations, for a number of years."

"Whatever."

The A.D.A. flashed Buddy a self-assured smile. "Don't worry, we'll still convict. The evidence is undeniable."

Buddy looked at A.D.A. Magnus in disgust and walked away.

ജ്ഞഇ

Unnerved by her run-in with Frank, Julia was hastening toward the double doors leading to the switchboard and security post when again there was a tap on her shoulder. Assuming it was the abrasive stagehand, she wheeled around to confront her aggressor.

"I'm out of your territory, what more do you wa—" When she saw Larry grinning at her she heaved a nervous sigh. "Don't you know you can terminally scare someone doing that?"

Larry regarded her with mild amusement. "A bit on edge, are we?"

"Wouldn't you be, if your best friend was in a heap of trouble?" she said, frustrated, and started to walk away.

"No time to chat? Just yesterday you couldn't wait to bend my ear."

"That was yesterday. Today I ..." She hesitated, realizing she was being needlessly snappish at him. "I'm just feeling hopeless, that's all."

He smiled in sympathy. "Yeah, I hear ya'."

Julia felt a sudden urge to confide more in Larry but thought better of it. "I'm sorry I can't stop and chat. I have to go home and get ready for a date."

"Oh? I'd have thought you too upset to be socializing just yet."

"It's not socializing, it's...business."

"I see." Larry regarded her, unfazed. "By the way, I interviewed that guy, what's his name...Geraldo." He paused to watch her reaction. "You know, the one who was arrested with your friend-in-a-heap-of-trouble."

Julia halted and cocked her head, intrigued. "And?"

"He and Sidney have been in cahoots for years, supplying drugs throughout the Met. It didn't just start yesterday."

Speechless, Julia stared at Larry in disbelief.

"Like I said before, you think you know someone—" He peered at her agitated face for a moment. "You okay?"

Julia was struggling with shock and an overwhelming feeling of hopelessness, but she was determined not to reveal this to Larry. He was finally doing his job, looking into the matters she had found the nerve to suggest to him.

I should be happy with that.

But all she felt was anger and bitterness. This was not the kind of news she had hoped to hear, but she made an effort to take it in stride. It was, without doubt, neither the right time to bring up her chessboard discovery, nor mention having found the missing page to Abel's song. She chose to gloss over her true feelings. "Yeah. I'm fine." She started to walk away and once again turned back to him. "By the way, thanks."

"For what?"

"For taking the trouble to follow up on a suggestion—from a 'kid.'"

With that, she left him standing in the middle of the hallway, having briefly caught the astonished smile on his face.

I bet he thinks I'm full of surprises, especially for a 'kid.'

Chapter 22

Perdon, perdono...quello non sono, sbaglia costei...
Il delitto mio non è. L'innocenza mi rubò

Oh, spare me, spare me...I'm not your man, you're mistaken...
The fault isn't mine. I was led astray.

Mozart, *Don Giovanni*, Act II

JUST AS SHE WAS RUSHING out the stage door, Julia bumped into Matt. She looked at him and shook her head. Matt gave her a puzzled grin.

"Gee, I thought you'd be happy to see me."

"I am, Matt. In fact, I was looking for you."

"You were? So there's hope after all."

Julia smiled. "No, I didn't mean...it was...I just had something I wanted to give you."

Matt's eyes grew wide. "Ooh, I love surprises. Lay it on me."

"Actually, I left it for you in your locker room."

"Uh-oh. Never do that, Julia. Nothing stays around there for long."

Julia checked her watch. "Oh. Sorry, Matt, I have to go home and practice."

"But what about my surprise?"

"Just look for a big white box from Anthony's."

Matt licked his lips. "Ah, Julia, you're a woman after my own heart."

"Yeah, I know. I've seen your rendition of it on the sign-in sheet."

Julia ran off, violin case in hand, and Matt headed for the locker room to retrieve his surprise.

঺ঙ

Larry sat at his desk, headphones over his ears, lost in thought. Even his favorite Verdi aria from *Luisa Miller, Quando le sere al placido*, in his preferred version sung by Jose Carreras, failed to distract him from his anxiety about the Trudeau case. Buddy, too, was not his usual upbeat self. Always ravenous, he tossed his sandwich into the trash uneaten. Seeing this, Larry slipped the headphones off his ears and looked at Buddy in surprise.

Buddy shot Larry a frustrated look. "So what do we do now, boss? Now Sidney Richter's out of jail, I mean."

"We'll still get him, I'm not worried. I'm thinking about Patricia, though."

"The general manager?" Buddy's expression turned mischievous. "You got a thing for her?"

"No, you dope. I meant she's been acting hostile to her employees, from what I hear." He paused, attempting a grin. "Hey, you know that the music world has the largest—"

"The largest number of sociopaths. I know." Buddy returned Larry's smile. "You like her for the murder? Accomplice, maybe?"

"Just a hunch. I want you to surveil her, just in case."

"Happy to. For how long?"

"As long as you can stand it."

"Sure."

They grinned at each other for a moment, but Buddy's expression soon returned to its former distressed look.

"Something bugging you, pal?" Larry asked.

"I was fine until you brought up the subject of women."

"Oh, I get it." Larry paused. "Well? Get if off your chest."

Buddy hesitated. "You sure, boss?"

"Go for it."

"Okay." Buddy took a deep breath. "I went to see my ex-girlfriend after work last night."

Larry raised his eyebrows. "Go on."

"I been carrying a torch for her for years. She broke up with me because I wanted to become a cop. Then she married a fireman."

Buddy wrinkled his brow. Larry was surprised to see his young colleague upset. And he had an uncomfortable feeling about what was coming next.

"He was one of the first guys to start up the staircase in the World Trade Center." Buddy's voice choked. "It's so ironic. She throws me over 'cuz she thinks my job is too dangerous, and then…"

Both detectives became silent, reliving their personal and collective traumas associated with the 9/11 catastrophe. Larry knew many of the several hundred lost from the Fire Station next to Lincoln Center, and he imagined Buddy did also.

Hoping to relieve the tension of the moment, Larry made an effort to brighten the atmosphere. "That's really nice of you to talk with her."

"Yeah, well…I'm afraid my intentions weren't completely unselfish. Ya' know what I mean?"

"I do. And I know you too well to believe that."

"Thanks." Buddy gave him a sheepish grin. "How about you, Lar? You have a girlfriend? You don't seem to get out much, with chicks, I mean."

"Not many 'chicks' like opera. I'd rather spend an evening with Mimi."

"'Mimi?'"

"She's an opera character, Buddy boy."

"So you mean like, you stay home and listen to opera?" Buddy sounded astonished. "That's sick, man. You should be out there meeting chicks. You're not gay, are you? You been holdin' out on me?"

"Nah, I just prefer the company of Carmen, or Lucia. Or Mimi."

"Maybe we should go out on a double date sometime, me and 'Carmen,' and you and 'Mimi.'"

Larry chuckled, and felt the tension ease. But this time, when he tensed up again, he appreciated Buddy's effort to lighten up the mood.

"Anyway, Mimi, Carmen, whatever twists your top. But do me a favor. Lose the sour face. I liked you much better when you were conducting along with Pavarotti."

৪ৎ

Julia stood in front of her music stand with a feeling of anticipation, like a novice violin student about to discover her first concerto. With Katie out of the house for an AA meeting, Julia had some uninterrupted time to plumb the depths of Abel's song. Even if Charles still had the first page, she had not yet explored the newly discovered second page. She eyed the pile of clothes in one corner of the room and the stack of books on the floor by her bed. Since Abel's death, she had lost her usual drive to keep things tidy and in place. She shrugged.

It'll all still be there tomorrow.

She placed the music on the stand and started to play through the second verse. But the second strain was even more jarring than the first. Julia let out a shriek of frustration.

What was Abel thinking? I'll never get this right.

Then a voice came to her as if from the grave.

You've got it right… You have the gift of an artist's soul.

She wanted to believe Abel. But she was doubtful she possessed that gift. And if she did, it was slowly trickling away.

ഇരുഗ

The atmosphere inside the Ginger Man was intimate, with subtle lighting and an air of privacy. Ensconced in a quiet corner booth, Julia and Charles lingered over cognacs. In general Julia stayed away from liquor, but she didn't want her companion to drink alone, and a sophisticated drink felt like a doable compromise. She had avoided bringing up the subject of Sidney's drug activities, but even after a few sips of the golden liquid had relaxed her nerves, it was still foremost in her mind.

"Did you know about Sid's…about his…" She paused. "His drug dealing?"

Charles flashed her a look of sympathy. "There were rumors. Among the company."

Julia's heart sank. "Oh my God. How could I not know?"

"You haven't been at the Met that long." Charles's voice was gentle and soothing. "Give it time, you'll learn all the secrets."

"But I trusted Sid. He was my best—" She choked back a lump in her throat.

He regarded her with compassion. "It's not good for you, being so preoccupied with this. Mind if I change the subject?"

Charles focused his attention on Julia's violin pin. "I see you wear it all the time. Abel would be pleased." He leaned toward her bodice to inspect the pin.

His closeness made her uncomfortable, but for some reason she didn't pull back. She began to fidget with the pin.

"You were about to tell me how you became so passionate about chess."

"Oh." Julia, suddenly self-conscious, let go of the pin and wrapped her hands around her glass. "My father and Abel were close friends.

Abel took me under his wing after my dad—" She paused for a moment, her eyes closing as the painful memory resurfaced. Swallowing hard, she blinked her eyes open, saw her companion's encouraging smile and, taking a deep breath, went on. "Abel taught me everything I know, about chess, about the violin, about music. He even showed me the different ways of naming notes in various languages."

Charles nodded in approval. "You and I will have to have a chess game someday. I'm always looking for a challenge."

Now in familiar territory, Julia began to unwind. She felt much better knowing she had something in common with Charles beside his penchant for attractive women.

"So…besides Scarpia, which roles are on your wish list?"

Charles gazed at her steadily, but she looked away, uncomfortable at his lack of subtlety.

"Scarpia forever." He modulated his voice from conversational to dramatic. "'*Tosca, finalmente mia*'… Julia, you are finally mine!"

Julia felt the color drain from her face. His operatic misquote made his intentions all too obvious.

Charles frowned in distress and made a hasty effort to make amends. "I'm sorry, of course I meant 'Tosca'—"

Julia rose, pulling her jacket around her shoulders. "You know, I suddenly feel so tired. I…I should go."

"But we haven't had a chance to look at the song." Charles reached beside him on the banquette and picked up the sheet of music. "Perhaps if you come back to my place, we can try it at the piano…"

"It's getting late, Charles. Why don't you just keep it for tonight and look it over. Then we can discuss it…tomorrow."

"Are you sure you don't mind my keeping it a while longer?"

"No problem. I can't make heads or tails out of it anyway."

Julia's jacket slipped off her shoulders. Charles leapt up to help her with it. "Would you like me to see you home?"

"No, thank you, I'll just grab a taxi." Her smile was tense. "Thanks for dinner." Clutching her purse, Julia beat a hasty retreat, leaving the song in Charles's possession. In spite of her inner turmoil, she felt relieved she had just brought the first page. And she was quite sure that Charles was cursing under his breath as he watched her go.

Chapter 23

Pervoi già possente la fiamma d'amore
inebria, conquide, distrugge il mio core

For you the flame of love, already powerfully kindled,
intoxicates, overwhelms, burns up my heart.

Verdi, *Rigoletto*, Act I

JULIA TIPTOED IN to find Katie curled up on the sofa, grinning at her from semi-darkness.

"So where have you been, Missy?"

Switching on a light, Julia dropped her bag on the table by the door and peered at Katie. "What are you doing sitting in the dark?"

"Unfair, answering a question with a question."

"No it's not, I'm Jewish, remember?" Julia considered Katie's query. "Okay, you win. I had dinner. With Charles."

A mischievous smile lit up Katie's face. "A date?"

"It wasn't a date, just a meeting. To discuss Abel's song."

"Oh, right." Katie smiled in satisfaction. "Where'd you go?"

"Ginger Man."

"Yep." Katie chortled. "It was a date."

Julia rolled her eyes. "Katie, the last thing I need right now is to 'date.'"

Katie regarded Julia's flushed face and tossed her a knowing smile. "Which reminds me, while you were out, not on a date, you got a call from the NYPD."

"I did?" Julia gasped. "What did they want?"

"They're letting Sid out on bail." Katie's expression turned sober. "But he's still sick, and they have to have a family member pick him up. He listed you as next of kin."

"Why didn't you tell me sooner?" Julia grabbed her bag.

Katie started to object. "Hey, you were the one who stayed out late—"

But Julia was already out the door.

ജയ

Julia looked around long enough to know Sidney's apartment was still in the same disarray as when the police had raided it. Sofa cushions, books haphazardly wrenched from shelves, notebooks and papers, and what looked like the contents of the front closet, were strewn on the floor. She quickly gathered the cushions and arranged them on the sofa as Sidney, too tired to complain about the mess, collapsed on it.

Julia perched next to him, searching his face. He appeared exhausted and ill. She hadn't liked the looks of him, so pale and thin, when she had picked him up from The Tombs. And he didn't look any better now.

"Can I get you anything, Sid?"

"A new life, maybe?"

The Jewish cadence usually made Julia grin, but today it had no effect on her worried expression. He attempted a smile but didn't say anything more, just shook his head. Julia tried to distract him with gossip about work.

"Do you believe Patricia threatened to dismiss me, just for talking to Matt backstage?"

"I don't want to talk about it."

The sudden abruptness in his manner startled Julia. "Oh. I understand. You must be so beat. We can talk about it later."

Julia waited a few seconds to speak again. She was afraid of tiring him, but she needed to stay long enough to make sure he was in good enough shape to spend the night alone. "You gonna be okay?"

"Sure."

But when he groaned in pain she frowned at him, concerned. "Why are you still sick, Sid? Is it your stomach?"

"I'm not sick, it's just those damn drugs they've been pumping into me. They make me woozy."

His eyelids fluttered and closed. Julia watched his face, her anxiety escalating.

"You look sick to me." She hesitated, waiting for him to respond. Then she leaned closer to him. "Sid, who do you think framed you?"

He sighed. "Stop with the questions already, kid. I've had enough of that in jail."

"But if we don't come up with an explanation before the grand jury decision—"

His eyes flew open. "For God's sake, Julia, you have no idea what you're getting into. Leave it alone!"

Julia was stunned. "What?"

"You heard me. And leave *me* alone, too!"

Sidney's petulant voice, so unlike his usual self, made her gasp.

He must have seen the look on her face, because he apologized immediately. "Oh, kid, I'm sorry. Forgive me, please."

Julia turned away from him, distraught.

"I shouldn't have jumped on you like that. I know you're only trying to help. I'm such an idiot."

A heavy silence fell over them. Sid fixed a remorseful gaze on her. "I'm sorry I yelled. You know I love you, kid."

He closed his eyes again, sighing. "Just let me sleep off the drugs. I'll be in great shape tomorrow, and I can answer all your questions. I promise."

Sidney's voice lowered to a murmur as he struggled to force his eyes open. Julia gazed at him in sympathy. His words had wounded her, but she was so fond of him and understood the magnitude of the strain he was under.

"I'd never do anything to harm Abel, you've got to believe me, Jul."

Julia covered him with the afghan throw she found on the arm of the sofa. Then she removed his shoes and planted a gentle kiss on his forehead. "Shhh, sleep now."

Pulling a notepad from her purse, Julia wrote down a number, ripped off a sheet of paper and placed it on the end table. "If you need me, just call. I left my cell phone number in case you have trouble remembering it. Good night, Sid."

He closed his eyes and murmured, "You touched me. I'll be damned."

Still smarting from his outburst, she left the room in silence.

଼ୠଔ

As soon as Julia arrived at the Met the next morning, she headed to the backstage area to look for Matt. She wanted to return the matchbook she had run off with, and fill him in on the unpleasant exchange between Frank and her in the stagehands' locker room. But she couldn't find him. Instead, she found Charles lingering in the wings at stage right, watching stagehands place the impressive backdrops for Act Three of *Tosca*. She, too, loved to gaze at this elaborate set, with its pre-dawn sky behind the terrace of Rome's *Castel Sant'Angelo* Prison and Saint Peter's Basilica in the background. Julia had no desire to see Charles at this particular moment, and turned to leave, but he must have caught sight of her.

"Julia, do you have a minute?"

She looked at him, wary. "Well, not really. Rehearsal's about to start, and—"

"You won't be late, I promise."

Julia nodded her assent and followed Charles to a far-off back corner.

"I wanted to apologize for coming on so strong to you last night, Julia. I couldn't help myself. But I feel I owe you an explanation."

"It's okay, Charles. Don't worry about it." Her tone was ambivalent, and she made no effort to hide her uncomfortable feelings.

"But I do worry. I care about what you think of me." He paused, searching her face for some sign of acknowledgment. "You know, I think fate brought us together."

"Oh? What makes you say that?" Julia's curiosity overcame her discomfort.

"You came to the Met exactly one year after me."

She smiled. "How do you know how long I've been here?"

"I noticed you the very first day you walked in the door."

"You did?" Julia blushed.

"Yes. And I remember it so clearly."

"You do?"

"I've been admiring you ever since." He paused. Julia showed no signs of warming to him. "But that's no excuse for being so forward. Please forgive me."

Julia was taken aback. She wasn't used to such overt male attention, even from Matt, and in general it made her ill at ease. But coming from Charles, she didn't mind it so much.

Maybe I've let the gossip about his 'wolf-like' tendencies influence me too much. Maybe I've been too quick in judging him.

He came off as genuine and sincere, and his compelling manner was too magnetic to ignore. There was something about him. *Something that makes me want to trust him. To let him care for me.*

Flushing with embarrassment, Julia glanced around to make sure no one was eavesdropping. "Nothing to forgive. I completely understand."

Charles searched her melancholy face. "Do you? You still seem upset."

"Oh, it's not you. I'm just worried about Matt. He's usually easy to find around here." Julia looked around in hopes of seeing some sign of the stagehand. "Have you seen him?"

"I haven't, but I wouldn't worry. He's probably off on some official 'head stagehand' business. Meanwhile, it looks like Frank's got things well in hand."

Julia turned toward the stage and spied Frank, barking orders to a number of crewmembers. She squirmed, uncomfortable, at the thought of their last encounter.

Why is he in charge? Matt's always here…

The P.A. system interrupted her thoughts.

"Fifteen minutes, ladies and gentlemen. Act Three *Tosca* rehearsal in fifteen."

"I'd better get to the pit, Charles."

"Are we okay?"

"Of course." She looked at him, smiling, and suddenly locked her gaze on his face. Something about Charles made her think of Abel. Perhaps it was his eyes, the same clear blue, or his look of intelligence. Julia wasn't sure, but she felt a sudden jolt of pain at this reminder of Abel and his death.

"What is it, Julia?"

"Oh, nothing." She hesitated. "I just thought I saw…Well, for a moment there was just something about your face. It reminded me of… Abel."

Charles laughed uneasily. "No one's ever told me that before."

"Maybe it was the light. Anyway, I really have to go."

With a suspicious look at Frank-in-charge, Julia took off and ran right into Larry and Buddy, who were just on their way in. Seeing Larry brought back the anger Julia had felt when he had told her about Sidney's drug dealing. She acknowledged Larry with a brief nod. Then she hurried away.

୫୦୯୨

Buddy raised his eyebrows at Larry. "What's her problem?"

"Damned if I know." Larry just shrugged and turned a fascinated eye on the stage as the cast members began to assemble for the dramatic last act of *Tosca*.

How lucky am I to be seeing this first hand?

He pinched himself to make sure it was real.

Chapter 24

È qui che voglio dirtelo, e tu m'ascolterai,
che t'amo e ti desidero, e che tu mia sarai!

Here and now I want to tell you, and you shall hear me say,
that I adore you and desire you and that you will be mine!

Leoncavallo, *I Pagliacci*

JULIA AND KATIE TUNED their instruments together, Julia struggling as usual with her violin pegs. Julia responded to Katie's sardonic smile with a defensive pout and shoved the recalcitrant pegs, casting a nervous eye on the *conductor-du-jour*, who was mounting the podium. Finally the pegs cooperated, and Julia sighed with relief.

The stage manager appeared in front of the curtain. "We start with the Act Three Firing Squad scene. Maestro?"

Act III of *Tosca* contained a great deal of violence, as did most of the rest of the opera. A squad of a dozen or so supernumerary soldiers bearing rifles filed onto the scene. Tenor Giuseppe, who had managed to get over his opening night trauma, positioned himself at stage left, where he awaited his "execution." Legendary diva Dorothy Muir, the Met's prima lyric soprano, crouched at stage right. Her role was to watch the action and sing *sotto* while she waited for her lover to fake his death and steal away with her after the firing squad had gone. Giuseppe had stood in front of this particular firing squad dozens of times and knew the supers carried dummy rifles. Dorothy, who stood in her spot at the side of the stage at least as many times, was also aware of that fact. Still, Julia knew that the tenor and soprano disliked the sound of the rifles. When fired, the shots distracted the audience from the music, and the noise frightened everyone, whether onstage, in the pit, or in the audience.

৪৩

The conductor raised his baton. From his position in the wings at stage right, Larry had a perfect view of Dorothy and could not help but gasp upon seeing her. Having listened to her recordings and watched her performances on TV for many years, he was in awe.

I can't believe I'm just a few yards away from her. Jeez...

He elbowed the stagehand standing next to him. "That's Dorothy Muir. Oh my God."

The stage manager flashed him a dirty look. Disturbing the respectful silence pervading the backstage milieu was obviously a cardinal sin in his book. Larry, embarrassed, responded with an apologetic glance and focused on the dirge the orchestra was playing. This scene, with its foreboding orchestra theme rising in crescendo to a passionate climax, was one of Larry's all-time favorite moments in opera. He girded himself for the crackling of rifles firing that always shattered the atmosphere and watched in hushed expectation as Giuseppe fell to the floor at the appropriate moment.

"*Là! Muori! Ecco un artista!*" Dorothy sang in triumph. "There! Die! Ah, what an actor!"

But when the supers took aim and blasted away and Giuseppe fell to the floor, the tenor did not fall in silence on cue. Instead, he uttered a blood-curdling scream.

The stage director scurried onstage from the wings, waved his arms in wide gestures and shrieked. "Cut!!"

Giuseppe clutched his leg, wincing with pain, as the infuriated director raced to his side.

"What's going on here? You're supposed to fall down. Dead, not screaming."

"What's going *on* here?" Giuseppe spat back at him. "I've been shot, that's what!" Giuseppe lifted his hand from his leg, revealing a large wound with blood gushing from it.

Gasps of shock emanated from the onstage company, as the thick red liquid spurted out in copious quantities. The director gaped, horrified. "Get a doctor!"

Buddy, who had been watching from the wings at stage left, joined Larry, who had raced onstage, in assessing the damage. "I've called EMS."

Larry shouted out the kind of orders he'd been taught to use in situations for crowd control. "Everybody stay where you are! We've got this under control."

But he hadn't had much call to use his training until now, and he sure as hell had never handled the all-hell-breaking-loose assemblage of theater people surrounding him. His commands were as useless as those of a Roman guard trying to keep Pompeian citizens from fleeing a wall of pyroplastic smoke and ash hurtling their way. Supers fled the stage in terror. Stage manager and stagehands came running. Giuseppe wailed. The director paced back and forth, head in hands, moaning.

"People, people!" the stage manager yelled in an effort to make order out of chaos. "We must continue!"

Dorothy spat fire. "Continue? Are you insane?"

Larry saw that the stage manager was trying his best to calm Dorothy, who was on the verge of a murderous diva-driven tantrum. The beleaguered manager seemed ready to insist, beg, or prostrate himself in order to persuade the intractable diva of her duty. "But Miss Muir, you must carry on."

"And get shot? I absolutely refuse!" Without waiting for a response, she stomped off the stage, her skirts rustling with each receding step.

In the midst of the onstage pandemonium, the music in the pit had stopped. Larry noted that the orchestra members, who he recalled had been unfortunate enough to witness not only this entire episode but Abel's murder as well, stood up in alarm. Some gawked at the stage, but most of the others either fled or looked up in paranoid fear in the direction of the balcony. Julia and Katie stayed rooted in their chairs, looking terrified, as stagehands carried the wounded Giuseppe offstage.

Larry, followed by Buddy, abandoned the stage to follow the large stream of company members making their exodus. "You go left, I'll take right," Larry directed, hoping between the two of them they could corral as many potential witnesses as possible.

ဆဝ

It wasn't long before Patricia hurried into the fray, waving her arms at the bedlam surrounding her and calling out. "Quiet, please! Rehearsal will continue." She motioned to the conductor with an authoritative glare. "Maestro, please."

The conductor gasped and stared, incredulous, at Patricia. "After what just happened?" He turned to the player closest to him and whispered. "*Is she crazy?*"

"It was only an accident. He'll be fine." Patricia lowered her voice to a normal tone, her eyes flashing with authority. "As you know, we've already closed the opera house once this week. The board of directors will not tolerate any further interruption in our usual schedule. Do I make myself clear?"

Patricia flashed a look of supercilious menace toward the conductor and all the other company members. The stage manager's face turned pale. He cleared his throat nervously.

"The show will go on. Understudies, please! Quiet onstage!" Everyone hushed as he continued his directive. "Covers for Tosca and Mario, please. Charles, Sarafina. On the double!"

Charles rushed onstage to take Giuseppe's place. "I'm already here, in case you hadn't noticed."

Flustered, the stage manager stammered an apology, after which Sarafina, a diva soprano of the "*Walküre*" body type, appeared onstage. Charles resumed Giuseppe's exact position on the floor with machinelike precision.

As the disgruntled conductor started to wave his arms at the staring, shell-shocked group in the pit, the musicians took their seats. Tony, who had been watching the action from the back of the pit, raced through the hallways and shepherded the players who had fled the scene back into their places. Once seated, the musicians began to play, albeit distractedly.

ഇരുൻ

Julia leaned over to Katie, murmuring. "How does she do it?"

"Patricia? With a little help from her *friends.*" Katie formed a small pill shape with her thumb and forefinger.

Julia gaped at Katie, eyes wide with astonishment. "You mean... antidepressants?"

"Maybe something stronger, if you get my drift."

Julia thrust the violin under her chin and obeyed the conductor's beat but was happy to be sidetracked when she looked up to see Charles onstage. All at once, her terror disappeared. She smiled, elated.

Finally, he's getting his chance. It's about time.

ଛୠ

Sarafina, happy to obtain her fifteen seconds of fame as well, belted out her last solo phrase with all the dramatic power she could muster. "*O Scarpia! Avanti a Dio!*" She turned to the nearest stagehand. "That means, 'Oh Scarpia! Before God!'" Unflustered, she proceeded to walk toward the wings.

The director screamed, throwing up his hands in disgust. "Cut!" He grabbed Sarafina's beefy arm before she could complete her exit. "What was that? You're supposed to throw yourself off the parapet!"

Sarafina was no fool. With her considerable girth and size, a leap off the edge of the parapet, even with stacks of mattresses waiting below, was dicey at best. After all, legendary hefty diva Monserrat Caballe was notorious for making her leisurely strolling exit to stage left without risking the precipitous vault. Why shouldn't she do the same? Sarafina fixed a determined stare on the open-mouthed stage manager.

"Are you kidding? There's no way I'm jumping off that Mother." And she continued to stroll offstage, smiling innocently.

ଛୠ

In the wings, chaos still ruled. Stagehands, choristers and non-speaking actors—supernumeraries in opera parlance—and other company members crowded the backstage area, talking among themselves in panicked whispers and driving the assistant stage manager mad. Larry, scoping out the chaos around him, noticed an attractive young man, not part of the company as far as he remembered, unobtrusively carrying a stage rifle toward the exit; he detained the man with a quick grab of the arm.

"Going somewhere, uh…what's your name?"

The young man regarded Larry with alarm. "P-Paolo."

Larry steered Paolo through a set of double doors into the foyer outside the wings. He whipped out a pair of plastic gloves, relieved Paolo of the rifle and, eyeing Paolo shrewdly, adeptly snapped a pair of handcuffs on his wrists with one hand. Then he buzzed Buddy on his cell. "Better get over here. And buzz crime scene to send some techs. We've got big time evidence to bag."

Buddy came running and stopped short when he saw Paolo. "What the—? Wait a minute, I know you," he said, pointing at the handcuffed young man, "you're the valet who was in Abel Trudeau's dressing room."

"I'm also a super."

"What?"

"It's short for supernumerary. A non-speaking actor."

Buddy groaned. "Oh, give me a break —"

Larry interrupted him. "You take our friend Paolo down to H.Q. I'll call for backup to handle the 'artistes' onstage."

Buddy looked at the super, puzzled. "Paolo? But I thought your name was Damon. Well, whatever."

As Buddy led Paolo away, Larry gestured toward him, holding the rifle carefully. "Whichever it is, someone took his stage duties too seriously."

"Valet and super?" Larry muttered after they had gone. "Someone is doing double duty."

Chapter 25

Badate! Questo è luogo di lacrime! Or basta!
Rispondete! Ed or la verità!

Beware! This is a place for tears! Enough now!
Answer me! And now the truth!

Puccini, *Tosca*, Act II

ALL THE COPS STARED, wide-eyed, at the sight of Buddy dragging the hapless Paolo/Damon up the stairs of the Precinct house and into the interrogation area. Even the straight cops seemed struck by the young man's uncommon good looks. Buddy, who imagined Paolo was accustomed to such attention, was surprised at how uncomfortable he looked.

"Aren't you used to being, shall we say, 'admired'?"

Paolo cast a withering glance in Buddy's direction. "I prefer being admired onstage to being gawked at in a police station."

"Oh, right. So many admirers, so little time."

Buddy shoved Paolo into a holding cell in an interrogation room and locked the door. "Stay here until my boss gets back."

"How long is that?"

"Ya' never know. Just whistle a few opera tunes to pass the time."

ಸಃಐ

Having interviewed dozens of company members and come up with little significant information, Larry arrived several hours later, more than ready to fire off some pointed questions at the young man with the loaded rifle.

Buddy released Paolo from his cell and gestured toward a chair by the table. Paolo sank down into it, glowering.

Larry took his notebook in hand. "So which is it, Paolo or Damon?"

"Paolo."

"Well, then, *Paolo*, would you like to tell me what you were doing with a loaded rifle on the stage?"

Paolo scowled. "I didn't know the bullets were real —"

Larry interrupted Paolo's protest. "I'm told you switched rifles with another guy, that his had your number on it."

Paolo was already bathed in sweat. "I didn't check the number, it… it must have been the prop master's mistake."

Larry, not fooled by Paolo's response, segued into another question. "Were you trying to kill the singer, or just wound him?"

Paolo's nervous silence made Larry even more suspicious. He decided to take a different tack. "Why don't you just tell me what you did before you got your job as a super?"

"I was Maestro Trudeau's valet."

"And before that?" Larry studied Paolo's face, his body language. He already knew the answer. He just wanted Paolo to admit it.

"I don't have to tell you anything!" Paolo jumped to his feet.

"Yes, you do. That is, if you don't want to see your so-called 'stage career' go down the tubes."

Paolo turned his face to the wall, speaking under his breath. "I turned tricks on the street." He wheeled, faced Larry and shouted. "I was a hooker, okay? I sold my body, to guys, some of them from the opera. One of them got me in."

"Which one?" Larry asked.

"I don't remember, I swear."

The detective paused for a moment, then eyed Paolo coolly. "We're booking you for first degree assault. DA'll probably add criminal assault with a firearm." Larry watched as Paolo's eyes widened with panic. "Don't complain, it's a class *B* felony instead of a class *A*."

Paolo turned pale. "But I didn't do anything, I was —"

"Set up? Just try and prove it. My advice, plead guilty to the first count and they'll likely drop the second one. First offense, they might even let you out without bail until your hearing." Larry motioned Paolo to the door. "Meanwhile, if that's the case, make yourself available for questioning. And keep your nose clean."

That guy shouldn't be out on the street.

In spite of his limited field experience, Larry knew the rights of a suspect counted for more than the rights of a victim at times. It was close to impossible to keep someone locked up for very long, and these days it was all the NYPD could do to detain a suspected perp overnight. However, once Paolo was back out on the street, Larry could at least have him surveiled. That was what his decided to do, as he steered Paolo to booking.

He'll slip up, sooner or later.

ೋೂೞ

Julia appeared at the stage door that evening in her concert attire and found Larry hovering near the security guard. Together, guard and detective were double-checking IDs. Both of them seemed surprised to see Julia.

"After what happened at rehearsal, I didn't expect to see you tonight." Larry sounded sympathetic. "I figured you'd be too upset."

"I still have to play, even under the worst circumstances. The show must—"

"Must go on, yada, yada. I had no idea you guys were so plucky." He cracked a friendly smile.

Encouraged, she took the opening. "So tell me about that super you collared today. Is it true his rifle had real bullets?"

"'Collared?'" Larry studied her eager expression. "My, aren't we the resourceful one?" He leaned toward her, lowering his voice. "As far as the ammo, I can't tell you that. You know what ammo means, right?"

Julia rolled her eyes, a *soupçon* of annoyance in her tone. "Of course. I watch *Law and Order*, just like everyone else. Not to mention *CSI.*"

"I have a feeling you do a lot more than just watch 'em." His voice took on a hint of admiration.

Julia handled the compliment with a knowing smile. "Thanks. Maybe you're not such a bad guy after all."

"Careful, I blush easily."

She was beginning to think the atmosphere between her and the detective had lightened up enough for her to share some of her recent finds. "In fact, if you promise to be very nice to me, I'll share a secret theory with you."

"I'm all ears."

She leaned close to him. "Somebody moved the pieces on Abel's chessboard in his dressing room."

"And?"

"*And,* don't you think it might have been Abel's killer, returning to the scene of the crime? You should at least dust for prints."

Larry narrowed his gaze. "You've been watching too much TV."

"Yeah, it just kills you, doesn't it?"

"I didn't ask you what you were doing in there," he cautioned. "So don't push me."

With a superior smirk, she showed the guard her ID and moved on.

଼ଠଓଃ

After the final curtain fell on the evening's performance of *Don Giovanni,* most of the musicians emitted a collective sigh of relief and made their hasty exits from the pit. But Julia just sat motionless in her chair, unaware of them. This opera always had a profound affect on her, even more so since Abel's demise. The sufferings of Donna Anna, the daughter of the murdered *Commendatore,* made Julia's heart break in empathy. She endured the agonies of the young woman's emotional torture as if they were her own. During the course of the opera, Julia mouthed the words of the libretto, which she knew from memory, sung by Anna when she finds her father's body:

Mal qual mai s'offre, oh Dei, spettacolo funesto agli occhi miei!...
Ah! l'assassino mel trucidò.

"But, oh God, what dreadful sight confronts my eyes!...

"Ah! The assassin has struck him down!"

These phrases alone were enough to bring tears to Julia's eyes, but the words that followed always brought Julia visions of her father expiring in her arms, when Anna intones:

Quel sangue...quella piaga...quel volto...tinto e coperto
dei color di morte...
Ei non respira più...fredde ha le membra.

"This blood...this wound...this face...discolored and covered with the pallor of death...

"He's not breathing anymore...his limbs are so cold..."

Julia often thought these brilliant and evocative words flowing from the pen of Mozart's librettist Lorenzo da Ponte accurately portrayed the agony of every daughter who has lost a father, in particular when the loss was sudden and violent. Now that she was mourning the loss of Abel as well, Julia could not help but be haunted by images of her mentor, his blood on her hands, being torn from her with as much brutality as Sol Kogan had been. It was as if she had lost her own father two times over.

Now, steeped in sorrow, she couldn't find the strength to budge from her spot. Not until after musicians and patrons had vacated the pit and the theater, respectively, did Julia manage to pack up her violin and make her way out of the comforting darkness of her orchestral womb.

The women's locker room was empty except for Katie, who had been waiting to walk home with Julia. To prevent Katie from intuiting her disconsolate mood, Julia tried to pretend casualness.

"What took you so long, Jul?"

Julia replied, a far-off look in her eyes. "Just needed to take my time. You know what that opera always does to me, especially now that Abel…"

Julia hesitated, biting her lip to stem her pain. Katie gave Julia a supportive smile, and Julia took comfort in Katie's affection. It was then that Julia noticed an envelope taped to her locker door. "What's that, K.?"

Katie shrugged. "I don't know."

Puzzled, Julia removed the envelope, opened it and scanned its contents. She studied it for a moment and gave a little "humph" of surprise. "It's from Larry. He wants me to come to the pit."

"What for?"

"Haven't got a clue." Julia thought for a moment. "He did seem a lot friendlier than usual when I saw him before the show —"

"Oo-o-h." Katie made no effort to hide the mischievous twinkle in her eye. "And I thought there was no love lost between you two."

Julia flashed Katie a look of warning. "I won't grace that with a response." She opened her locker and stuffed the envelope inside. "I'll be right back."

As she stood at the pit entrance, Julia scoured the dark, empty space. Larry was nowhere in sight. Passing the music stands and chairs, she ascended onto the podium and peeked over the pit rail into the audience.

At that moment, a protrusion from the ventilation hole in the pit wall caught her attention. Clambering down, she peered into the opening. Something was stuffed into the opening. A bloodied body. Matt.

ເ০০৪

Julia's screams echoing through the halls brought Katie racing into the pit. Collapsed on the floor in shock next to the pit wall, Julia allowed Katie to pull her to her feet, just as a flock of security guards and stagehands descended on the scene. Then Tony, who had finally appeared, helped Katie escort Julia out of the pit and walk her to the locker room, where Julia crumpled onto a sofa in a distraught heap.

Julia did not even remember that Katie and Tony had carried her to the sofa, where she lay prostrate. As she moaned, traumatized, Katie grabbed some paper towels, ran cold water over them and applied the improvised compress to Julia's forehead. Julia was in such a state of shock she didn't try to push Katie's hand away as she would have under normal circumstances.

"How did I get here? Where's Charles?" Julia half-cried, half-groaned.

Katie whispered. "Shhh, Julia, it'll be okay."

"Charles. I want Charles."

Katie arched her eyebrow at the name of the attractive understudy. "He'll be here soon. Just try to relax."

There was a soft knock at the door, and Larry appeared. He spoke to Katie in a low whisper. "Poor kid. She found the body?"

Katie responded with a somber nod. Larry knelt by Julia, murmuring in a gentle tone. "Julia, can you get up?"

She shook her head, moaning with agitation.

ເ০০৪

Larry turned back to Katie. "I have to go check out the murder scene. Anything I can do for her?"

"She's asked for Charles Tremaine. Could you find out if he's still in the opera house? He might be able to calm her down."

"I'll call upstairs."

Larry strode to the door, signaling Katie to follow him. Again he lowered his voice, leaning over her ear.

"Her friend Richter's been arrested again. They're accusing him of this murder, too, on top of the other one."

Katie gasped. "Oh, no."

"Soon as he's out on bail, this has to happen."

"But... wasn't he too sick to go right out and commit... murder?"

"D.A. says he may have been faking it after the first day or so. She's really had it in for him, ever since this whole mess began. Unless he has a good alibi, it looks bad." Larry shook his head, his expression sober. "Make sure Julia doesn't find out about Richter, not until she's in better shape. She doesn't need to know yet."

Katie nodded in understanding.

"I'll have to ask her a few questions about the victim."

Larry made his way out the door and down the hall toward the pit. *Yet another murder. This place is unbelievable.*

ഇരുൽ

Katie turned back to Julia and continued dabbing her forehead with the towels. After a long moment, Charles tiptoed in. He approached the two women, leaned over Julia, and regarded her with concern. She looked up at him, her eyes glazed over.

"Julia, do you want me to take you to my apartment?"

Katie frowned at Charles. "I don't think that's a good idea. I mean, going to a strange man's place ..."

"But she did ask for me, didn't she? I offered her consolation if she ever needed it, and now she wants me to take care of her." He turned to Julia. "Do you want to come with me?"

Julia managed a shaky nod.

Unfastening the chain around her neck, Katie removed the delicate gold cross from it. Then she unclasped the chain holding Julia's "*J*" pendant and slid the cross onto it, whispering to Charles. "She needs all the help she can get right now." Then she turned to Julia. "For protection and strength. I know you're Jewish, but I don't think God will mind."

Julia managed a weary but grateful smile and allowed Charles and Katie to help her up. The untouchable Julia let Charles hold tight to her waist and lead her to the door.

"Charles. Wait." Whispering into Charles's ear, Katie revealed to him the terrible news Larry had confided to her about Sidney. "It's what the detective told me." She held Charles's gaze. "Keep it under your hat."

Charles acknowledged Katie with a somber look. Taking great pains to be gentle, he guided Julia out the door. Katie watched them depart. "Take care of her."

Down the alley behind the Met loading dock, a face was obscured in shadow inside a ratty phone booth. A gloved hand picked up the phone receiver, dropped coins in the slot with an incongruously musical tinkle, and dialed.

"Condition corrected."

Chapter 26

Soglio in cittade uccidere, oppure nel mio tetto.
L'uomo di sera aspetto; una stoccata e muor

I kill my man in the town or under my own roof.
I wait for him at night; one thrust, and he's dead.

Verdi, *Rigoletto*, Act I

IN THE PIT, Larry conferred with the medical examiner as Matt's body, still *in situ*, was being photographed. Larry's calm exterior belied the emotions raging inside of him. Julia's reaction to losing a second important person in her life within a matter of days had rattled him. Seeing Matt's remains stuffed into the crack in the pit wall gave him even more cause to feel unbridled anger toward the killer and immense sympathy toward the poor, naïve young violinist. It was hard to imagine what she must be going through.

"Anything?" Larry asked the M.E.

"Can't tell much, not until we get the body out of that crack."

"So we have an appointment tomorrow morning, I presume?"

"You bring the espresso. And make it strong."

Larry acknowledged his colleague with a frown and somehow found his way to Patricia's office. Calmly, he watched the general manager standing by the window, hunched over a cigarette and looking distraught.

"Tense, are we, Ms. Wells?"

Patricia took three hasty puffs. Then she crushed out the cigarette with a nervous twist. "Wouldn't you be, with such hideous goings-on?"

As she drew another cigarette from her silver case, Larry shot a disapproving glance in her direction. She returned it with a defiant look.

"Yes, I'm breaking the law. Are you going to arrest me?"

Larry picked up the matching lighter from Patricia's desk and lit her cigarette. "On the contrary. As long as you don't cause anyone else physical harm."

"That's very benevolent of you."

Placing the lit stick in an ashtray, Patricia carefully polished the lighter with a soft cloth. Then she began puffing again, blowing the smoke out the window.

"And who do you think might clue me in to these 'hideous goings-on?'" Larry asked.

Patricia shot him a venomous look. "Why don't you talk to that little vixen with the innocent face...Julia?"

"Come on, Ms. Wells, we both know Julia is no 'vixen.' Someone else is behind these murders." He had a thought. "Who are you trying to protect?"

"I have no idea what you're talking about," snapped Patricia, a little too hurried.

The abrupt jangle of Larry's cell phone—the "Anvil Chorus" from Verdi's *Il Trovatore*—disrupted their conversation. He picked up. "Yeah, Buddy. I'm on my way down. Come up and keep our manager company, okay?" Larry hung up the phone and turned to Patricia. "Don't try to go anywhere. There are cops all over the place."

"So I would imagine," she said. "Thank God, I feel all safe and squishy now."

"Yeah, right." He walked out of the office with the air of a man trying not to punch someone.

ଽୠଔ

Patricia finished off the cigarette, exhaling forcefully, just as Buddy knocked. She gritted her teeth. "Come in." He and that other guy, the opera fan, must have passed each other in the hall.

The silence between them was palpable as Buddy watched Patricia quash the embers in the ashtray.

"I'm afraid I have to ask you more questions, Ms. Wells."

"Oh? Am I a suspect now?"

"From now on, Ms. Wells, everyone is."

ଽୠଔ

Larry hated to view the body of anyone he had known, if only for a brief time, while they were still alive. But here he and Buddy were in

the Medical Examiner's office, bright and early, doing just that.
No matter how many years of experience I might end up with, this is
one part of the job that'll always leave a bad taste in my mouth.
Larry and Buddy stood next to the M.E., who had Matt's body
stretched out on a gurney. Larry tried to concentrate on the exam-
iner's words, but all he could think of was Julia's agonized face.
Two dead bodies in one week. The poor girl's suffered enough.
"Blunt metallic object to the head," the examiner said. "Shape of
the wound suggests a tool of some kind."
Larry forced himself to attention. "Like…what kind?"
"Hard to tell. Looks like he put up a real fight, too. Torn fingernails.
No fingerprints on the body, a very careful job. Could have been two
people working together."
"A tool?" Larry thought for a moment. "Maybe a…a stagehand's
wrench?"
"Possibly. I wouldn't rule it out. But it could be any other kind of
blunt object."
Larry nodded in understanding, trying to decide what to do next.
He and Buddy left the M.E. to his studies and stepped outside.
After a long silence, Buddy, as though intuiting Larry's thoughts,
spoke. "So what now, boss? Richter's still the prime suspect, right?"
"Yeah, Richter had motive, there's no doubt of that. It's a classic set
of circumstances."
"Plus the stagehand's murder happened within hours of Sidney's re-
lease. And if he was faking being sick, like the D.A. says —"
"Right," Larry agreed. "Aside from the fact Abel was about to throw
over Sidney for Matt, the so-called jealousy factor, Matt may have
had known something about Sidney that would implicate him in
Trudeau's murder. Sidney wanted to make sure Matt was silenced be-
fore it got out."
"But if Reynolds knew something he could use to point the finger
at Richter, wouldn't he have revealed it during his interview right after
Trudeau's murder?"
"Not necessarily," replied Larry. "It wouldn't be the first time someone lied by omission in a prelim. Unless…"
"Unless what?"

"Unless Richter had something on Reynolds he could hold over him."

"Like what?"

"I don't know. I just have a hunch." Larry paused, contemplating. Something just wasn't clicking. In spite of the overwhelming evidence against Richter, he couldn't rule out accomplices. "Go search the stagehands' locker room again, Buddy. I've got a date with *Tosca*."

"Meaning?"

"Meaning, it's time to look into possible conspiracies."

Buddy eyed Larry. "You sure you want to bother? Richter's gonna fry no matter what."

Larry summoned up his best look of authority and flashed it at the younger detective. "Humor me."

"You got it." With a mock salute, Buddy departed, leaving Larry to his contemplation.

This isn't going to be easy. With Giuseppe back in commission, we've got to be extra alert. Too bad he had no clue about his attacker. And the stagehands won't be any help, either.

The Met employed countless numbers of crewmembers, and he was sure they all looked out for each other as far as alibis were concerned. The International Alliance of Theatrical and Stage Employees, or I.A.T.S.E. to those in the loop, was a powerful union, under the benevolent and far-reaching umbrella of the Teamsters. Everyone knew it was no fun messing with those guys.

Meanwhile, Larry was beginning to consider Julia's claim that the song Abel had written for her might well contain a clue to the conductor's murder. Larry was not educated in the nitty-gritty of music theory. He didn't even read music. But at the very least he might cheer Julia up and distract her from her grief if he showed a bit of interest in her hypothesis. Plus he still had to question her about the murder. She was, after all, a witness. He decided to call her as soon as he could free himself from the dank confines of the M.E.'s domain.

Chapter 27

Entrava ella, fragrante, mi cadea fra le braccia…
e non ho amato mai tanto la vita!

Fragrant, she entered and fell into my arms…
and never have I loved life so much!

Puccini, *Tosca*, Act III

JULIA LAY WEAKLY on the sofa in Charles's living room. Her face was still tear-streaked, but she was a good deal calmer than she had been before they left the Met. Charles departed to the bedroom, returned with a comforter, and laid it over her with great care. As he seated himself by her side, she regarded him with grateful eyes.

He gazed for a long moment at her tortured face. "How do you feel? Can I do anything for you?"

"Thank you. For being there for me."

"I promised you consolation, didn't I? I'm a man of my word."

She hesitated, as if speaking would mean Matt really was dead. Then a stubborn tear escaped from her eye and traveled down her cheek. "Matt was so sweet, so thoughtful. He didn't deserve this." Julia felt her eyelids, heavy with fatigue, wanting to shut off the world. But haunting images forced them open after an instant. "Every time I close my eyes, I see him, crammed into that crack like one of his matchbooks. Oh, God…"

Charles threaded his arms around her in a consoling gesture. She didn't pull away. "Shhh, just rest now. There's nothing you can do."

She began to cry. He held her, comforting her, until her bitter sobs diminished and she was calmer and more coherent. She sat up, panicked. "Poor Sid, he'll be so upset. I've got to see him, to tell him—"

Charles gently lowered her back onto the sofa, watching her face. He hesitated a moment. "Julia, he…Sid's back in jail."

"What?" Julia's eyes widened in distress. "But he's been out for less than a day."

"They…they've accused him of killing Matt."

"No! No, they can't! "Why would Sid—"

"It was a triangle …" Charles did his best to keep his voice soft and steady. "I didn't want to tell you, for fear of hurting you. But everyone backstage knew Sidney was jealous of Matt."

"Jealous? I don't understand, Matt wasn't…"

"Gay? Oh yes, he was. It just so happened he couldn't resist you. No one can." He held her gaze.

"But Sid was so sick, he couldn't have been so violent."

"The police must have thought he was faking his illness."

Julia broke down again, her body wracked with sobs.

"I'm so sorry, Julia, so sorry."

He clasped her, rocking her with soothing tenderness.

She wrapped her arms around his neck, as if hanging on for dear life. "Oh, God, what am I going to do?"

"Just lean on me. Let me take care of you." He held her, his strong arms encircling her, consoling her, and planted tender kisses on her forehead.

Julia responded by holding him tighter, clinging to him. As his embrace became more powerful, more forceful, she did not resist him but allowed his lips to find her mouth, covering it with passionate kisses. She felt the same fervor that Tosca did when she dared to embrace her lover in front of the Virgin Mary's watchful eye. Overwhelmed with emotion, she melted into him, finding solace in his arms. It felt wonderful, being in his powerful grasp, protected and cared for.

This can't be happening. Not Matt's murder, not Charles's kisses. No, no. I shouldn't allow myself this…comfort."

But it only took a moment of hesitation before her resistance dissolved like perfumed crystals in a tub of warm, soothing water. He was her rock, her strength, her safe haven in this tempest raging all around her, threatening her sanity. He was, truly, a man of his word.

৪০৫৪

Charles awakened Julia with a gentle kiss. Disoriented and still sleepy, she allowed his embrace, until the morning light illuminated Charles's face. Then she sat bolt upright in the bed, drawing away from him, distressed.

What have I done?

In a moment of weakness, she had given in and let herself be seduced. Her vulnerability had caused her to let her guard down, to allow herself the consolation of the physical contact she had shunned for half her life, to betray her resolve not to let anyone in. She had opened herself to emotional anguish.

What was I thinking?

Charles pulled her back into his arms, as if holding her close would remove any of the obvious doubt her uncertain face revealed. A quote from *Tosca* popped into her mind: *"Nel tuo cuor s'annida Scarpia!..."* *He's nested inside my heart.*

As if reading her thoughts, he leaned over her ear and murmured. "Good morning, my darling."

Julia regarded him with misgiving and regret, berating herself for what had happened the night before.

It was my fault, not his.

A ringing phone jarred her out of her thoughts. Extricating herself from Charles's embrace, she fumbled in her purse for her cell phone.

"Don't answer it, Julia."

Ignoring his frown of disapproval, she clicked it open. "Hello?"

"Julia, it's Larry."

"Larry?" She heard the urgency in his voice. "What's wrong?"

"I need you to come down to the Met right away. It's important."

Julia voice trembled as she suddenly remembered the revelation that had precipitated her distress of the previous night. "If it's about Sid's arrest, I already know—"

"Oh, that's too bad, I wanted to tell you myself." Larry paused but continued. "But no, it's something else."

Julia sighed, tired. After all, it had been a long night. "Okay, okay. I'll be right there, I promise."

Puzzled and still groggy, Julia clicked off the phone and started to rise, pulling the bedclothes around her. She looked at Charles with a mixture of regret and embarrassment. "I...I have to go to the Met. The police need to ask me some questions."

Charles tugged her back toward the bed, trying to mask his discontent. "Now? Is it that important?"

"When it's about Sid, it is."

Offended, he let go of her. "You're being foolish, Julia. It's time you faced facts about Sidney."

"What facts?" Julia was wary.

Charles took a deep breath. She could sense he was about to tell her something she didn't want to hear.

"He's taken advantage of your good will. You're becoming an emotional wreck over him."

"How can you say that?" Julia said, outraged. "He's my best friend."

"But you can't go on fighting battles for him." Charles softened his tone. "Not if you want to give *us* a chance."

Warning bells went off in Julia's head.

'Us?' Is he hinting at the 'R' word?

The last thing she wanted was to become part of a relationship, even if she felt the tug of attraction. She felt drawn to him with an overwhelming force, and when he reached for her and pulled her down on the bed, clasping her to him, her resolve began to melt.

"I've been so proud of you, for being such a survivor through all of this." His voice soothed her, mesmerized her. "Why don't you stay another hour? They can wait."

"I…But it sounds urgent."

"Your loyalty to your friend is admirable, Julia."

Again Julia untangled herself, before Charles's persuasive abilities could win her over. This time, he didn't try to prevent her. She rose, scooping up her clothes, and dressed with haste behind the bathroom door. Then she returned to gather up her belongings.

"If Abel had been about to throw over Sidney for Matt, it would have given Sidney motives for both murders. You've got to face that possibility."

"No! That can't possibly be true!" She paused, conflicted.

What if he's right?

Charles, as though recognizing she was wavering, reached out his arms toward her. "Julia, don't go. Stay with me. I want to hold you once more, to feel your softness, your heart beating against mine."

Anguished, Julia tore herself away.

"I have to go."

She left and did not turn back.

Chapter 28

Bello e fatale un giovane offriarsi al guardo mio…
se i labbri nostri tacquero dagliocchi il cor parlò.
Furtivo fra le tenebre sol ieri a me guingeva …

A fatally handsome young man met my gaze…
Though our lips were silent, our hearts spoke through our eyes.
Secretly among the shadows last night he came to see me…

Verdi, *Rigoletto*, Act II

JULIA EYED THE ORGANIZED CHAOS in the pit, cops stationed at each corner and crime techs sweeping the pit wall for fingerprints, and headed straight for Larry, who was inspecting the bloodstained floor. He looked up at her.

"Sorry, Julia, but I have to ask you some questions about Matt."

Julia's face darkened. "Oh. So that's what this is for?"

"Only partly." He nodded toward two chairs in a corner. She followed him and sat down. "How long did you know him?"

"Only since the beginning of pre-season rehearsals. About a month."

"And did you notice any conflicts between him and other company members?"

Julia thought for a moment. "Well, I've seen Patricia mouthing off at him, but she does that to everybody. And that guy Frank seemed to resent Matt. But Frank has it in for everyone."

"Did you see Matt the night he was murdered?"

"No." Julia shuddered. "I went looking for him but never found him."

"I see." Larry hesitated. "About Matt, Abel, and Sidney—"

"I know about the love triangle between them."

His eyebrows shot up. "Just where do you get your information?"

"I have my sources."

"Well, I'll bet you didn't know about this."

Reaching into his pocket, Larry pulled out a plastic baggie with a scrawled note in it and held it up for her to read. Julia scanned it, recognizing Abel's handwriting, and read aloud.

"'Sid, I'm sorry I had to bring Julia in on it. She has to know the truth now. It's the only way. Please forgive me. Abel.'"

She took in a sharp breath. "Where'd you get this?"

"Your boss Tony just happened to recall Sidney had a second locker. We found it there." He peered at her in suspicion and continued. "So, what did Abel 'bring you in on?'"

Julia was stunned. "I…I have no clue."

"Think again." Larry paused. "You told me about it in the bookstore."

Julia thought for a moment and gasped. "The song?!"

"You've known all along what was in there, haven't you?"

Julia bristled with indignation. "No! I still haven't figured it out, I swear."

"Then it's about time you did."

"But I can't, I don't have it." She hesitated, reluctant to admit the truth to Larry. "I loaned it to someone."

"Who?"

Julia hesitated. "I—"

I don't even want to think about how he wangled it out of me.

"Charles."

Larry shook his head. "You'd better get it back, pronto, it's evidence. Or do I officially have to ask you?"

Julia considered his demand. The thought of going back to Charles made her squirm.

Should I go ask him to give it back? Should I just bring Larry the second page? Should I even tell Larry about the second page?

Deciding against it, she nodded, grudging, and stood up to leave. Then she faced Larry once more. "Speaking of notes, I never did find out why you left the one for me last night."

His eyes narrowed. "Note? What note?"

"The one that…that brought me back to the pit when I found …" Her face contorted in anguished memory.

Larry frowned, puzzled. "I didn't leave you a—"

They eyed each other for an instant. Then Julia raced out of the pit toward the women's locker room, Larry following close behind her. Once there, Julia wrenched open her locker door. The contents were in disarray.

"Someone's been rifling through my things. Damn!"

"That someone might also be watching you, which upsets *me*."

She sifted through her locker several times and gave up in frustration.

"Are you sure you left it there, Julia? You were probably in a big rush."

"No, I distinctly remember stuffing it in." She sighed.

Julia closed the locker door and allowed Larry to escort her out of the locker room. She accompanied him as far as the pit.

"When you get the song back from Charles, bring it down to H.Q. I want to have a closer look at those notes. I'll be there if you need me."

"Do you know anything about reading music?"

"No. But you do. And no note should be left unturned." He paused, then chuckled at his little pun. "Note unturned - stone unturned. Ha."

Julia wasn't amused. She was merely dreading the thought of having to seek out Charles after their little confrontation earlier that morning.

৪০০৪

Julia navigated the crowded backstage wings, active with stagehands and other members preparing for rehearsal, and reluctantly scanned the space. Spying Charles in a huddle with the stage manager, she walked toward them. Charles eyed her with unconcealed aloofness, and she shifted with discomfort. Nodding to the stage manager, Charles motioned Julia to a quiet corner.

"Did you want something, Julia?"

His cool manner undermined her courage. "I...I was wondering if...if you...had Abel's song with you?"

"Regretfully, I left it in my apartment."

Her look of disappointment must have melted his frosty expression. She was relieved to see it soften.

"Under normal circumstances, I'd pop back home and get it for you. But I'm needed onstage for today's rehearsal." He paused, unable to hide a glow of excitement in his eyes. "I may actually be replacing

Giuseppe in Abel's tribute performance tomorrow night. He's still limping and not really up to stage work yet."

Julia uttered a cry of delight. "Oh, Charles, that's fantastic! Why didn't you tell me sooner?"

"I wanted it to keep it a secret, so you'd look up at me onstage and drop your bow from astonishment."

"I'm so proud of you."

Throwing her arms around him, she gave him an impulsive squeeze. Then, embarrassed, she looked around to make sure no one was looking. He embraced her for a long moment, and she reveled in their feeling of closeness.

He lowered his voice. "I'll be in very intense rehearsing all day, closed session away from the opera house. They won't even tell me where it's going to be."

Julia was impressed. "Charles, you're finally beginning to get the VIP treatment you so deserve."

"Then they're rushing me straight to the post-performance gala tonight. But after that, I'll swing by your place, and we can go over the song. Is that okay?"

"Yes, of course. That would be great." Julia felt aglow with excitement for Charles's good luck, even though it rode on the coattails of poor Giuseppe's misfortune.

"Wonderful. Will you walk me to the stage?"

Eyes moist with tears of happiness, Julia followed him closer to the stage, where together they watched Frank supervise the stagehands' maneuvers. They were using a rope and pulley to haul a seventy-five-pound face-shaped plaster mask up to a rail fifty feet above. Charles pointed upward, where a stagehand attached the mask to the rail and then came shimmying down.

"That's for the new production of *Butterfly*. They're going to make it like a Japanese *Noh* play, with masks attached to the proscenium."

"Wow. I'm impressed." Spying a matchbook on the floor, Julia bent down to retrieve it, her eyes misting over again.

Poor Matt.

But her reflections were interrupted by a cracking sound. Small particles dusted the air from above. Charles looked up just in time to see the mask high above them come loose.

"Julia, watch out!"

Julia looked overhead, terror-stricken, as the mask came crashing toward her. With a split-second response, Charles grabbed her and yanked her out of the way, just as the mask smashed onto the floor, breaking into jagged shards.

Stagehands immediately swarmed the area. Frank cornered the stagehand who had attached the mask and began to scream at him.

The stage manager strode onto the scene, yelling. "Clear the stage, everyone!"

Terrified, Julia crouched on the floor. She struggled to catch her breath and clutched Charles's arm as if it were the only thing saving her from falling off a cliff. He took her by the shoulders, holding her close.

She moaned as he rocked her. "Oh my God, oh my God."

"Are you hurt, Julia?"

"No...just...very...shaken up..." She forced herself to take deep, slow breaths. "It...It was just an accident. Wasn't it?"

"Things like this always happen in theaters," Charles told her.

His reassuring voice did nothing to soothe the troubles nagging at her brain. She remembered one of her very first rehearsals, when a similar incident had taken place. A piece of scenery had come loose from the top of the proscenium, and the very alert lead soprano saw it hurtling toward the stage. She had enough presence of mind to shout a warning for everyone onstage to scatter before it came crashing down, avoiding disaster and perhaps even saving someone's life. Then there was the time when some poor unsuspecting chorister fell down an open elevator shaft.

But still...

Julia began to tremble.

Charles gazed at her in concern. "You'd better go home. You can't rehearse in this condition."

She was quick to protest. "But I've got to. I've never missed a rehearsal— "

"Nonsense. It's more important that you be up for the performance tonight, don't you think?"

Julia opened her mouth to object, but his chastising look stopped her. She nodded, resigned. In her battle-weary state, his suggestion made perfect sense. But the thought of confronting her boss made her quake with anxiety. "Tony will have a fit."

"Don't worry, I'll talk to him."

"You will? I suppose that would be okay..."

She felt too traumatized to argue further. Charles helped her up and led her through the onstage chaos and toward the exit. Once out of the opera house, he walked her to Amsterdam Avenue, where he hailed a taxi with a practiced whistle. Within seconds, a cab pulled up to the curb Charles helped her inside.

"I'll try to catch a moment and call you later, okay?" He kissed her on the cheek.

Smiling bravely up at him, she leaned back into the seat as Charles closed the door. She saw him watch with concern as the cab zoomed away.

Chapter 29

Recitar! Mentre preso dal delirio non so più
quel che dico e quel che faccio!
Eppur...è duopo...sforzati!

Perform! While I am racked with grief, not knowing
what I'm saying or doing!
And yet...I must force myself to do it.

Leoncavallo, *I Pagliacci*

JULIA TOOK MINCING STEPS as she climbed the outside stairs of her
brownstone. She was still feeling shaky from her near-miss backstage.
The temperature was nippier than it had been thus far this autumn
and, feeling a slight chill, she pulled her jacket closer around her.

She berated herself for being so unsteady, so fragile. The show was
supposed to go on, no matter what. She could have, no—she *should*
have stayed and done her work, even after her close call. Where was
her strength, her inner power?

Abel would not have been proud of my showing this morning. It was
a disgrace to his memory.

Too mentally fatigued to chastise herself further, she turned the
key to the outer door, entered the foyer, and took the stairs to her
apartment. It was empty, of course, since Katie was back at the Met
rehearsing. Once inside and alone, Julia curled up on the sofa and
again began to think self-castigating thoughts. She hated missing any
of her obligations at the Met so soon after her opening night, even if
it had been a disaster. But she also knew Charles was right. She was
much too shaken up to do justice to the rehearsal, and she needed to
be in shape for the performance of *Rigoletto* that evening.

Rigoletto was not the most difficult opera to play, but it was one of
her favorites.

The scenes between the devoted father and his doomed daughter always gave Julia goose bumps. Unlike *Don Giovanni*, where a young woman mourns the loss of her father, *Rigoletto* told the tale of a father's anguish when he inadvertently causes the death of his beloved daughter, his only remaining family member after his wife dies. There was a certain tragic justice in that, Julia had often thought, a parallel to her own life. Her own brush with death earlier in the day brought this home in a way she had never experienced before.

Her ringing cell phone came as a welcome distraction from her thoughts.

"Hello?"

"Is this Julia? Julia Kogan?"

"Yes. Who is this?"

"Herb Cafferty. Sidney Richter's attorney."

Julia became suddenly alert. "Oh, my God. Is everything… did something… is he okay?"

"He's okay. At least for the moment." Herb's booming voice rattled Julia's nerves. "Sid wanted me to bring you up to date. About the grand jury today."

"Oh." Julia gulped. "What…what happened?"

Herb's voice took on a grim tone. "Well, it doesn't look so good. Ya' see, this D.A., Carolyn Pike—we call her 'six feet tall and bullet-proof'—she was elected on a 'D.P.' ticket."

"'D.P.?'" Julia was confused.

"'Death Penalty.'"

Julia swallowed hard.

Herb continued. "So that means she's hot to get a quick indictment in Sid's case and move it through the system ASAP, like before Sid knew what hit him. Well, when I pointed that out to her, she said anyone who killed a beloved public figure in cold blood, not to mention in view of three or four thousand of the conductor's devoted fans, deserved to have the full wrath of God meted out to him."

"But Sid didn't do it," Julia protested.

"You know that, and I know that. But the D.A. thinks he's guilty. And that means she's angling for the sentence to be carried out in a timely manner, in other words, immediately if not sooner."

Julia, feeling faint, remained silent.

"You still there, Julia?"

"Yes. I'm here."

"So bottom line, after the final witness of the day testified, Carolyn told the judge—he's a real *alte cocker*, if you know what I mean, old and bored—she told him the State had shown probable cause. He agreed, so he handed down an indictment."

"So, now what will happen?"

"The trial." Herb paused. "I gotta go, Julia. Any questions, feel free to call. My name's in the book."

"Okay. Thank you."

Julia clicked off and sank into the sofa. The day kept getting worse, first the near miss onstage, and now this. She felt herself being sucked into a vortex of swirling confusion and dark thoughts, like Violetta after her confrontation with Germont in Act II of *La Traviata*.

The downstairs buzzer jarred her from her brooding, however, and with reluctance she rose from the comfortable womb of her sofa. At door, she pressed the intercom. "Who is it?"

"It's Larry. Can I come up?"

Julia pressed the buzzer and opened the door, watching as Larry strode down the hall toward her. As she motioned him inside, she noticed he was agitated.

"So, do you have the song? It's time we had a look at it."

"I…I couldn't get it. But I will as soon as—"

"'As soon as' is not soon enough. We need it now."

Julia regarded him, annoyed. After what she had been through that morning, she just didn't feel like being pushed. She thought about telling him about the accident at work, but put it out of her mind. Her patience was escaping her like a cascade of rapid notes in a bravura violin passage. "Is it that big a deal if I don't have it this minute? I'm having a really bad day."

"Yes, I just heard what happened, and it's under investigation." Larry's voice became more urgent. "But I have to warn you. The case is super high profile. And believe me, I know this judge. He'll want to show that he's not soft on violent crime. If anyone can put it on a fast track, he can."

Julia used the table by the door to steady herself. "What do you mean?"

"Sidney'll plead not guilty, leaving no room for bargaining. And the judge will lose no time pushing things into high gear with that hot-to-trot D.A. on his tail. Even with the usual delays, and Sidney's lawyer pushing for continuances, a trial date could be set pretty quickly."

"Oh my God."

"Once the trial starts, bringing in new evidence will be practically impossible. This new D.A. will see to that. She got elected on a death penalty ticket."

"Yes. I know. Sid's attorney just called me."

"And here it is, election year again. Just our luck."

Julia swayed, suddenly dizzy. Larry led her to the sofa and took a seat beside her, eyeing her with concern. There was urgency in his voice as he spoke. "That song is your only hope. You need to get it ASAP."

"I can't. Charles has it. And he's unreachable for the rest of the day."

"What do you mean, 'unreachable'? No one is *unreachable* for police business."

"He's getting intense coaching all day today for the performance tomorrow night, in an undisclosed location. It's his debut, very crucial for his career."

"'Undisclosed location?' What is this, the Met Opera or the International Monetary Fund?"

"It's what they do when someone is being replaced at the last minute for a really important performance." Julia tried her best to enlighten the disbelieving detective. "But he'll be at the post-performance gala tonight."

"Fine. You can weasel it out of him there."

"Are you kidding? Lowly musicians aren't invited to those shindigs."

"Oh?" Larry thought for a moment. "Well, maybe low-on-the-totem-pole detectives are. I'll look into it. In any case, I think it's time Charles and I had a chat."

He reached over to give her a reassuring pat. She pulled back.

"I gotta go. You gonna be okay? Can I get you anything?"

Julia shook her head. "No, but thank you. And thanks for taking my theory seriously."

Larry looked at her, smiled crookedly, and let himself out.

೫೦೦೪

Larry viewed the post-opera gala as a microcosm of the opera world, at least the Met's own version of it. From his post to the side of the entrance, he watched as the elegantly dressed patrons and members of the board of directors encountered one another and interacted as if they were characters in a play. He took advantage of the opportunity to speculate on the subtext between the lines of the actions he observed.

Charles would want them to be toasting him this evening. Fat chance. Larry sensed Patricia would see to it all the attention was focused on her. But he imagined Charles would garner all the notice he could possibly want the following evening for his stage debut. From what he had perceived about Charles, Larry had no doubt the singer's every desire for attention and longed-for praise would be accorded to him, during his curtain calls and long afterward.

The privileged attendees sipped champagne in the immense, high-ceilinged Belmont Room with its sumptuous furnishings, while a six-piece orchestra played cocktail music on a platform at one end. The ensemble was led by a conductor no doubt pulled from the ranks of the myriad of assistants who hung out at the Met just waiting for a chance to do something besides conduct the backstage bands, or *bandas* as they were usually called.

Larry glanced around the room and spied Patricia. At that moment she noticed him and headed his way. Appraising her striking appearance, he adopted his most cordial social manner. "Swell gathering, Ms. Wells."

"Thank you, Detective. Do enjoy yourself," she responded with exaggerated politeness.

Larry scrutinized his surroundings. "Who are all these people, anyway?"

"Oh, patrons, benefactors, board members. The usual."

Patricia's neutral expression morphed into solicitousness when she spied Sophia Tallman, the elegant dowager and most important patroness of the Met, approaching with Charles in her wake.

"Patricia, my dear, you've outdone yourself tonight," gushed the woman. "This party is exquisite."

"My sentiments exactly," Charles said.

Larry recognized Charles's earnest attempt at echoing the dowager for the posturing it was, but he sensed Patricia was determined to convey only the utmost social refinement.

"Thank you both." She gestured to Larry. "Allow me to introduce you to Detective Somers. Mrs. Sophia Tallman, of the Tallman Foundation—"

"How do you do?" Larry managed his most urbane tone.

"…And you know Charles Tremaine, the tenor."

"Yes, from the memorial service for Maestro Trudeau." Larry turned to Charles. "I'm a great fan of your Schubert art song recordings. Hope you get a chance to do more."

Larry hoped his sincerity was not lost on Charles. The recording in question was little known, and he thought he detected a bit of surprise in the tenor's reaction.

"Thank you. I'm just waiting for some…luck. To make me a household name."

Once again Patricia deflected attention from Charles. "Mrs. Tallman's foundation has made all of Abel's most brilliant productions possible, Detective."

"Is that so?"

"You're too kind, Patricia."

Mrs. Tallman protested with such convincing modesty, Larry couldn't decide for sure whether she was being genuine or not.

Charles was not about to be outclassed. "And she's promised me a new production as well, haven't you, Sophia?"

"As I've already told you, Charles, I'll have to speak to my board about it."

Patricia flashed an admonishing glance at Charles and addressed the patroness. "Detective Somers is the one who's been investigating the shocking events here as of late, Sophia."

"We are all so distressed about Abel's death, Detective. I hope you can, how do you say it, 'sew up the case' soon."

"I'm doing my best, Ma'am."

This uncomfortable dialogue was interrupted as a woman Larry recognized as Dorothy Muir swept grandly into the room. Statuesque, black, stunning, dressed to the nines, she was the embodiment of

"Diva." All eyes turned toward her, as everyone in attendance began to applaud.

Larry watched as an overdressed matron dripping with jewels rushed over to the *prima donna*, grabbing the singer's hands in an intimate gesture. "Dorothy, how nice to see you again."

The haughty soprano regarded the gushing woman with a cold stare. "Likewise, *Miss* van Dam," she responded, putting the overfriendly patron in her place.

Registering alarm at Dorothy's brazen, discourteous behavior, Patricia blanched and hurried over to her, and smiling an apology to Miss Van Dam, took Dorothy by the arm and drew her toward Larry. With a nod, Mrs. Tallman excused herself, and Patricia hurried to cover up Dorothy's gaffe.

"Dorothy Muir, Detective Somers. He's investigating the murders."

Larry nodded at the diva, impressed. "I'm a great admirer of yours, Miss Muir."

Dorothy didn't offer her hand, so Larry didn't try to shake it. She ignored Larry's admiring comment and looked him over with a supercilious eye. "And did that violinist do it?"

"I'm not at liberty to comment on that." Taken aback at her directness and slight sneer, he watched the singer lean over Patricia and whisper in her ear.

Patricia smiled politely and turned to Larry. "Would you excuse us, please?"

Larry nodded.

She's honed her charm into an art form, there's no question about that.

As Patricia and Dorothy moved out of his earshot, Charles turned toward the detective with a sardonic expression. "Maybe by tomorrow, I'll be getting all that attention."

Larry was of two minds on the subject. On one hand, Charles was an accomplished tenor who did not often get to display his talent. On the other hand Dorothy was a recognized diva with a worldwide following.

I imagine she gets her own way—in everything.

৪০০৪

At that moment, in fact, the renowned soprano was exercising her customary and accepted right to make the general manager's life miserable by making demands of Patricia. "Why are you being so nice to that cop?"

"So he'll stay out of my way, of course." Patricia smiled with her usual confidence. "I've got an opera house to run, after all."

කාශ

As the opera scene's beautiful people caroused without a care in their rarefied world, Julia and Katie were sitting at the long, exquisite mahogany bar in the Maestro Café on Sixty-Fifth Street across from Lincoln Center, where *après*-performance customers filled every one of the small tables. Still spooked by the disastrous experience backstage that morning, Julia had begged Katie to keep her company at the bar after the performance. Charles was otherwise engaged. Sidney was being held without visitor privileges, and was not even allowed a phone call from the outside. Julia needed moral support. The fact Katie was a recovering alcoholic and a card-carrying member of AA didn't prevent Julia from prevailing on her friend that evening.

Julia felt badly about roping Katie into a situation she generally tried to avoid, but she knew Katie wouldn't have the heart to refuse. Julia drained her first glass of scotch in one long swallow and noticed Katie staring at her.

She should have no problem figuring out why I'm taking to the bottle.

In the matter of a few days, Julia had been subjected to an ordeal that had left her buckling under the strain. She admired Katie's efforts to steer the conversation away from Abel and Sidney. But she wasn't surprised when Katie voiced her concern over that near miss before rehearsal, and she was ready with a response. "Scenery falls sometimes, especially in new productions. Charles said so."

"*Charles said so.* What's up with that? You're beginning to sound like his press agent."

Julia gave Katie a hostile look. "And you're starting to act like a mother hen."

"Hey, I only said it out of concern over you."

"I'm sorry, K. It's just that lately, I've been—"

"That's okay, Jul, I understand. I'm just worried about you."

"Well, don't be. Sid's the one we should be worrying about. He's been in that freaking jail for three nights already." Julia's face took on a determined air. "Besides, between Charles and Larry, I've got plenty of protection."

Katie took the opportunity to satisfy her curiosity. "Speaking of Charles, what is going on between you two?"

"I'd love to tell you." Julia flashed Katie a sly smile. "But it will have to take second place to nature's call."

After her uncharacteristic imbibing of two shots of whiskey, Julia was feeling all too relaxed and flubbed her first attempt to rise from the barstool. Smiling in embarrassment, she managed to slide from her perch on her second try and walked unsteadily toward the back of the bar, making an effort to move in as normal a way as possible in her tipsy condition. Convinced that Katie would be anxious, Julia willed herself to walk a straight line. At least until she reached the restroom.

Chapter 30

Di che fulgor, che musiche esulteran le soglie

With what magnificence and music the ballroom shall resound.

Verdi, *Un Ballo in Maschera*, Act III

LARRY USED HIS BEST GUMSHOE stealth to approach Patricia and Dorothy without their noticing him. He was not about to miss the juicy conversation between the two egocentric women. An ungraceful and unwanted exit from the star of the evening would not be welcomed, by Patricia or by the patrons. He couldn't help but feel admiration as he observed Patricia's efforts to keep the temperamental diva's disposition in check.

"I've got to get out of here, Patricia. Now."

Patricia tried to hide her panic. "But Dorothy, dearest, they're expecting you to—"

"I don't care. I've made my appearance. Look at these hypocritical philistines!" Dorothy cast a disparaging glance at the room full of buoyant patrons who were becoming more boisterous by the minute. "Makes me feel positively nauseated. Abel hardly cold, and—"

Patricia looked around, worried. "Shhh, they'll hear you."

"Let them," spat Dorothy. "This ball is not happening, at least for me. I'm out of here."

"But what will I tell them?"

"Tell them I'm…unwell."

Not waiting for either a response or a protest from Patricia, Dorothy turned toward the door. Patricia managed to catch her by the arm, but Dorothy gave her a chilling "don't mess with me" look, shook her arm free and took off with a flurry of long skirts.

Meanwhile, Larry, who had noticed the orchestra conductor waving in Patricia's direction, approached the general manager. "Looks like you're on, Ms. Wells."

"Yes, thank you, Detective." She made an effort at sincerity. "Please excuse me. I hope you won't be too bored."

Larry reached into his coat pocket, retrieved his memo book and pencil, and flashed her a bright smile. "Oh, don't worry about me. I'll just take notes, in case there's a quiz later."

Ignoring his attempt at repartee, Patricia glided across the room with Mrs. Tallman, mounted the platform and waved delicately at the crowd. The room became hushed, as all faces turned toward her.

"My dear friends, I'll be brief. We are all aware of the sadness that mars this momentous occasion, yet I feel sure Abel would not have wanted the traditional festivities to be canceled."

Patricia paused, taking in the engrossed expressions of her captive audience.

"I'm certain his genius will live on, through the generosity of his greatest patrons…" She cast a gratified look in Mrs. Tallman's direction. "… So let us all drink a toast to your continuing and renewed support of the greatest opera house in the Western Hemisphere, if not the world!"

Larry watched intently, scrutinizing Patricia's face as she raised her glass for her triumphant finish. Even he found her apparent sincerity touching, though he remained skeptical about the reasons behind it.

With Abel out of the way, she's got no competition for the top of the heap. No one left to question her authority. She can afford to be sincere.

"And to the memory of its guiding genius, Abel Trudeau, whom we honor here tonight."

The patrons, in unison, echoed the general manager's tribute.

"To Abel Trudeau."

Patricia gestured to the waiting conductor, who raised his baton. The orchestra launched into the spirited waltz from the second act of *Die Fledermaus*, as Patricia had requested earlier that evening. It was appropriate for the occasion: cheerful, yet dignified. As the guests danced, Patricia watched, sipping champagne and smiling.

Larry could see that Patricia was savoring the moment, but he was more intent on eyeing Charles, who was drinking a tall glass of bubbly in one long gulp. "Thirsty, Mr. Tremaine?"

"These affairs always make me want to get drunk," Charles said, more than a little grumpy. "Useless political pandering. I'm so under-appreciated here." He turned his gaze on the detective, frowning. "Ever tried lobbying for something you want desperately, in a hopeless bureaucracy?"

Larry felt a brief *frisson* of sympathy for the under-recognized singer. "You've just described the NYPD, friend." He watched as the tenor smiled wryly, grabbed another glass of champagne from a passing waiter, waved his glass, and drank in deep swallows.

"But aren't you that Italian stallion tenor's replacement? Giuseppe?"

"For now, yes." Charles replied between gulps. "But that's today, or tomorrow. With Abel gone, Patricia's taken the reins. She could throw in a wrench any time. You can never count chickens in this place."

Larry eyed Charles with curiosity.

What a strange guy, and what a weird world. People here are either unreachable or in your face. One day you're on top, the next you're on Amsterdam Avenue.

Turning toward Patricia, Larry studied her easy, self-confident poise. He caught her eye and held her gaze while he scribbled a few notes in his memo book. Meanwhile, Charles was working his way through another glass of champagne. Larry turned away from Patricia and gave Charles a sympathetic look.

"Speaking of Maestro Trudeau, I've heard he wrote a song—"

But a fanfare from the orchestra interrupted him. All eyes turned toward the doorway, where Giuseppe the Stallion was bravely making his grand entrance, still limping from his leg wound. Admiring "bravos" emanated from the crowd.

Charles watched with unbridled envy and turned back to Larry. "You were saying, Detective?"

"Never mind, it can wait."

Larry continued to put pen to paper.

Julia was right. Helluva way to make a living.

&0C3

Julia leaned over the sink in the ladies' room and threw water on her face in an effort to regain her equilibrium. Blinking her eyes, she tried to focus on the mirror. In the dim light, she thought at first the shadowy form reflected behind her was a hallucination, a product of liquor-induced overindulgence. But when the masked person turned out to be real and seized her arm, Julia became suddenly alert—and terrified.

With the odd clarity of fear, Julia reached her hands under the faucet, turned it on full blast, pivoted around abruptly and pointed the spray attachment at the figure, who got drenched. Then, with a violent jerk, Julia pulled her arm free and raced toward the door. Shaking off the deluge, the person went after her but slipped in a puddle of water and sprawled on the floor. Julia catapulted out the door. When she had reached the hallway, she paused next to the Ladies' Room door, gulping for air, until she heard the door open. Twisting around, Julia gasped as she caught sight of the figure coming out.

Gotta escape. Gotta…run!

But at that moment the terror hit her full force, paralyzing her. Or was it the alcohol? She'd only had two drinks… She couldn't move. As in her childhood nightmares when she'd tried to flee a terrifying, unknown assailant, her legs felt heavy and leaden, and despite a Herculean effort, she could not lift them. Whimpering, she stood rooted to the spot.

She received a reprieve, however, when two chattering women approached from the far end of the hallway on their way to the ladies' room. The menacing person turned and darted through the fire exit. Heaving a sigh of relief, Julia caught her breath and, panting, rushed back to Katie.

Katie gaped at her, astonished. "Julia, what happened? You look like you just saw some weird creature from M. Night Shyamalan."

"S-someone was after me." Julia stammered between gasps for air.

"After you? But why?"

"D-Don't know, K. But I'm…I'm scared."

ଈଔ

After the stir over Giuseppe wound down, Larry sidled closer to Charles. This time he was determined not to be further disrupted, even if the ghost of Pavarotti himself showed up.

"As I was saying, Mr. Tremaine—"

"Please. Call me Charles."

"Charles. That song, the one that the maestro—" A jangling cell phone interrupted him. Grimacing in frustration, he yanked the phone from his pocket. "Somers here...She was...*what?*" Larry felt alarm pierce through him.

Charles regarded him, puzzled.

"Emergency. Please excuse me, Mr....uh, Charles."

Larry elbowed his way through the crowd to reach the exit, while Charles drained the last of his champagne and reached for another.

ಐಞ

Larry tore across Broadway to the bar, hastened inside and found Julia, with Katie glued to her. The flashing lights of two NYPD cruisers filtering through the window facing the street bathed Katie's face in a blue-red glow.

"Thanks for calling me, Katie."

"No problem."

Larry moved to the agitated Julia. Buddy, who had arrived in a cruiser already on the scene, joined Larry.

Katie moved to the far end of bar and ordered two cups of black coffee. Larry nodded his appreciation to her and gestured to Buddy to interview the bartender. Then he leaned over Julia. "Are you okay?" he asked.

Her voice trembled. "I...I...don't know."

"Did you get a look at the face? Male, female?"

"Couldn't...tell."

He noticed she was slurring her speech. "Don't worry, we'll find this creep. Trust me on that."

Seeming calmer, she nodded. Katie placed a cup of coffee in front of Julia and started sipping her own.

Larry lowered his voice. "I'll bring you two back to your apartment and ask for a police guard to watch your door tonight. It's kind of atypical, but then everything about this case is. And by the way," Larry added, "we'll stop at the hospital for some tests. Someone could have slipped something into Julia's drink."

Katie gasped. "Oh my God. Is that possible?"

"Unfortunately. It's a way of incapacitating an unsuspecting victim. If someone was going to attack her, she'd be unlikely to fight back if she was drugged."

"But how ..." Katie shook her head in disbelief. "How could someone just ..."

Larry grimaced. "That's why Buddy here is interrogating the bartender. Shall we go?"

Katie nodded and retrieved Julia's violin from its perch next to the barstool. Signaling an officer stationed at the door, Larry led the two young women toward the exit and noticed with admiration that Julia attempted to carry herself with dignity.

That poor kid. She's really had it tough.

Chapter 31

Ah, mi si aggela il core!
Sino il rumor de' passi miei, qui tutto m'empie
di raccapriccio e di terrore!

Ah, but my heart freezes within me!
Even the noise of my own steps fills me
with dread and fear!

Verdi, *Un Ballo in Maschera*, Act II

TO LARRY, Julia and Katie's living room looked like the classic dwelling of two single women. With its cushiony furnishings, softly draped window treatments, and muted rosy color scheme, it broadcast femininity. The stuffed animals decorating the mantelpiece over the non-working fireplace completed the effect.

Removing her shoes, Julia sank down into the sofa, legs tucked up under her. Katie carefully placed Julia's violin case on the floor next to the sofa and exchanged glances with Larry. They had both noticed Julia's face was weary and strained.

Katie grabbed the comforter folded over the back of the sofa, gently laid it over Julia, and turned to Larry. "I'm off to bed. Let me know if you need anything."

Larry nodded and watched Katie retreat to her room. He gazed at Julia. "You want me to stay for a bit?"

"That's really nice of you, but I'll be fine—" She faltered, suddenly self-conscious, even in her battle weariness.

Her tone sounded exhausted to him. He felt tremendous sympathy. "Don't mention it. Just try to relax, okay? Maybe listen to some music."

Julia attempted a smile. "That won't be a problem. Just look around."

When he did so, Larry was astonished to find himself gazing at an impressive array of shelves packed with opera CDs and LPs in every possible edition, arranged in alphabetical order, and walls plastered with covers from old copies of *Opera News*. He gasped, awestruck.

"You weren't kidding when you said you were hooked on opera." He grinned. "My mom would'a loved to see all this."

He couldn't take his eyes off the astounding wall display. All the latest CDs of Domingo, Pavarotti, Te Kanawa, Bocelli. Vintage LP's of Bergonzi, Callas, di Stefano, Siepi. Mozart, Verdi, Puccini, Donizetti, Bellini. Historical performances of *Ernani*, and *Madama Butterfly*...

Larry ambled to a shelf and studied the titles. "All right if I pick something?"

Julia nodded.

Larry pulled out a CD. "Speaking of relaxing, how 'bout the Vickers *Otello*." Not waiting for her response, he placed it in the CD player. "I take it you approve?"

"How could I not?"

He hoped his discriminating taste would impress her. In some ways, Larry thought *Otello* was the greatest opera ever written, the crowning achievement of Verdi's career. Of course, many opera aficionados considered his next and final opera, *Falstaff*, the zenith of the composer's lifework. But *Falstaff* was a comedy, and Larry thought dramas were always taken more seriously in the opera world. Thus, in his estimation, *Otello* remained the be-all and end-all of opera.

Something told him Julia felt the same. The music from the first act love duet washed over them, its intimate, steamy quality wrapping them in its mantle of lush and passionate tenderness.

"No matter how many times I play or listen to it, I could never get tired of this opera," Julia sighed.

"Me, neither."

Larry was pleased to see that his guess about her tastes had been correct, and that she showed signs of starting to unwind. "That's it, make yourself comfy. If you need anything, just ask your friendly officer-in-residence, Sammy. He's right outside the door. I'll come check on you later." He started to leave.

"Detective ..."

He turned back to her, smiling. "Please. Call me Larry. Now I've seen your entire opera collection, I think it's permissible."

She grinned back. "Would you like me to play something for you?"

"After what you've just been through?"

"I feel badly about not playing for you during that *Tosca* rehearsal. You've been so kind and generous. I could at least return the favor."

"You're just full of surprises."

Julia's expression turned serious. "When Abel died, I…I tried to pour my heart out to my violin, but I couldn't. Playing for you now will make me feel better, trust me."

Before he could respond, Julia reached down for her violin case, opened it, and removed her violin. Larry reached over to turn off the stereo, but otherwise he didn't move from his spot, even as she tuned. He watched, transfixed, as she rendered the poignant melodies of the "Meditation" from Massenet's opera *Thaïs* on her instrument, which seemed a mere extension of her body and soul. She played with a rapturous expression on her face, caressing every note and nuance, building phrase upon phrase, until the haunting melody soared into dizzying heights he had never believed attainable.

After the last note had faded away, she put down the violin. For once, he was at a loss for words, at least for a brief moment.

When he found his voice, it was full of emotion. "That was…wonderful."

"My father taught it to me." She lowered her head in a modest gesture and returned the violin to its case.

"And it was definitely concertmaster quality, in my unbiased opinion."

"You really think so?" In spite of his praise, he could see she was still filled with doubt. "Abel thought so. But Sid says I'm far too sensitive a person to handle the pressure of being the lead violinist in the Met orchestra."

"*Sid* didn't see the tiger in you."

Julia's face darkened. "He…He's all right, isn't he? I mean…if there were only some way I could speak to him …"

"I wish there were, but he's the focus of a double murder investigation now. No contact allowed with the outside world."

"Oh."

She raised her face toward him. Their eyes met for a moment, a sympathetic vibration flowing between them. But when he caught sight of her worn out face, he took the role of concerned older brother. "You should get to bed. Here, I'll help you up ..."

Julia pulled back from him and tugged the comforter tighter around her body. "Thanks, I...I think I'll just stay here."

"You sure?"

She nodded. He dimmed the lamp beside the sofa.

"Get some rest now. I'll check on you later."

"But I'm not sleepy. I've got too much to think about. There's Abel's song, and—"

"You're a stubborn one, Julia." He replaced his authoritarian tone with an admiring one. "And I really respect your determination. I just hope it doesn't get you into *real* trouble someday."

"I've heard that before," she murmured, as much to herself as to him. She reached into her purse, extracted a key and held it out to him. Then she allowed her eyes to fall shut.

With a quick but soft step, Larry gently took the key, departed and closed the door without a sound.

&OCR

In spite of her efforts and Larry's orders, Julia tossed on the sofa in a fitful sleep until the wee hours. Then at 3:00 a.m. the door opened. She sat upright, heart hammering, until Larry peeked his head in.

"It's only me. I said I'd check on you, didn't I?"

She sighed with relief. Closing the door behind him, Larry inspected her heavy-lidded, worn-out face. "Have you slept at all?"

"Does it look like I have?"

Larry smiled, good-natured. "Hey, I'm the detective here. You answer the questions, not ask them."

"I'm Jewish, it's my birthright to answer a question with a question."

Julia tried to return his smile, but she couldn't seem to manage it. Larry regarded her with sympathy.

"Looks like some more music is on order. But something different this time ..." He pulled a CD from his jacket pocket and brandished it to her.

"Herbie Hancock?"

Noting her disappointment, he extracted two others. "Dave Brubeck? Stan Kenton?"

"I'd rather listen to *La Bohème.*"

"Opera didn't do anything for you tonight. Herbie Hancock will."

He loaded the CDs into the player and started them. Julia grimaced, but as the music filtered through the room, he saw her begin to relax. She leaned back and closed her eyes.

"This stuff's not half bad."

Larry grinned, gratified, as he watched her drift off to sleep. Covering her again with the comforter, he stole away.

And this time, maybe she'll manage to get through the night.

Chapter 32

L'on m'avait même dit de craindre pour ma vie;
mais je suis brave! Je n'ai pas voulu fuir!

I was even told to fear for my life;
but I'm brave! I didn't want to run away!

Bizet, *Carmen,* Act IV

Sidney and his attorney occupied a table on the aisle opposite the district attorney. All three rose as the judge ambled in. He looked closely at Sidney and then addressed Sidney's attorney, without a trace of emotion. "Does the suspect's plea remain unchanged?"

Sidney, his teeth clenched, flashed Herb a sober look and nodded. "My client still pleads not guilty, Your Honor." Herb lowered his usual booming voice. "If I may point out, Your Honor, he was too ill to have committed murder at the time of —"

"Well, he looks healthy enough now." The Judge peered at the lawyer. "Grand Jury selection ASAP, motion schedule, yada, yada. You know the drill. Let's move this along, Counselor, there are too many hoops to jump through. We don't want to wait too long to set a trial date. This case is too hot."

"But Your Honor, I need time for discovery," Herb protested.

"You'll have plenty," the Judge snapped. "Better yet, see if you can get together on a plea agreement."

Sidney shook his head vehemently. The district attorney flashed an imperious look at both Sidney and his attorney. Sidney glared at her in defiance as he was led from the room. The D.A. leaned over to Herb. "Let him glower away," she murmured. "It won't help."

৪০৩

Early afternoon light streamed into Julia's living room as she wakened and stretched her arms overhead. But she was alarmed when she caught a glimpse of the clock.

Twelve p.m.! It's noon! How could I have slept so late?

Sitting up, she reached for her purse, pulled out her cell phone and dialed. A voice picked up on the other end.

"Hello?"

"Charles, it's Julia."

"Julia! Where have you been? I've been frantic. I tried calling you, but—"

"I'm home, I must not have heard the phone. I…I …" She hesitated. "There was an incident last night after the performance. Someone… someone attacked me."

"Good God! Where?"

"I'll explain later. Just come here, I need you." Julia tried not to lose her composure. "And I need you to bring over Abel's song, too, ASAP."

"Of course, my darling, I was planning on it. I'll be right there."

ಏಂಬ

By the time Charles arrived, Julia had already been pacing back and forth for some time. In the meantime, overwrought about her lack of communication with Sidney, she had dialed information to find out the number for The Tombs. It took some doing, but she was finally able to get through.

"Switchboard, may I help you?"

"Hello? Yes, I'm calling to check on a pri…a detainee. Sidney Richter."

"I'll look him up. Please hold." There was a pause. "I'm sorry, his information is not available at this time."

"Are you sure?"

"Yes, I'm sorry."

With a frustrated sigh, Julia clicked off. Her phone rang immediately. It was Larry.

"How you doing this morning, kid?"

"I…I feel like I got hit by a truck."

"No surprise, since they found 'roofies' in your blood."

Julia was bewildered. "What?"

"Rohypnol, ten times more potent than Valium. Makes you look drunk, slurred speech, dizziness and such. Then it disrupts your sleep." He paused. "Supposed to be visible in a drink, but copycat versions from other countries aren't."

"So, you mean I was...drugged?"

"Yep. Bartender says he didn't see anything. We're still looking into it."

Julia didn't know what to say.

"You okay, Julia?"

"Yes. It's just...why would someone do this?"

"That's what we're trying to find out. Meanwhile, I gotta go. Check with you later."

She hung up, puzzled, her mind racing.

Someone drugged me, but who? Why?

After what seemed like hours, there was a faint knock at the door, and Sammy the police guard peeked in. "This guy says you asked him here, is that right, Miss?"

Julia glimpsed Charles poised behind the guard and nodded. "Yes, I did. It's okay."

The guard stepped aside, let Charles pass, and closed the door. Charles dashed over to Julia and pulled her to him. After a lifetime of shying away from physical contact, Charles's touch felt to Julia like the first drop of water after a near-fatal deprivation, and she drank from his caress thirstily. The envelope he was carrying fluttered to the floor.

"Thank God you're safe!" he exclaimed.

She clung to him like a shipwrecked passenger awash at sea, hanging on to the last piece of debris from the sinking vessel. "Oh, Charles, it was horrible."

"Shhh, darling, I'm here now."

They kissed slowly. But instead of feeling invigorated from these new sensations, she felt worn out. Then Julia sat down, hard, onto the sofa.

Oh, God, why did I sleep so late? Is that what drugs do?

"Charles, we have to look at the song."

Charles picked up the envelope and placed it in her hands. He eyed her agitated face.

"Julia, I'm worried about you. I'm afraid you're beginning to obsess about—"

Julia thought about telling him she had been drugged, but deciphering the song was her first priority. "This…this is Sid's only chance!" She opened the envelope and gazed at the music. "Sing it with me, Charles."

Charles hesitated, reluctant, but her commanding tone made him obey. "You're the one with perfect pitch. Give me the first note."

Julia looked at the note, hummed a tone and took a deep breath. Then, in a tentative voice, she began to sing. Charles joined in, but by the time they reached the scribbled notes at the bottom of the page, they both stopped.

"It's no use, that gets me every time, Charles." Then she remembered.

"Charles! There's a second page. It's in my violin case."

"What? Why didn't you tell me?"

"I…I just forgot."

She reached for her violin case on the floor beside the sofa, unzipped the outer compartment, pulled out the missing page, and handed it to him. They began to put together the music on both pages, but the melody was just as incoherent.

Charles thought for a moment. "There must be another way. Have you tried transposing it to another clef? It might sound completely different."

She gasped. "Of course, why didn't I think of that? I'm no good at transposition, though, without a piano …"

"We could go to the Met."

"Now? But I'm under house arrest until tonight's performance."

Charles checked his watch. "Actually, it's now or never. I'm kind of short on time."

"Oh." Julia's face fell. "I thought we could spend some time together."

"There's some last-minute coaching for tonight. I'm sorry, I meant to tell you, but in all the confusion …"

Julia nodded. "Of course. I understand."

"So if we're going to the Met together, we should leave now."

"But if I'm supposed to stay here, how will we get past Sammy the 'gatekeeper'?"

"Not a problem." He flashed a reassuring smile. "Just watch me."

Sammy the police guard looked up as Charles opened the door and approached with Julia by his side. When Julia explained she wanted to go to the Met to practice, he gave her a skeptical look. But Charles assured Sammy he was going to accompany Julia there and asked him to call Larry for permission. The guard agreed and pulled out his cell phone. After he had clicked off, Sammy addressed Julia.

"Detective Somers says it's okay as long as your friend goes along with you. He'll be waiting at the women's locker room, he says."

"Thank you, Officer."

Charles winked at Julia and, taking her by the arm, shepherded her down the hall. She clutched music and violin under her other arm. For the first time since her terrifying encounter at the bar the night before, she felt safe.

Chapter 33

Il passo è periglioso, può nascer qualche imbroglio

The step we take is dangerous, I fear for you.

Mozart, *Don Giovanni*, Act I

PATRICIA HEARD through the opera house grapevine about Julia's potentially fatal encounter the night before, and how she'd acted with considerable courage. She herself wondered if she could have gotten safely out of such a scrape, though she considered herself clever enough to squeeze out of difficulty if it presented itself. After all, she was Patricia.

Nonetheless, she admired the young woman's pluck.

Perhaps Julia isn't such a pain in the ass after all.

In fact, Patricia had to admit Julia was just the type of female whom she generally found attractive. Those coal-black, smoky eyes, luscious sweetheart lips, slender curvaceous body and magnificent *derrière* made Patricia salivate.

She stopped herself from fantasizing about Julia, though, when she thought about Dorothy, with whom she had been having a long-standing love affair. The Junoesque diva was a stark contrast to the youthful violinist: more mature and, most likely, more experienced in bed, though Patricia imagined Julia to be every bit as temperamental as Dorothy was, musically and otherwise. Underneath the young musician's reserved exterior probably lay a tiger's passion.

At least the girl was reputed to play the violin with that kind of dynamism and intensity. Not that it mattered. Julia was probably as straight as they come, at least in her present undeveloped state. But in a few years, when the girl had ripened and evolved a bit…

Well, who knows?

Patricia remembered the strained meeting they had had in her office shortly after Abel was murdered. Yes, indeed, the girl had shown her spunk, in spite of her controlled speech and mannerisms. She had great dignity. Patricia admired that.

In any case, she was beginning to rethink her harsh treatment of Julia, and her own behavior as well. Abel was dead, and now that cute stagehand Matt. The whole drug thing was getting out of hand, and the temptation would always be there. Maybe it was time to end her forays into the drug underworld, permanently. Even with Geraldo locked up, there was always going to be a reliable source for the white powder—"happy dust," they called it, in *Porgy and Bess*. Imagine that, confronting that subject onstage, in an opera, decades ago...

Well, perhaps that's overstating the case. Everyone knows Porgy *isn't real opera.*

Patricia reined in her wandering thoughts and summoned up her full aristocratic demeanor. It was time to move to the catacombs of the theater and deal with the descending hordes of patrons and company members who would soon be gathering for Abel's tribute performance. It was a splendid occasion, and she intended to shine like the beacon of cultured dignity she represented, in every fiber of her being. As she filtered through her cache of jewels to find the perfect pair of earrings, her mind began to wander again.

Too bad Matt got caught in the crossfire of the entire mess.

She missed his handsome, macho presence. He was without doubt her type, as far as men were concerned. If only he hadn't spied her walking hand in hand with Dorothy one golden afternoon in Central Park, she might not have had to contemplate firing him.

Of course, that's all moot, now that he's dead.

She turned her thoughts to Matt's replacement, Frank. With his surly attitude, he was not going to be as easy to manage as Matt, nor with those looks, as pleasant. But she was never one to shirk from a challenge. And as far as that was concerned, Charles was proving to be a stronger force than she had reckoned with. She had observed the body language between him and Julia, and it occurred to her that Charles might have found his way into the violinist's affections. Patricia was surprised to find herself a little envious.

How interesting. Well, there's no doubt he has taste.

෴

Patricia watched Julia and Charles make their way through the Security checkpoint and flashed Julia a smile of approval. Julia looked at Patricia with a brief glance of surprise. Then she returned the smile, wondering what the friendly pretense was all about.

Patricia just smiled at me. Maybe I'm hallucinating. After effects of the drugs?

Whatever the reason, Julia was not about to look askance at any sign of favor from the general manager. Such things were all too rare.

Julia followed Charles through the gate. He reached for her hand and led her through a door toward the rear of the security area. Here they arrived at a quiet, intimate carpeted hallway, devoid of people, where Julia rarely ventured. She felt intimidated by these lush trappings of opera glamour reserved for a well-heeled clientele: subtle lighting; plush love seats made for comfortable lounging between acts; glass cases perched on pedestals, containing historical opera lore; paintings of former opera greats and distinguished-looking former Met dignitaries and luminaries. It was all rather daunting for Julia. Charles, however, seemed quite at home in this atmosphere.

When he had determined they were alone, Charles leaned over Julia, pulled her to him, and kissed her with fervor. Anxious about being seen, she was afraid to respond at first, but she could not resist the urgency of his embrace and gave in to the delicious and exciting feelings his passion elicited from her.

After a long moment, Charles let go of her and held her face close to his and murmured. "I can't tell you what it means to me, knowing you'll be there, playing for me tonight." He sang a snippet from *Tosca* in a soft voice. "*L'ardente amante mia…il mio solo pensiero…sei tu!*"

Heart fluttering, Julia held his gaze until she perceived the sound of a hallway door opening. She gave Charles one last elated hug. Then she extricated herself.

"I'll be with you on every single note." She turned to go, quoting the phrase often used by opera aficionados for wishing luck. "And… *Bocca al lupo.*"

৪০৪৪

Charles watched her take off down the hall, flushing with pleasure. He contemplated the aptness of the analogy. Being on the Met stage in front of an audience at long last would indeed feel like being in the jaws of the wolf.

But it's also going to feel like being at the top of the world. Of that, there's no doubt. No doubt at all.

৪৩৫৪

Halfway to her destination, Julia remembered they had planned to look for a piano. But she was reluctant to distract Charles when he had his all-important debut foremost in his mind. It didn't matter. She could always find a piano in one of the practice rooms on orchestra level.

Or maybe I'll get lucky and figure out the song without a piano. It can happen.

৪৩৫৪

Larry was waiting in front of the women's locker room door when he spied Julia striding down the hallway carrying her violin case and Abel's song. At the sight of her glowing face, he had an impulse to make a comment, but he decided against it.

Whatever caused her afternoon blush is none of my business. Guess she got the drug out of her system.

Instead, he just glanced at the wall clock above their heads: 3:30 pm. Julia nodded and held up the sheet of music.

"I'm going to work on this thing the rest of the day if I have to. I'll even change into my concert clothes first, so I can optimize my time."

"Right. I'll be around. Beep me if you find anything."

Julia frowned at Larry. "This is Sid's fourth night locked up. Can't you do something?"

Larry gestured at the music. "Nope. Only you can." He strode away and Julia slipped through the locker room door.

৪৩৫৪

In her concert clothes, black slacks and blouse, Julia searched among the practice rooms along the hallway outside the locker room for a free room with a piano. No luck; they were all occupied. So she settled for a room without one. Outside the door, an officer stood guard.

The studio was a sterile cubicle with gray walls and concrete floor. A table and a black metal music stand were its sole furnishings. Julia poised herself in front of the music stand, opened the music, and began to play. She tried the song in every possible key and transposition, varying the notes to make sense of them. Every so often, she gave up out of frustration and played some Bach or Mozart or noodled at the Sibelius Concerto just to keep from breaking a string in exasperation. Before she knew it, her watch alerted her to the fact that it was seven-thirty p.m. and time to get ready for the pit.

Exhausted, Julia laid her violin in the open case on the table and sighed.

How could Abel have composed such a baffling piece?

Even with the missing page fitting into the puzzle, there was no way to figure it out. Perhaps he intended to decipher it for her at some later date.

It wasn't his fault he died.

Julia berated herself, upset at her own disturbing thoughts, and stared at the music, idly fidgeting with the violin pin Abel gave her, which was fastened to her blouse as usual. In her state of distress, she didn't realize the pin was coming loose. Suddenly, it broke apart, and before she could catch it, the pin went crashing to the floor. Devastated at losing this beloved vestige of Abel's faith and trust in her, Julia cried out in dismay.

"Oh, no!"

The precious object had shattered into unrecognizable shards. Julia bent over to retrieve the pieces, tears welling up in her eyes. But she was astonished to find among the fragments a minuscule plastic square. She inspected it for a moment, puzzled. Then she pulled out her cell phone and dialed.

"Larry, I think I found someth—"

The two detectives appeared before Julia finished her sentence. Larry, finding her still crouched on the floor, became alarmed.

"What is it? What happened?"

Julia stood up and showed him the plastic square. "I don't know, I… my pin broke and then I found this."

ಬೃಜ

It took Larry only a brief moment to identify the little plastic square. He looked up at Julia's perplexed expression. "Haven't you ever seen a flash card from a digital camera?"

"Uh-uh. Those are for left-brained people."

Buddy flashed an incredulous look at Larry. "Is this girl for real?"

Julia ignored his jibe. "Besides, when do I have time to take pictures? But I always wondered how Abel found time for it. I guess he needed a hobby to divert his attention from his work-related stress. He was always bugging me to become interested in digital pho—"

Larry interrupted her. "Why didn't you tell me that before?" Then he addressed Buddy. "Get this to H.Q. and have it uploaded."

Buddy took the flash card and hurried off. Julia, meanwhile, gathered the remnants of the pin and regarded them with sadness.

Her touching emotion elicited a sympathetic glance from Larry. "Take heart, Julia. That card is an important piece of the puzzle. The pin... well, that can be fixed."

Julia looked up at him with a hopeful expression. They held each other's gaze for a brief moment. Then Larry held open the practice room door.

"I'll assign an officer to keep watch over you for the performance."

"Thanks."

She tucked her violin case and the music under her arm and gently placed the remains of her beloved pin inside her violin case. Then she headed for the pit.

Chapter 34

*Ah di quegli occhi vittoriosi veder la fiamma illanguidir
con spasimo d'amor fra le mie braccia...*

Ah, to see the flame of those imperious eyes grow faint and languid
with passion in my arms...

Puccini, *Tosca*, Act I

As she slid into her assigned chair, Julia noticed Katie eyeing the
gold cross still nestled at Julia's throat.

"Well, I'm happy to see you're still wearing my protective charm,"
Katie said. "You never know when vampires are going to attack."

Julia was glad for a bit of Katie's wry humor to distract her. "It's so
good to know you have such faith in my ability to take care of myself."

The two women grinned at one another with affection.

"Speaking of which, how's Charles?"

Ignoring Katie's innuendo, Julia leaned down and placed her violin
case next to her chair. Then she opened the music on the stand and
gazed at the title: *Tosca*, by Giacomo Puccini. Now, with her involvement with the leading man, the opera had taken on a whole new
meaning for her. She just wasn't sure what that meaning was.

Not yet.

Julia glanced at a bug mashed into the top of the page. Someone
had drawn an arrow pointing to it and labeled it, "Mario," after the
tenor lead in the evening's opera. She smiled with nostalgia, remembering the person responsible for the graffiti. "There's the mosquito
Sid squashed at the Parks Concert, remember, K.?"

Katie grinned in sympathy but didn't comment. Julia appreciated
that. At the moment, she just needed a friendly ear when it came to
the subject of Sidney. She and Katie had both sat with him enough
times during the outdoor concerts the Met played every summer in

the parks in and around New York City to know how bored and antsy he became. Sidney didn't consider sitting on a stage behind a row of solo singers in searing heat and relentless humidity to be a lot of fun, and as a result he fidgeted nonstop. In his non-playing moments, he alternated looking out into the audience seated on the lawn for interesting faces with searching up into the sky for low-flying airplanes, or squashing any errant insects that may have been unfortunate enough to cross his path.

"He always complains about the bugs dive-bombing us in the great outdoors—"

Julia's voice trailed off. She didn't want to dissolve into tears again. Instead, she focused her attention on the music. But when she turned the page over, she caught her finger on a paper clip attached to it. The finger began to bleed, and she sucked on it, murmuring under her breath.

The last thing I need is another injury, physical or emotional, to keep me from playing the violin.

But the finger was beginning to hurt, and her muttering became more vocal. "Ouch! They know they're not supposed to put paper clips in the music. What were they thinking? Damn!" Julia saw Katie cringe. "Oh, sorry, K. I'm swearing an awful lot these days. Not that you're all that virtuous."

Katie pretended to be offended. "Maybe, but cursing is discouraged in my church group."

"I know. I'll try to be more careful …"

Meanwhile, Julia was reading to herself the typewritten note she'd found attached to the clip.

MIND YOUR OWN BUSINESS. OR NEXT TIME YOU'LL BE SQUASHED LIKE A BUG.

Julia gasped, then noticed that Katie was regarding her with apprehension.

"What is it?"

Julia replied with little conviction. "Nothing. I…I'll be right back."

Distraught, Julia grabbed the note and raced out of the pit. She approached the officer stationed at the pit entrance and told him about the note. Together they went in search of Larry. When they found the detective in the wings, she showed him the note. He read it, frowning.

"Where did you find this?"

"It was attached to my music."

"Any idea where it came from?"

Julia shook her head.

Larry pocketed the note. "We'll try to analyze it. Dust for finger-prints." Seeing her distressed expression he added, "I'll send it down to the station right away. Maybe the lab can get some prints off of it."

Larry nodded to the officer, who escorted Julia back to the pit and resumed his position at the door. Still shaken by the less than veiled threat, Julia put on a brave face for Katie when she re-entered the pit, sat down, and took out her violin.

Katie looked over at Julia, concern written all over her face. "I've never seen you leave the pit so close to curtain time. It's bizarre, even for you. What's going on?"

"I can't start explaining, K. Not now."

"But—"

At that moment, the concertmaster stepped up on the podium and put a crimp in any further discussion. The first oboist gave the "*A*" for the orchestra to tune, and Julia and Katie added their tuning to that of the other musicians. Sensing Katie's eyes burning into her, Julia felt obligated to come up with some idle chitchat while she struggled with her cantankerous violin pegs and waited for the conductor to appear. "I spent all afternoon on Abel's song and I still can't make sense of it. What am I going to do?"

"It's gonna be okay. You'll figure it out, I know you will."

"But time's running out for Sid."

She was forced into silence, as the audience became hushed for the conductor's entrance. By the time he reached the podium, Julia's brow was still furrowed with anxiety.

Katie held her bow in readiness for their clicking ritual. "To Sidney. Solidarity."

Julia returned Katie's encouraging smile with a look of gratitude. "And hope."

The conductor raised his baton to give the upbeat, and the musicians blasted their way through the dramatic opening bars of *Tosca*. Julia willed herself to concentrate, but at the moment of Charles's first entrance she allowed her eyes to stray to the stage and focus on him. As a result she missed a note, and Katie flashed her a mock chastising look. With a sheepish smile, Julia went back to her music and made an extra effort to concentrate.

But Julia could not hide her distress from Katie, who saw the distracted look on Julia's face out of the corner of her eye. Julia sat motionless as she played, not swaying to the music as she tended to, and not even bothering to mouth the words of her favorite passages. Her face was creased in an agitated expression. And even if Katie were to ask Julia what was going on, Julia was not about to tell her.

ഇരു

Larry, meanwhile, had found a niche in the wings with a clear view of the stage, which was set as an enormous Baroque church. He had never been so close to the mammoth sets, even when he had watched that *Tosca* rehearsal from the first row of orchestra seats. Other than that, he had only seen the sets from a sky-scraping perch in the Family Circle.

He gazed in wonder at the church of *Sant'Andrea della Valle*, reproduced in gorgeous detail, which he imagined must have duplicated the real one in Rome, with its lofty ceilings, huge pillars, and magnificent artwork. He tried to envision himself as the painter Cavaradossi, in a precarious position on that towering ladder toward the back of the stage.

That thing is high enough to give anyone a serious case of vertigo.

After a brief moment, Larry turned his gaze back to the monitor screen showing the conductor and the musicians in the pit and made sure Julia was there. Once he established Julia's presence, Larry diverted his attention to the action onstage, which he found mesmerizing.

Larry thought back to the rehearsal he had attended, when he had asked Julia to play for him, and remembered her arrogant reaction. At the time, he had thought she was a snob, but he realized now she had been responding to the pressures and emotions of her situation.

She's really a good kid at heart.

He reflected on the exquisite *Thaïs* excerpt she had played for him in his apartment and smiled to himself.

Guess I'll have to sing for her at some point. How the heck am I going to manage that?

Charles's first entrance brought Larry back to attention, however, as the tenor's appearance elicited a fit of enthusiastic audience applause. Heartened by the spectators' response, Charles sang his exchange with the Sacristan with utmost self-confidence.

Got to admit the guy has stage presence out the wazoo.

The performance went along smoothly through the first two acts, and when Charles and several other singers, Dorothy included, returned to the wings from their Act Two curtain calls, Larry couldn't help staring at them. Dorothy, of course, reacted to Larry's presence with her usual hauteur. But Charles acknowledged Larry with a friendly smile, which made Larry feel like he was "in the loop," or at least on its fringes.

"Very lifelike." Larry eyed Charles's blood-red stage makeup. "If I didn't know any better, I'd say you were tortured for real in that last act."

"What a way to make a living, right?" With an amused grin, Charles made his way to the exit.

Larry smiled to himself. This nonchalant little quote of Julia's was about to fix itself permanently in his personal lexicon of quips.

Coming from a rising star in his hour of glory, that's pretty cool.

Despite the ego boost stemming from the singer's attention, Larry knew he should maintain some distance in order to be professional. Before he became involved in all the hubbub at the Met, Larry had no idea how integral the individual personalities were to the workings of the theater. In tandem with the adversity he had witnessed behind the "golden curtain," he had also become privy to an insider's view of the place he had worshipped since he was a child. He blessed his luck in being chosen for this assignment.

How many people experience that in the course of a lifetime?

But when he looked over at the doors leading to the foyer and saw a breathless Buddy headed straight toward him, Larry knew his happy moment was only a temporary one.

"These…were just…faxed…over…from H.Q." Buddy's voice

came in short gasps as he held out the papers to Larry. "Printout of the flashcard."

Still basking in his recent moment of pleasure, Larry forced himself to alertness. "What?"

"That flashcard you sent over to the precinct, boss." Buddy flashed an aggravated grimace at Larry.

"Ah."

Larry nodded and began to study the papers, which contained reproductions of photos and newspaper articles, dating back to past decades. He scanned the documents for a moment and eyed Buddy, puzzled. "What does a drowning at a music camp twenty-odd years ago have to do with anything?"

"Read on, boss."

As Larry continued, his eyes opened wide. He whistled in surprise. "This is unbelievable, Buddy."

"Yep."

Grabbing Buddy by the arm, Larry led him to the hallway outside the entrance to the wings. He waited for the always-beleaguered stage manager to pass by before he started to read aloud. He didn't even notice the irritated look the stage manager flashed toward Buddy.

"July, Nineteen Eighty-Two: 'Trudeau Brothers, Abel and Carl, brilliant young pianist-singer duo, perform at prestigious Upstate Willowstream Music Camp under guidance of renowned music pedagogue Haim Ghent...'"

Larry turned to Buddy in disbelief. "Wait a minute, 'Trudeau... brothers... ?'"

With a sober nod, Buddy motioned to Larry to continue.

"August 'Nineteen Eighty-Two: Mysterious Death of Camper at Summer Music Festival Goes Unsolved.'"

Larry's mouth dropped in astonishment.

"Don't stop there, boss."

Larry examined the entire document before turning back to the first page. He reread the passage. "'Renowned music pedagogue Haim Ghent'...Is this guy still alive?"

"He's old but still going strong." Buddy paused. "And waiting for you at the Ansonia."

Chapter 35

Ore di morte e di vendetta…ormai t'affretta!
Incancellabile il fato ha scritto:
l'impresa compier deve il delitto
poichè col sangue s'inagurò

Hours of death and of vengeance…come swiftly now!
Immutable fate has writ:
the enterprise by crime must end,
since with blood it was begun.

Verdi, *Macbeth*, Act I

JULIA FELT OVERJOYED for Charles. What a spectacular showing in the first act. She couldn't wait to see him afterwards and lavish some well-deserved praise on him. During the second act she diverted herself from troubled thoughts of Sidney by speculating on just what she would say to Charles.

Meanwhile, I still have to get through Acts Two and Three.

During the first intermission, Julia was too exhausted to do anything but crumple onto the sofa in the ladies' locker room with her eyes closed. She figured Katie would understand she needed some time to chill out before revealing the details about the threatening note. By the time Act Two drew to a close, however, Julia felt Katie would be anxious for an explanation. Julia had a plan to thwart Katie's curiosity.

Onstage, Dorothy as Tosca was placing a crucifix on the chest of the character of Scarpia - played by the ubiquitous Roberto - who was lying prostrate on the floor, having just been assassinated by Dorothy. She uttered her final line of the act in solemn tones.

"*È avanti a lui tremava tutta Roma.*"

Julia translated in her mind. *And before him all Rome trembled.*

At that moment, it dawned on Julia the parallel between this stage drama and the events that had occurred since Abel's murder was astonishing. At the Met, Abel had been the power behind the throne, so to speak, at least in the musical sense. Patricia had tried to usurp Abel's authority and made every pretense of dominating their operatic world. But in fact, the opera house revolved around music, Julia knew, and in this sense Abel was the undisputed ruler—at least he had been until his murder. In *Tosca*, the fiery diva held reign over the villainous police chief Scarpia for only a brief part of the action, just as Patricia was doing. Thinking of this, Julia began to wonder.

Is Patricia involved in Abel's murder?

Then Julia brought herself back to reality with a shudder.

Dear God, what was I thinking? None of this makes any sense. I can't let my emotions carry me away into this ridiculous fantasy world. I have to make a conscious decision not to do that. But how?

One way to do that, she realized, was to hold on, in as fierce a manner as possible, to any elements in her life that were concrete and real.

Yes. Like helping Sid, or appreciating Katie's friendship. Or Charles's love?

Act Two ended to thunderous applause. By this time, Julia's anxiety about finding the secret she was convinced lay within the notes of Abel's song was at full tilt. She held onto her violin and bow as she was leaving the pit, balancing them in one hand as she extracted the song from the zipper compartment of her instrument case.

Katie caught up with Julia at the pit entrance. "Are you sure you want to spend the intermission practicing?"

Julia fixed Katie with a determined look. "I've got to give the song one more go. Otherwise I'll never get through the damned last act of *Tosca*."

"There you go swearing again. We've got to have a heart-to-heart once the present insanity is all over and done with," Katie declared.

But the ever-present boom of the P.A. system, like Big Brother reminding the worker ants of their ultimate duty, interrupted any possible retort from Julia.

"Act Two intermission, twenty-five minutes, ladies and gentlemen."

The officer standing guard at the pit entrance accompanied Julia and Katie into the hallway.

"Anyway, it's just a short intermission, Jul. You won't have much time."

"It doesn't matter. Now that I've unearthed that…whatever it was, hidden in the violin pin, I'm going for Abel's song, big-time."

"Okay. But I think you'd be better off relaxing in the lounge."

Julia ignored her friend's advice. "There's something hidden somewhere in that piece of music, and I'll be damned if I'm not going to figure it out."

"You know, you're awful tense."

"Wouldn't you be?" she snapped. Julia immediately felt contrite at Katie's wounded expression. "Sorry, I didn't mean to say it that way. You know that, right?"

"That's okay, I understand. You're under some heavy pressure. It's a lot for you."

"Thanks, K., you're the best."

Julia flashed Katie a smile of gratitude and informed the officer of her plan to sequester herself in a practice room during the intermission. He escorted Katie as far as the women's locker room and followed Julia to the practice room where she had labored before the performance.

"I'll be right outside, Miss Kogan." The officer smiled at her, adding, "You must be pretty devoted to your music to want to practice while everyone else is drinking coffee in the cafeteria."

Stepping inside the room, Julia closed the door.

಄಄಄

The grand piano took up most of the space in the small parlor of Dr. Haim Ghent's Upper West Side apartment in the historical landmark Ansonia Building on Seventy-Third Street just off Broadway. Larry had heard the Ansonia was the last bastion of New York's former musical and artistic glory, housing famous musicians of all generations whose names evoked either past prominence or present renown.

In the case of Dr. Ghent, a benevolent relic of a man, the celebrity involved was from times long past. That's what Larry gathered, as he gazed at the ancient photographs covering the walls: Dr. Ghent at various ages, with Pablo Casals, Arturo Toscanini, Jascha Heifetz, and other luminaries of the music world who had long since passed away. The old professor himself was a rarity, one last remaining vestige of a golden generation of performers who could never quite be replaced.

Dr. Ghent squinted with difficulty as he perused Larry's papers. Larry understood the old man was of an age where a computer's reproduction of old newsprint must be a real bear to make out, but it was all he could do to keep his patience. He needed to find out something, anything, to fill in the gap in his existing chain of information. That missing link was preventing him from solving two murders. And he hated to be so far away from Julia when she could be in danger.

"Ah, yes, the Trudeau Brothers, I remember them well." Dr. Ghent, having at last deciphered the troublesome print on the page, smiled in triumph. "They were prodigiously gifted, and in constant intense competition with one another."

"What else do you recall about them, sir?"

The professor's voice became tinged with regret. "Carl was always in his older brother's shadow, poor child, looking for an outlet for his frustration. He was perpetually jealous of Abel, always trying to catch up with the other's achievements, as if he had to prove by his one-upmanship that he could be as good as, or even superior to, Abel."

"And did Carl ever overcome that gap between them?"

"No, I'm afraid not. It was an insurmountable task to outshine his brother. Abel was a number of years older, and always more adept at capturing people's attention." Dr. Ghent shook his head. "Blessed as he was with his lovely voice, Carl could never come close to Abel's success."

"What do you know about that camper's mysterious death?"

"Ah, yes. Unfortunate incident. Carl was the sole witness."

Larry's guard went up. "Did you say, 'sole witness?'"

"Indeed. The poor boy drowned. It was deemed an accident, but frankly, I was never quite convinced..." His voice trailed off, as if he were struggling to remember an ancient place and time.

"What do you mean?"

"According to Carl's version of the story, he saw the boy drowning and jumped in after him but was too late to save him. The coroner found a skull contusion, but decided the boy must have hit his head on the rocks at the bottom of the lake. At least, that was what was ruled at the inquest."

Dr. Ghent looked at Larry with a faint, quizzical smile.

"Interestingly, the boy and Carl were both up for the lead role in the camp musical ..." The Professor paused in an effort to focus his mind on the long-ago occurrence. "In any case, because of the power and prestige of the distinguished Trudeau family, the entire affair was kept as quiet as possible, though not entirely out of the media."

"Professor, do you remember the names of any of the other campers that year?"

"Oh dear, it was so very long ago. But I might remember the most talented ones. Let's see—"

The professor contemplated for what seemed like an eternity to Larry. As the minutes ticked by, Larry prayed Dr. Ghent's failing memory was capable of dredging up a few more facts. Finally, the old man showed a pleased expression.

"Yes, I remember now. Other than Abel and Carl, There were... ah, excuse me...Yes, Sidney Richter and Matt...Matt Reynolds. They were inseparable, those four. Thick as thieves, but as different as night and day."

Taken aback, Larry stared, open-mouthed, at the professor. After he had recovered, he continued his line of questioning. "No one else seems to know Trudeau even had a brother, Dr. Ghent. How is that possible?"

"After the, ah...incident, Carl was sent to Europe, and stayed there to pursue a singing career, I'm told. Changed his name, in fact."

"Did he ever come back?"

"Not to my knowledge. But then, I've been retired and 'out of the loop,' as they say."

"What if he did come back? Would anyone know who he was?"

"After so many years? I doubt anyone would recognize him. Except, perhaps, the maestro."

Larry flipped his notebook shut and peered at Dr. Ghent. "By the way, what did Carl change his name to?"

Dr. Ghent contemplated for a long moment.

"It was something like...excuse me, a 'senior moment'— "

He paused, as Larry waited breathlessly.

"Ah, I remember now. It was Charles. Charles Tremaine."

Chapter 36

Ma v'ha fra loro il tradito; più d'uno forse

But among them there is a traitor; more than one perhaps.

Verdi, *Un Ballo in Maschera*, Act I

JULIA WATCHED THE WALL CLOCK out of the corner of her eye as she played. She repeated notes, tried playing every other note, and played the notes out of sequence, over and over again. Finally, shrieking in frustration, she turned the music upside down and tried once more. This time, a coherent melody emerged. But it stopped at the bottom of the page. She groaned.

Oh, no, not again.

Then she had a sudden flash of recognition and turned the second page upside down as well. The melody continued and resolved in a familiar-sounding melody. She stopped, flabbergasted, and sang the tune to herself, adding the words she knew belonged to it. Recalling the line from the first act of *Tosca*, she exclaimed it aloud in Italian.

"'*Va, Tosca, nel tuo cor s'annida Scarpia!*'"

Then she translated it into English. "'I've nested inside your heart...' But who... and why...?"

Glancing at the tops of the pages, formerly the bottoms, where Abel had scribbled his last-minute changes, she took a closer look and noticed the notes looked different upside down. She leaned in even nearer to the page and inspected the notes with care, slowly repeating them out loud. "C, *B-flat*, no, *B-natural*..."

Julia paused, conjuring up the image of Abel saying to her, "Remember, always think *beyond* the notes," and realized this could be an opportunity to utilize his advice. She closed her eyes, trying to recapture what he had taught her about translating musical notes into letters and recalled that, in some foreign languages, the letters converted to non-musical ones. Thus, "*B* natural" in English became "*H*" in German.

"Yes, that must be it." The picture started to become clearer. "C, H, then, A..."

Julia turned ghostly pale. She gasped, staring at her music with disbelief and shock.

"Oh, no! It can't be!" Then she remembered. "'*Nel tuo cuor s'annida Scarpia* ...' Oh my God, that's what Charles said to me the night we—"

A sudden declaration coming from the P.A. system jolted Julia. She jumped, startled.

"Five minutes, ladies and gentlemen. Orchestra to the pit, please."

Heaving an anxious sigh, Julia headed for the door, violin in hand. She was torn between her duty to the Met and her pressing need to reveal her new discovery to Larry.

There just isn't time to think about it right now. I'll have to wait until after the opera and make sure Larry knows about it then.

Throwing open the door, Julia looked around. The hallway was empty, since everyone was in the pit. But the officer was nowhere in sight. Puzzled, Julia paused. But when she heard sounds of the orchestra tuning up, she panicked.

I'd better hustle if I don't want to miss the beginning of Act Three.

She was just about to break into a run when she felt an arm grab her from behind. Frowning in annoyance, she stopped and jerked her head to look behind her.

"Larry, didn't I tell you what an irritating habit that is, grabbing someone—"

But it wasn't Larry.

જીન્દ

Larry rose abruptly from Dr. Ghent's sofa. He had heard enough.

"Dr. Ghent, you've been very helpful."

Nodding his thanks, Larry departed in haste. It was time to get back to the Met and do some very aggressive questioning, even if it meant disrupting a performance in progress.

It's not as if that's never happened before.

જીન્દ

Before Julia could turn around fully, however, she felt something wedged in her back. Something cold and hard, like metal. She found herself facing Frank, wielding a pistol. She gasped. He wasted no time reacting to her shock.

"Leave it inside the room."

Frank pointed with his Beretta at her violin. Without a word, Julia stepped back inside the room and placed her violin and bow on the table. She hesitated.

"Hurry it up, I haven't got all night," he growled at her.

Turning Julia around roughly and jamming the gun into her back, Frank shoved her out the door and headed with her down the hall toward the rear stairway. Once they turned the corner, Julia spied the unconscious form of the officer, prostrate on the floor. She shuddered in terror.

"Is...is he ...?"

Frank forced her to step over the body and move on. "No. But that don't mean it won't happen to you."

Without waiting for her response, Frank led Julia through the maze of dim hallways and back stairways into territory she found disturbingly unfamiliar. The sounds of the orchestra playing the Prelude to Act Three of *Tosca* filtering through the P.A. system kept her from losing her grip on her emotions. The idyllic shepherd's song, accompanied by the innocent cow's bell ringing in the background, wafted through the hallways of the opera house, followed by the sound of a thousand church bells awakening the Eternal City of Rome from its pre-dawn slumber.

Julia strained to listen to the reassuring sounds of the opera music, sounds that became more distant with each nudge of Frank's revolver. After a few minutes, she had trouble perceiving the rich resonance of the four cellos accompanying the dialogue between Charles and the jailer, or the plaintive tones of the clarinet's introduction to Charles's poignant aria, *E lucevan le stelle.*

Charles. Finding his name in Abel's song had rocked her world off its axis.

What did it mean? Why did Abel take such pains to write Charles's name into his song for me and then encrypt it to the point of its being undecipherable?

Julia feared she might never find out the answer to this puzzle. And as the music faded further into the background, her apprehension escalated into sheer terror.

ಬಂಡ

Larry cursed to himself as he shoved his way through the throngs of people clogging the streets. The crowds pouring out from Lincoln Center were always a bitch to navigate. But on weekends, when the theater bunch started to pour from their respective venues at the same time as the after-dinner hordes, the chaos resembled thoroughfare gridlock.

He had abandoned his police cruiser at the traffic-choked corner of Broadway and Seventy-Second when he realized he would not make it to the Met unless he hoofed his way there. Walking down any of these congested streets and avenues beat driving on them in most instances, but with this mob, going on foot was proving to be a slow and painstaking process.

Since operas lasted longer than any other type of performance, the Met multitudes were always the last to get out from the theater. Larry thanked his lucky stars *Tosca* was still going on when the Philharmonic, State Theater and Vivian Beaumont were already dark. Otherwise, negotiating the journey down Broadway would have been more like jockeying for space in front of the Saks Fifth Avenue window displays before the Christmas holidays. As it was, he realized every moment was precious, and he checked his watch.

I need to find out more about Charles. Immediately.

While he waited for the light to change at 70th Street, he whipped out his cell phone and called Buddy, who was at the Met, keeping an eye on things.

His partner was irate. "Where the hell have you been?"

Larry had no time. "Get up to the stage and make sure Tremaine doesn't go anywhere."

"Where's he gonna go, boss, he's on sta—"

"I don't have time to explain, just do it."

Without another word, Buddy clicked off and rushed up to the stage.

ಬಂಡ

Patricia stood poised over the gleaming stainless steel toilet in her private executive bathroom. Everything in this lavatory had been custom ordered in stainless steel, from the washbasin to the tiles on the wall. It seemed much cleaner, more sanitary somehow. No one else ever used it, and thus no one had to know its uniqueness, except for her. She took a long look at her silver vial filled with the precious white powder, the object of her obsessive desire, and rolled it sensuously between her long fingers.

I will, after all, have to give this up someday. It's as inevitable as giving up a married lover.

Now was as good a time as any to take care of her little "problem." But how she was going to get along without the cocaine, she had no idea.

More sex, I imagine, with more "admirers."

She had no lack of them. Perhaps a nice young boy-toy. That might help her forget the comforting rush of the drug seeping into every pore of her body and mind, satisfying a need she thought must have dated from her early childhood. Those fine white particles were the only remedy for the pain: the shame of growing up in a disgraceful, sordid lower class environment, the wrong side of the tracks in a western Massachusetts mill town. The recollection of that anguish stayed with her night and day, plaguing her with discomforting memories.

Emptying the contents of the vial into the toilet, she watched them flush away and disappear, as if they had never been there. Then she reached her index finger into the vial to extract the last few grains and placed them delicately on her tongue. As she felt the last of the granules disintegrate into the moistness of her taste buds, she sighed a regretful farewell.

"Ah…How I will miss you all."

ಬೃಠಿ

As Frank led her up darkened back stairways and down secluded hallways with the gun jabbed in her back, Julia quaked with fear. She had never realized how extensive and remote the maze of isolated back corridors and passageways snaking through the Metropolitan Opera House were. They reminded her of the tunnels leading into and through the Egyptian pyramids, or the network of channels comprising a macroscopic human anthill. The vastness of it all… how would anyone find her?

No one but a stagehand would be familiar enough with the opera house to find his way in this labyrinth.

Most frightening of all, she had no idea where she was. But she knew she had to maintain whatever composure she could to keep her wits about her. Her very survival depended on it.

"Where are you taking me?"

Frank didn't respond.

"They've got cops all over the opera house, you know."

He poked the gun with more force into Julia's back and snarled. "Where we're going, they'll never find you. Now move."

Julia stumbled up steep stairs as Frank pushed her along, through a door and over a catwalk with a sheer drop of fifty feet below them, and through another door into yet another darkened hallway. She strained to hear the sounds of the opera coming over the P.A. system, and barely detected Charles and Dorothy Muir singing to each other onstage with passion.

Gradually the music faded further into the background, becoming more distant, until Julia no longer heard them. This music was the one thing connecting Julia to her world, the world she considered her home away from home: the world of opera. Deprived of the music's familiarity and proximity, Julia felt hopeless, cut off from everything she knew and loved. And her fear turned into blind panic.

Chapter 37

L'effroi me pénètre

I'm filled with terror.

Offenbach, *Les Contes d'Hoffman*, Act III

JULIA GOT AN ANSWER to her question when she and Frank ended up in front of a door marked "Roof: Caution." Kicking the door open with his foot, he shoved her outside. She stumbled out onto the roof and looked out at the glittering lights of Lincoln Plaza seven dizzying stories below, overcome with vertigo. Frank trained his gun on her, sneering.

"I tol' ya' they'd never find ya'."

Trying to mask her fear, Julia faced him with defiance. "Oh yes, they will. And you'll be caught red-handed."

Frank sneered. "Too late for you, chickie. Much too late."

Is he going to shoot me? Or something worse...?

Julia tried to think of some way to buy time, to forestall the inevitable.

If I can hold him off, someone will come. I have to believe that...

She pretended bravado. "I'm missing the third act finale, you know."

"Don't worry, you'll get your finale all right. Your last." He chortled. "More dramatic than strangling you in the bar. Operatic, ya' might say."

Her stomach sank.

"Now you mention it, good things come in threes. First Trudeau, then Reynolds, then—"

Julia gasped. "Abel...and Matt...it was you?" Staring at him in disbelief, she tried to wrap her mind around his revelation. "I know you were jealous of Matt, but...murder? For a...a job?"

Frank smirked. "Are you kiddin' me? It's the best job in the opera house. The head stagehand has more power than the general manager.

I'm on top of the world in that job. And I deserve it, too. Reynolds didn't."

"But…Abel?…"

"Abel was the one who appointed Matt, just because he liked him in bed. God, I hated that Trudeau."

Julia cried out in agony. "Enough to…to kill him?" She choked back a sob. "But…but how—?"

"You can thank the US Army. They only train the best. Killing was easy. So was planting the evidence against Richter and polluting his coffee so he'd have to leave the pit just before the murder. Too bad that orderly in The Tombs didn't use enough poison to kill him. But I had to make sure that greaser Geraldo didn't put too much roofie in your drink. That'd deprive me of the pleasure of your company."

"Oh my God," Julia voice was now a throaty whisper.

Frank's satisfied smirk spooked Julia even further. "As I was sayin', Trudeau and Reynolds were easy, compared to you. You're a feisty piece of ass."

"M-me?"

"'Me?'" he mocked. "Why dy'a think I brought you here?"

He began to drag her toward the edge of the roof. She resisted, kicking and panting from the effort. He tightened his grip. "See what I mean? Feisty."

As they reached the brink, she averted her eyes from the dizzying height. "But why me? What have I done?"

"Nothing personal. We would' a done the same to any busybody who got in our way."

"We…?" Her confusion was now complete. "We?"

೩಄ಣ

Meanwhile, the third act was progressing at its normal pace. It was time for the mock fusillade. In the wings, the stage manager spoke into his microphone.

"Firing squad to wings, stage right."

As if with military precision, an array of supers in firing squad costumes filtered in and took their positions at the entrance to the stage. They all kept their eyes glued to the stage, as Dorothy and Charles sang their last farewells onstage before Cavaradossi's final ascent to his doom on the flanks of the Castel Sant'Angelo. The stage director had coached them to stand in readiness for the dramatic shooting to follow, no matter how impassioned the exchange between the two protagonists.

"*Tiene a mente: al primo colpo, giù...E cadi bene,*" Tosca reminded Mario. "Keep in mind: at the first shot, down...And fall in the proper way."

"*Come la Tosca in teatro...*like Tosca on the stage."

To his jest, she replied, "*Non ridere.* Mustn't laugh."

The stage manager approached the prop master. "You've checked all the rifles—and the bullets?" he asked, his teeth clenched with tension.

The prop master nodded. Since the "accidental" shooting onstage of Giuseppe, he had been warned repeatedly to make doubly sure of the company members' safety. It was enough to make anyone contemplate early retirement, especially someone who had been in his position as long as he had.

The firing squad took aim at Charles and fired. He fell to the floor with convincing bravado, just as Tosca had asked him to. She exclaimed in triumph.

"*Ecco un artista*—what an actor!"

The dramatic tension of the third act *dénouement* continued to rise. Dorothy crept to Charles's side, singing to his prostrate form in hushed, urgent tones, casting furtive glances at the firing squad.

"*Mario, non ti muovere...*You mustn't move, not yet."

ෂ⬥ඥ

The squadron moved off scene just as Buddy reached the wings at stage left. He stopped short of the stage, readying himself to detain Charles as soon as the curtain fell. He couldn't wait to find out what Larry must have learned from the old musician he had interviewed, something that pointed to Tremaine as a source of information for the investigation. Maybe Larry even liked Charles for a perp, but whatever the reason for Larry's orders to apprehend the guy, there was no escape for Charles, nowhere he could go but into Buddy's custody.

There was only one problem. The guy lying on the floor wasn't Charles.

Chapter 38

Quegli è il carnefice...!

He is the murderer...!

Mozart, *Don Giovanni*, Act I

FRANK GAVE JULIA a cryptic smile when Charles, still in costume, stepped out onto the roof and surveyed the scene.

"Good work, partner."

In her struggle against Frank, Julia was stunned to hear Charles's voice. She jerked her head back toward the door and stared at him in shock.

"You're wondering why I'm not onstage for the climax, are you, Julia? How thoughtful. Right, Frankie?"

Frank nodded, tightening his hold on the revolver.

"I had a super take my place," Charles continued. "But not to worry—I'm willing to give up my curtain calls, if it means I can have the privilege of personally getting rid of you."

Julia was incredulous. "Get rid of me! But, why?"

Charles smiled. "I'm disappointed in you, Julia. As an artist, you of all people should understand my humiliation, my bitterness, at seeing my brother Abel get *all* the kudos through the years."

Julia was overwhelmed with confusion. "Your...brother? But your name is—"

He allowed a moment to let the revelation sink in. "I changed it after Abel sank my career. Frankly, I didn't want to share his name anymore, after all the leading roles he'd promised and not delivered."

Julia backed up in slow steps toward the roof's edge, regarding Charles in horror as he approached her and Frank.

Charles sneered. "Leading roles... That conniving liar." He turned his head toward Frank. "Your work is done here. No more sneaking around hallways or making phone calls on the sly. Give me the gun, Frankie."

The intensity of Charles's expression must have been enough to convince Frank to relinquish the weapon. Without a moment's hesitation, Charles fired at Frank, one clean shot, aimed straight to the heart. Frank crumpled to the ground in a lifeless heap.

Gaping in disbelief, Julia uttered a sharp cry of distress and was overcome with a wave of nausea.

Within a few days, I've witnessed the murders of the two most important people in my life. And now, this?

Julia summoned up her last remaining shred of calm. "Charles, I do understand your feelings of frustration about Abel, but...murder?"

Charles raised his eyebrows.

"Just think about it, Julia. All my life, it was always Abel. From the time I was a kid, he did everything he could to assure I would remain in his shadow. He had all our parents' attention, all the public's adulation...and all of Mrs. Tallman's money."

Frantic, Julia tried to think.

By now Larry must know I'm missing. He must have been able to figure out where I am, if not now, then within a few minutes. If I'm going to survive, I have to keep Charles talking.

But Charles was in a garrulous mood, as if he'd been waiting for a chance to unload his burden of hate. "My greatest desire was to see Abel pay. He did. In front of three thousand of his most adoring fans, thanks to Frank's military training."

"But you still made it to the top."

"No thanks to Abel. He would have done *anything* to keep me off the stage!"

In his fury, Charles's face turned red and he began to tremble.

Oh my God, what if the gun goes off, just from the fallout of his anger?

She tried a different tack, softening her voice and summoning up her last shreds of composure. "That night...the one we spent together—"

"Ah, yes, paradise, my darling." He allowed himself a shiver of remembrance, then returned to his former steeliness. "But Abel chose you over me for his protégée, while he made *me* suffer as an understudy. I just couldn't live with that."

"I let you into my heart. I thought you cared."

"Of course I did." Charles flashed her a derisive look. "I cared about Abel, too. Just as Cain cared about *his* brother. But— " He stepped closer to Julia.

She cringed.

"Abel knew his days were numbered. After I stole the song from Patricia's interoffice mail, he went and gave the only other copy to you, with my name encrypted in it, the bastard. I knew then it was just a matter of time until you figured it out and took it to the police to save Sidney's neck."

Julia's knew she couldn't deny his claim. She saw his face glow with a surge of what she guessed were feelings—gratification or resentment, or both. He pinned her arms behind her back, making her wince, but she kept her mouth in a tight line to keep from crying out.

I'm not going to give him the satisfaction of knowing I'm in pain.

"But enough about me. It's time we turned our attention to you, Julia."

Without missing a beat, Charles grabbed Julia by the shoulders and inched her toward the edge. She resisted with all her strength.

"Charles, stop!"

"Ah, the girl has spirit, she tries to thwart me." He gave an appreciative little laugh. "*Ha più forte sapore la conquista violenta…*How much stronger the taste of a violent conquest."

Julia shuddered at his reference to Scarpia's speech, extolling the virtues of taking love by force. Suddenly she understood Charles's identification with the villainous character from Puccini's *Tosca*. Like Scarpia, Charles had a taste for beautiful women, and also happened to be a ruthless, cold-hearted killer. Julia struggled to extricate herself from his ever-tightening grip. He laughed at her helplessness.

"Think! You won't get away with this."

"When the police interview me, I'll tell them I knew Frank had it in for you. It was well documented, the conflicts between you. There were even witnesses. Frank even confided to me he might do you harm."

Julia breathed in short gasps. "You know that's not true."

Charles went on. "When I looked down at the pit during the firing squad scene and saw you were missing, I ordered that super, Paolo, to take my place and I rushed up to the roof. But it was too late to save you. Frank and I struggled for the gun, it went off, he was a goner."

"You're insane!"

Despite Julia's escalating distress, Charles maintained his calm. "Am I? Well, perhaps. All performers are insane, one way or another. Or didn't you know that. Who was it that said the music world has the largest number of sociopaths?"

Charles wrenched her around to face the drop-off and leaned on her shoulders. The lights of Lincoln Center radiated below them, their brilliant glow blinding Julia. She made a Herculean effort to keep her balance.

"What a shame. A pretty, talented girl like you, murdered by a deranged stagehand."

Charles turned Julia around to face him and forced a kiss on her lips. Then he positioned himself to give the ultimate push. "Jump, Julia. This is your final performance."

Chapter 39

Dieu me préserve de ton conseil,
misérable assassin!
God save me from your advice,
you wretched murderer!...

Il serait dommage en vérité de laisser
à la mort une si belle proie
It would indeed be a shame to hand
such a pretty victim over to death...

A la mort qui t'attend je saurai, pauvre enfant,
t'arracher, je l'éspère.
From the death that waits for you, you poor child,
I hope I shall know how to save you.

Offenbach, *Les Contes d'Hoffman*, Act III

LINCOLN PLAZA WAS QUIET, empty of theater-going patrons. The evening's Philharmonic and New York City Opera performances were long over, and the spaces surrounding the fountain stood at the ready to receive the post-*Tosca* crowd from the Met.

Winded from his sprint down Broadway, Larry darted past the fountain toward the glass revolving doors to the opera house, past the street violinist holding down his usual position. Larry made his way toward the revolving front doors of the Met. But before Larry could reach the doors, the violinist grabbed Larry's elbow and pointed up to the roof, where Larry could make out the forms of Julia and Charles.

"Jesus!"

Larry ran inside the lobby. He shouted to the security guard. "Get me to the roof! Pronto!"

ಎಃಚಿ

In her discovery that her lover was dead, Tosca/Dorothy became hysterical. A platoon of supers dressed as armed guards charged toward her. She thrust back the leader and made a run for the steep stairs of the parapet.

As Tosca mimed her fatal leap, Larry followed the security guard through hallways, up stairways, through one door after another, across catwalks perched precariously above forty or fifty foot gaps—all in the pursuit of Julia. Larry could not believe how complex and convoluted the opera house landscape was, a veritable network of passageways, back-alley type paths evoking images of Babylon or a futuristic mini-metropolis housing an intricate mob hideout.

Still, they had not yet made their way to the roof. And time was running out.

ℰℭ

On the rooftop, Charles was basking in his moment of glory.

"Seeing your demise will be just as pleasurable as seeing Frank blow away my brother," he boasted, swaggering in his self-important arrogance. "Poor child. If you hadn't antagonized Frank, he wouldn't have pushed you off."

"He didn't push me!"

Charles ignored her outburst. He turned her to face him, taking a step back for one last admiring glance.

"Let me look at you once more." He sighed. "So naïve, so ingenuous…"

Gazing at her, Charles caught a glimpse of Katie's gold cross, nestled at Julia's throat, reflecting the city lights from Lincoln Plaza. He laughed in disdain. "A cross. How touching. But you won't need it anymore, Julia. Even God can't save you now." With a malevolent smile, he reached over to pluck the necklace from Julia's throat. "You don't mind if I take it as a souvenir of our passion?"

Julia clutched the cross. "Don't touch me, you vile—"

"*Non toccarmi, demonio, vile Scarpia!*" Charles laughed mockingly. "How well you've learned your libretto. And how you flatter me, comparing me to that most admirable of villains. I've been waiting for that all my life."

He paused, brushing her neck with his lips. She shuddered in response. Then he drew himself up, shouting in triumph. "*Tosca - finalmente mia!*"

ℰℭ

Caught up in the fervor of his performance, Charles was distracted for a split second. Julia took in the ecstatic expression, the faraway look in his eyes. It was long enough for her to seize her opportunity. With a sudden jerk, she jammed her elbow into Charles's stomach with brute force. He stumbled, losing his footing. Julia thrust her body at him, with every shred of her strength.

"O, *Scarpia, avanti a Dio!*" screeched Dorothy, her final line, as she leapt off the parapet on stage.

At that precise moment Charles Trudeau plunged to the plaza of Lincoln Center, his body shattering on the pavement.

ഇരുന്നു

Julia looked down from her precarious position on the roof's edge, gasping for breath, as Dorothy/Tosca's last line echoed through her mind.

"Oh, Scarpia, before God!"

The cry, loud and clear, pulsated throughout Julia's overwhelmed psyche, as if Dorothy's onstage shriek had carried from the theater through the hallways and up the stairways to the soaring heights of the roof.

Julia was still in shock when Larry burst through the door. He ran to her. "Julia, thank God!"

Julia sobbed. "It was Frank and Charles! They're dead. They —"

She clung to him, sobbing in terror and relief. But when the shock of her encounter with Charles wore off, she pulled back from him. "Where were you? What took you so long?" she asked, her expression suddenly childlike.

"I'm sorry." He laughed with relief. "I had no idea how tough it would be to find my way up here. Are you okay?"

"I am now."

She wavered for a moment. Then she threw her arms around him, hugging him tightly.

ഇരുന്നു

Larry was astonished at her spontaneous show of affection, but he had no problem returning the gesture. He was surprised at how comfortable he felt holding her. He just squeezed her as hard as he could without cutting off her oxygen supply and allowed himself to feel wonderful.

ℰℭ

Lincoln Plaza was crowded with onlookers. The opera patrons just exiting the Met, unaware of what had transpired outdoors, came upon a scene surpassing the one they had just witnessed on the stage. Security guards and NYPD officers were forced to hold them back, along with the bystanders who gathered from the street, from the center of the upheaval.

Larry and Buddy discussed the evening's shocking events with two detectives and a police officer from the Twentieth Precinct.

Julia stood between them, feeling stunned and drained. She watched, shaken, as paramedics loaded a stretcher carrying Charles's covered body into one waiting ambulance and placed Frank's body in another.

As the E.M.S. vans drove away across the Plaza, lights flashing, Julia felt a chill and shivered. Larry took off his jacket and placed it around her shoulders, gazing at her catatonic face.

He smiled at her. "How about a nice, hot cup of tea and *La Bohème*—the Carreras recording?"

"Sure, but,..." She managed a weary smile. "even Herbie Hancock would do."

Larry draped his arm across her shoulders, and Julia, glad to entrust herself to him, did not pull away. As they walked away together, he began to sing in a tentative voice.

"*Dammi il braccio, mia piccina...*"

"Give me your arm, my little one ..."

"Ah, so you're finally singing in public."

He stopped singing and took his arm away. "Not 'in public.' Just with you."

"You have quite a nice voice, after all." She grinned.

"So? Are you going to respond?"

She gave him her arm and joined in, melding Mimi's voice with Rodolfo's.

"*Obbedisco, Signor...*"

"I obey, Sir ..."

Their singing dissolved into the voices of the two lovers pledging their mutual adoration at the end of Act I of Puccini's *La Bohème*. Julia was surprised how easy it was, how comfortable for them to harmonize together. She wondered why Larry, whose voice sounded so mellifluous, had kept it to himself for so long. She was overjoyed that Larry had chosen to share this intimate aspect of his being, and she sang along with enthusiasm.

We're just like Mimi and Rodolfo...well, not quite. We're not poor artists, but we do have a lot in common after all.

Rehearsals for *La Bohème* were due to start the following week. And she had obviously studied her libretto.

Epilogue

È avanti a lui tremava tutta Roma!

And before him, all Rome trembled!

Puccini, *Tosca*, Act II

THE LIGHTS IN LINCOLN PLAZA sparkled. Julia ambled past the fountain toward the Met front entrance and stopped to listen to the street violinist's performance. As he finished his cadenza she reached into her violin case, pulled out her cherished libretto of *Tosca* and placed it in his instrument case. He acknowledged her gracious smile with a deep bow. Blushing, she nodded her to him and followed the crowds through the glass revolving doors.

At the switchboard inside the stage door, the security guard greeted Julia with a radiant grin. She reached for her ID, but he waved it aside and ushered her through the gate.

Julia made her way downstairs to Pit Level and started to sign the attendance sheet. Noticing a small "heart symbol" scrawled next to her name, she looked up to see Sidney, close by her side, beaming at her. She gave his arm an affectionate squeeze.

"Thank God you're here, Sid."

"No." His voice was gentle and caring. "I have you to thank for that."

"Stop it, Sid. How many times do you have to tell me?"

As they bantered, Tony appeared by their side and pointed to his watch with a sour expression. They both groaned. But he just grinned at them and walked away, waving his baton at the empty air. Julia and Sidney looked at each other. Then they burst out laughing.

Julia wandered into the women's locker room to find Katie seated on a bench, a sly smile emanating from her face, pointing at a small box taped to Julia's locker. Opening the box, Julia discovered her violin pin, repaired to perfection, along with a handwritten note.

Katie looked at her, expectant. "Well, read it already."

Julia read aloud. "'Here's to your real, much overdue debut performance. From Larry.'"

Katie flashed a knowing grin. "I once had a fling with a cop. Very hot."

Without missing a beat, Julia fastened the pin to her blouse. Pulling her violin case from her locker, she hoisted it onto her shoulder, smiled at Katie and sauntered toward the door.

Once ensconced in the pit, Julia tuned her violin, working her brand-new pegs without a problem. Sidney, beside her, watched with approval. Katie, right behind them, made a "thumbs up" gesture. All three of them clicked their bows together, chorusing in perfect unison.

"Solidarity."

Sidney nodded in the direction of the pit rail. Looking up at the first row of orchestra seats, Julia saw Larry leaning over, beaming at her. She smiled back.

Then the lights dimmed, and the crystal chandeliers rose to the ceiling, heralding yet another enthralling performance. Outside, in the shadow of Lincoln Center, the immense, brilliantly colored Chagall murals stood witness to the greatness of the Metropolitan Opera House.

Questo è il fin di chi fa mal!
E de' perfidi La morte all' vita è sempre ugual!

This is the fate of those who do wrong!
Evildoers always come to an equally evil end!

Mozart, *Don Giovanni*, Act II Finale

About the author

Violinist turned author Erica Miner has had a multi-faceted career as an award-winning screenwriter, author, lecturer and poet. A native of Detroit, she studied music at Boston University, the New England Conservatory of Music, and the Tanglewood Music Center. After experiencing a variety of highs and lows in her quest to forge a career in New York City, Erica won the coveted position of violinist with the Metropolitan Opera Company, a high-pressured milieu but the pinnacle of her field.

Her life became even more challenging, however, when injuries from a car accident spelled the end of her musical career. Searching for a new creative outlet, she drew upon her lifelong love of writing for inspiration and studied poetry and screenwriting, winning a number of awards in both categories. After moving to the West coast, Erica honed her screenwriting skills with author and script guru Linda Seger of *Making a Good Script Great* fame and with Ken Rotcop, the author of *Perfect Pitch.* Erica's screenplays, one of which is based on her award-winning debut novel, *Travels with My Lovers,* have won awards and/or placed in such competitions as WinFemme, Santa Fe and the Writer's Digest. Her essays and articles have appeared in Vision Magazine, WORD San Diego and numerous newsletters and E-zines.

Erica has completed both the novel and screenplay of her suspense thriller, *Murder in the Pit,* which takes place at the Met, and currently is at work on the second novel in her "FourEver Friends" series chronicling four young girls' coming of age in the volatile 60s and 70s.

In addition Erica has developed a number of writing lectures and seminars, which she has presented at various venues across the West Coast and on the High Seas, where she is a "top-rated" speaker for Royal Caribbean Cruise Lines. Topics range from "The Art of Self Re-Invention" to "Opera Meets Hollywood" and "Journaling for Writers: Mining the Gold of Your Own Experiences." Details about Erica's novels, screenplays, seminars and interviews can be found on her website, http://www.ericaminer.com.

Don't miss any of these other
exciting mainstream novels

➤ Death on Delivery
(1-931201-60-9, $16.50 US)

➤ Death to the Centurion
(1-931201-26-9, $16.95 US)

➤ Mazurka
(1-60619-160-8, $16.95 US)

➤ Murder Past, Murder Present
(1-60619-206-X, $19.95 US)

➤ The Golden Crusader
(1-933353-91-0, $16.95 US)

➤ The Vandenberg Diamonds
(1-933353-83-X, $18.95 US)

➤ Tremolo
(1-933353-08-2, $16.95 US)

Twilight Times Books
Kingsport, Tennessee

Order Form

If not available from your local bookstore or favorite online bookstore, send this coupon and a check or money order for the retail price plus $3.50 s&h to Twilight Times Books, Dept. CS610 POB 3340 Kingsport TN 37664. Delivery may take up to two weeks.

Name: _____

Address: _____

_____

Email: _____

I have enclosed a check or money order in the amount of

$_____

for _____ .

Synopsis

On the night of her first performance at the Metropolitan Opera, prodigious young violinist Julia accepts two gifts from her mentor, Maestro Abel Trudeau: a jeweled violin pin and a song dedicated to her. Then an assassin's bullet strikes down Abel on the podium, and Julia's close friend and colleague Sidney is accused of the murder. Despite her grief and compelling evidence pointing to Sidney's guilt, according to unsympathetic NYPD Detective Larry, Julia resolves to clear Sidney's name.

Julia enlists support from tenor understudy Charles and head stage-hand Matt, but encounters resistance from Matt's disagreeable assistant Frank. She senses danger, however, when toppling scenery barely misses crushing her and threatening notes appear on her music. And when she discovers Matt's bludgeoned body stuffed in a crack in the pit wall, she finds consolation in Charles's embrace.

The story unfolds with clues from the violin pin and Abel's song, abduction, and a series of shocking revelations that ultimately force Julia to save her own life and to learn whom—and whom not—to trust.

Made in the USA
Middletown, DE
13 June 2018